BEER

Jim leafed throug _____ e came across a spell _____ gold. "Look," he told Willy. "I'm going to show you what the book does." He looked around the room, and settled on his almost-full beer can. Might as well drink my beer out of a gold can as an aluminum one, he decided.

He set the can in front of him, and said, "Watch, okay?" and started reading the spell. As he read, the light over the kitchen table dimmed and flickered, and the room started to fill with fog.

Will stared over Jim's left shoulder and grew pale. "Uh . . . Jim," he squeaked. His eyes were round and white-edged. "Jim, man . . . you've gotta stop."

Jim heard a pop in the air right behind him. The beer can sat there, gleaming gold from pop top to base. He reached out to pick it up . . . and it slipped out of his hand and *thunked* on the table.

The beer had turned into gold, too.

"Solid gold?" he whispered. He owned a tall-boy-sized lump of solid gold? "Wow," he murmured, and looked up at his friend again.

Willy looked like he was about to throw up. "Look . . . behind . . . you," he gasped. He was sitting in the chair, shaking, pale as a dead man, sweating bullets.

Jim turned around—and screamed. A leathery cat-like face with fangs long as his hand and white, pupilless eyes grinned at him. The thing stood up straight . . . and kept standing—up, and up. Its head touched the ceiling, and it was still crouched over. And then the thing grinned even more broadly, and started toward him . . . .

Baen Books By Holly Lisle

Fire in the Mist
Bones of the Past
Mind of the Magic
Minerva Wakes
When the Bough Breaks
with Mercedes Lackey
The Rose Sea with S. M. Stirling
Mall, Mayhem & Magic
with Chris Guin

Mall, Mayhem and Magic

Holly Lisle & Chris Guin

BAEN

MALL, MAYHEM AND MAGIC

This is a work of fiction. All the characters and events portrayed in this book are purely fictional, and any resemblance to real people or incidents is purely coincidental.

A Baen Books Original

Baen Publishing Enterprises
P.O. Box 1403
Riverdale, NY 10471

ISBN: 0-671-87678-3

Cover art by Darrell K. Sweet

First printing, August 1995

Distributed by Simon & Schuster
1230 Avenue of the Americas
New York, NY 10020

Typeset by Windhaven Press: Editorial Services, Auburn, NH
Printed in the United States of America

Dedication

This one is for Holly
For thinking I could do it when I didn't
For making me do it when I wouldn't.
And for helping me do it when I couldn't.

So much of what I am I owe to you.
You gave me back my dreams,
And showed me how to make them real.
I will always love you.

Acknowledgements

I'd like to thank everyone who helped me in the writing of this book, most especially the members of Schrödinger's Petshop writers' group, who were there at the beginning, and Grendel's Lab, who were there at the end.

I'd like to thank my stepdad, Mike Phillips, for the gun information on the Davidson 10-gauge in Chapter 38—any errors are mine.

And I'd like to thank Jim Baen, for giving me the chance to write this book with Holly, and Toni Weisskopf for giving me two extra days on the revisions, and for not killing me for needing them. I'd like to thank Holly for giving me correct anatomical details of the innards of the Barbie doll—which she assures me were gleaned from hours of childhood experimentation.

And I'd like to thank my mom and my dad, for years of putting up with my fascination with fantasy and science fiction—and you said it would never get me anywhere.

Chris Guin

Chapter One

FRIDAY

Feels like a storm coming.

That was all Jim could think of to explain his edgy tension and the nervous anticipation he was feeling. The back of his neck tingled as though someone was watching him, which was ridiculous. The stretch of road leading to the mall was completely empty.

The radio blared out the opening bars of Creedence Clearwater Revival's "Bad Moon Rising," and the snake that coiled around Jim's stomach tightened its grip. The way he felt, the song seemed like an omen.

He wrestled his battered Chevy Nova into the mall parking lot and turned off the ignition; sat for a moment, listening to the engine ping as it cooled. The parking lot was still empty—would be for another hour. The place was as peaceful now as it ever got, and about as likable. He sighed and grabbed his backpack from behind the passenger seat.

Sharra was working today—that was something to be grateful for, anyway. He sighed again. At least it would be if she ever noticed him.

Jim swung the car door open, frowning as it dropped six inches on its bent hinges. He unfolded his legs and squeezed out of the Nova, then set the backpack down and braced one hand firmly against the car window so it wouldn't fall down when he lifted up on the door and slammed it shut. Someday soon, he thought, I'm going to have to get that fixed.

He didn't lock the car. He kept hoping some idiot would steal it.

The relative coolness of night was disappearing beneath the early onslaught of the August sun. Q-103 weather predicted temperatures in the high nineties with humidity to match. There were days when working inside, completely isolated from the outdoors, drove Jim crazy. Today was not going to be one of those days. The air felt wrong. He wasn't sure why—heat and humidity were normal enough for North Carolina summers—but *something* wasn't right.

There's definitely a storm building, he thought. Out of sight, but still too close for comfort.

He went in the back way, through the high-ceilinged access corridor, and came out beside Shoe Towne. His footsteps echoed back to him as he entered the cool silence of the main mall. In the early morning, before the mass of humanity filled it, Greentraile Mall had an eerie, tomb-like quality about it. If it was a tomb, Jim thought, then I'd know where people with bad taste came to die.

He grimaced at the results of the recent remodeling. The floors were tiled in a large black-and-white checkerboard pattern, bordered with a narrow row of alternating lime green and peach. The wrought iron and wood slat benches were now painted lime green, sherbet orange, and violent purple. The "decorator" who had come up with that color scheme was also the genius who had decided faux black marble on the columns would be just the right accent touch to finish it all off. Jim had seen faux painted finishes that looked good, but these weren't them.

Down by the Chick-Fil-A, Franklin Ray, the sheriff's

deputy who worked part-time as the night security guard was finishing his rounds.

"Hey, Jim! Ready to sell a million?" The guard waved.

Jim waved back and said, "You bet, Frank."

The guard said the same thing every time Jim saw him. After a while it became routine, familiar. But today, the familiar felt dangerous; something was wrong, and Jim didn't know what.

Maybe I'm just coming down with something, he thought.

He rounded a gentle bend in the hallway, saw the store, and smiled. G. Galloway Bookshop was a welcome change from the bathroom-tile-and-Day-Glo nightmare of the mall. The walnut floors gleamed, and the rich brass trim along the woodwork and down the sides of the shelves glowed with the soft richness of understated class.

Every single one of the 146 G. Galloways was the same—from floor plan to stock—but it was a comforting sameness. Jim closed the store's rickety metal gate behind him, and breathed in deeply. There was nothing like the smell of a bookstore; new ink, dust, and slowly decaying paper mingled together into a perfume fit for the gods.

If heaven doesn't smell like a bookstore, he thought, then I don't want to go.

He walked slowly through the store, picking up fallen books and stray magazines, straightening the leftover mess from the previous night and enjoying the presence of the store. His morning ritual complete, Jim headed for the downstairs stockroom.

The manager had left behind a long "to-do" list for the morning staff. Jim's first job was unpacking the bargain assortments, which had been languishing in the back since Luisa went on vacation. Jim sighed. Luisa was their receiving clerk. She was a feisty, fiftyish

Mexican lady who moved like eight-armed lightning. Whenever she went on vacation, the shipments went to hell until some poor soul got delegated to try and restore order.

Looks like I'm the lucky one, Jim thought, and sighed. Just my luck.

He tossed the first box on the table, brandished his box cutter like a rapier, and sliced the packing tape open with a practiced motion. He began checking in the books, sorting them by title and stacking them on the carts to be shelved. Piles of the previous year's not-quite-bestsellers sat on the cart next to the Oprah Winfrey dysfunction-of-the-month for last April.

Jim usually loved unpacking books. It was like having Christmas all year round. Boxes of books came in every day, loaded with new tales, freshly spun and bursting with the promises of new worlds to see, new people to meet. Somehow, bargain books just weren't the same.

He settled into the routine, and worked steadily for about an hour—until a loud banging on the back door broke his concentration.

"I'm coming, I'm coming," he yelled. He looked through the peephole. It was Kent, the delivery man for R.P.S., and he had a stack of boxes on the cart beside him.

"We don't want any!" Jim yelled. Usually, he was joking when he said that—but this time, in spite of his smile, he meant it. That same sick feeling was back in the pit of his stomach, gnawing away at him like it had been in the parking lot—only this time it was stronger.

Kent yelled back at him through the closed door. "Yeah, sure, that's what you said yesterday, too." He grinned and waved the clipboard at the peephole in the door.

I'm definitely coming down with something, Jim thought. Or else there *is* a storm brewing—and it's getting closer.

He opened the back door. Kent's cart was loaded down—with another huge selection of bargain books. "This time I really mean it," Jim said. "I can't deal with any more bargain books today. If I give you twenty bucks, will you take this garbage and shove it off a cliff somewhere?"

"Luisa usually makes me a better offer than that." Kent started pulling boxes off the cart. "When's she comin' back, anyway?"

"I think she's got four more days of vacation," Jim answered. "So she should get back on Tuesday. And when she does," he motioned towards the stack of boxes, and a blissful smile crossed his face, "all of this will be hers again."

Kent handed over his clipboard; Jim signed for the shipment and passed it back.

"I'll see you tomorrow," Kent said.

Jim winced. "Not if I see you first."

Jim closed the door, and stacked the new shipment off to one side. He went back to unpacking the first shipment.

His heart raced, and his fingertips tingled. Storm, the back of his mind kept saying. Close. Something in the back of his mind insisted that the storm was ready to strike—and that this time, the storm wasn't outside. Then, in the bottom of the last box, beneath twenty more hardbacks of the *T-Factor Diet*, he found a book that clearly didn't belong.

The first thing he noticed was the weight of it. The book had a solidity that Jim never associated with bargain books—the feel of good, heavy paper and a sewn binding. The leather covers were old and cracked, worn smooth and white in places. The front cover was completely blank, so Jim opened to the title page, and the sharp scent of ink and paper mixed with the smell of old leather. He closed his eyes and breathed deeply. He found the title inside, written in a thin, spidery script. The spellings were archaic, and it took Jim a moment to figure them out.

ᚦHE GRYMOIRE OF LUKAS SMALLING
A Collexion of Certain Spelles and Summonings
1773

He held it and stroked the old pages. Must not have invented spell-checkers yet, Jim thought. He smiled slowly, studying the title. Then again, I guess that's what this book is.

He traced a finger over the name at the top. Lukas Smalling. Interesting. Jim had a Grandfather Smalling on his mother's side—about three generations back. He wondered if they were related. Probably not, of course. The whole area was up to its armpits in Smallings. Still, the possibility was kind of neat.

The book was an enigma. The title page was blank— it listed no publisher, no copyright notice or printing history. He checked the next page, but it too was blank. After that was the table of contents, then the main body of the text. He flipped through the pages in amazement, as he began to realize the book wasn't a very good copy of a hand-calligraphed manuscript. It was the real thing.

He didn't recognize the lettering style. Jim had once tried to learn calligraphy, but this script hadn't been in his Speedball text. It was a long, narrow hand, with heavy thick-and-thin strokes and a lot of very pretty, very aggravating interlocking loops.

The only thing he could say for sure was that the book was in English, though it was the English of a very creative speller. It seemed to be divided into sections, grouped by type of magic. There were sections on Lesser Summonings, Greater Summonings, Sympathetic Magic and Totems, On Weather and

Binding the Elements, and a long section titled "Love Spells and Bindings."

Jim found that last section intriguing.

Maybe I should check out one of those. Sharra hasn't paid attention to anything else I've tried. A love spell would at least have the virtue of being different.

He carefully closed the book, caressing the worn leather of the cover. I wonder how much it costs, he thought. But along with the other things it didn't have, he also couldn't find a price.

He sniffed the leather again, happily, and sighed. He couldn't believe anything so cool had arrived in a bargain shipment.

He checked the invoice, but the book wasn't listed. No ISBN number, of course—that would have been on the back, next to the also-nonexistent bar code and price, and on the equally nonexistent copyright page. Jim ran the title through the computer—another dead end.

He decided to put it on his "wish list" shelf of books he was eventually going to buy, until he found out more about it. He climbed the stockroom ladder, moved a stack of romance novels that were waiting to be stripped, and carefully set the book on the highest shelf, next to a signed and slipcased leather Asimov *Forward the Foundation* and the leather-bound *Complete Sturgeon* he hoped to have enough money to someday take home. He moved the romance novels back in place. All the G. Galloway booksellers had hiding places for those special books they were going to buy someday. Getting first pick of the new books made up some for the weird hours and lousy pay.

With the book safely tucked away for later, Jim got back to work. He suddenly realized that he was humming to himself, and smiled. Whatever had turned his stomach before was gone. He'd probably been trying to get some sort of a stomach virus, and his system had managed to kill the bug before it could make him sick.

He was finishing the next shipment when he heard the clattering of the front gate. A few minutes later Michael Gilmore came in the stockroom door, his daily planner under one arm.

"Morning, Michael." Jim kept moving. The manager didn't believe talking was one of those things that needed to be done standing still.

"Yes, I suppose it is, isn't it?" Michael stared gloomily. at his planner. "Listen, Jim, I hate to ask you to do this, but Catherine called me at home this morning, and she's got a stomach virus or something. I was wondering if you'd mind going home at noon and coming back in at six to close up the store."

There, Jim thought, I knew it. There's just something going around.

He frowned. He hated working split shifts. A succession of possible excuses ran through his head—and right on out the other side. None of them were likely to convince Michael, and Jim had always been a lousy liar. Besides, Mike was a decent manager, and a nice guy.

"Well, I guess so," Jim answered.

"Thanks, Jim. I really appreciate you helping out like this."

Jim said, "No problem." And really, if he were going to be honest with himself, it *wasn't* a problem.

Michael picked up a copy of the *T-Factor Diet* between his thumb and forefinger and wrinkled his nose. He held it at arm's length, rolled his eyes, and put it back down.

Jim grinned. "They must have printed ten million copies of that book," he said.

Michael said, "The sad part is that it's actually a pretty good book. But we'll never get rid of all the bargain copies we've already got, and every shipment brings in more."

Michael turned and left the stockroom, and Jim sighed, resigning himself to the idea of having to close the store.

Hell, it's not like I had plans, he thought. Even if it is Friday night. It just makes for a long day.

The last time he'd been on a real date had been over six months ago. The girl had turned out to be only slightly smarter than a block of granite. He wanted pretty, and she'd been gorgeous—but Jim was tired of Dates From Hell. He also wanted someone he could talk to, someone who could honestly say that the last book she read didn't have Fabio on the cover. Someone like Sharra.

Sharra Mills had been running the literature and poetry sections of the store since the middle of June. She was a junior at Methodist College, majoring in English Literature—and she was gorgeous. She read, too, though unlike him she actively preferred the classics. Jim liked everything, and was as happy discussing Gibson or Sturgeon or L'Amour as Keats or Shelley or Wilde. Sharra, if she talked to him at all, discussed his "other" reading with a slight sniff and an expression of distaste, as if she'd just smelled something rancid.

But beautiful and smart weren't the easiest combination to come up with, and Jim figured she'd come around if he ever got her to read anything besides her lit list. He imagined discussing the themes of transcendence and futility that ran parallel in Clifford Simak's work with her, or spending a happy evening trying to run down the origins of some of the words in Gene Wolfe's *Book of the New Sun*. He thought she'd like Wolfe—he was literary enough to satisfy even readers of James Joyce, but he told a better story.

And then Jim imagined running his fingers through her long, black hair, staring into those deep blue eyes, kissing her—

He shoved his glasses back up on the bridge of his nose

with one finger and sighed. Get real, Jim, he thought. She was more than just not interested in him. She really seemed to dislike him—though he couldn't understand why. Most people liked him, though he'd never been wildly popular. He was always nice to her, he didn't stare or drool or paw—he was, he guessed, pretty decent-looking. A lot of intellectual girls despised jocks, but he'd never said anything about his failed hopes for a career in baseball, and no one at the store knew, either.

He rubbed his shoulder absently. If he thought about it, the ache was still there; most of the time, he tried not to think about it. What was that stupid line? *I coulda been a contenda.* Yeah, he thought, I could have been. Could have been. Those were bitter words. Fast ball, slider, changeup—a really nasty curveball that broke deep in the pocket—he'd had them all. A full scholarship had been in the wings, with three different big schools scouting him and a dozen lesser ones; he could have gone on, even with the first injury. His torn ligaments would have healed with time and rest, and he had given them time and rest.

But he'd been stupid—he'd seen four guys in an alley behind a bar beating up on another, who was alone, and he'd waded into that fight without stopping to think or ask questions, because the guy in the middle wasn't going to get out alive. It had taken all of about five minutes for the four he was fighting to notice that he was favoring his right side. They exploited the weakness in his shoulder and when they finally got him down, they pounded him until there wasn't much left of it but mush. Meanwhile, the one they'd all been fighting had seen his chance and run like hell.

For Jim, what followed were months of reconstructive surgery and physical therapy and medication that had cost his mom and stepdad a fortune they couldn't afford. Squeeze the ball, the doctors said. Wiggle your fingers. Can you feel anything here when I do this?

He'd suffered a lot of pain, only some of it in his arm. His baseball hopes died that night, and with them, his chances of going to college. Might as well say his entire future had died, too. The guy he'd saved had never said thank you.

And even that wouldn't have mattered so much, except that the guy in the alley had deserved the beating he was getting. The creep had dated one of the other men's sisters—once. Took her out, took advantage of her, and from all accounts, roughed her up pretty badly when he was done. The brother and three of his friends were just evening the score for the girl.

Jim stared off at nothing, rubbing his shoulder, trying to make the hurt—all the hurts—go away. It had all been a big, expensive lesson. Don't jump in on somebody else's fight. Leave do-gooder deeds to the heroes. Keep your head down and mind your own business. One big, expensive lesson, but now that he'd learned it, he didn't get a second chance. Baseball was gone, college was gone, the future had narrowed down to an almost-minimum-wage job in a bookstore in a mall, and lonely nights in a crummy apartment. If there was anyone in the world who needed a bit of magic, it was him.

He wished his imagined romance with Sharra didn't feel like his last chance for a real life. But then, he thought glumly, he *wished* a lot of things.

"Jim!" Ann leaned into the stockroom. "A couple of your regulars are out on the floor, dying to know about some weird book I never heard of, and they don't know the title, but they sort of think they know who the author is." She shook her head, dismayed. "Can you handle it for me?"

"Sure, I'll take care of them." He pushed back the darkness, grinned at her, and stopped rubbing his shoulder. "I needed to get out of here for a few minutes, anyway."

Chapter Two

Sharra frowned at herself in the mirror. She looked exactly the same as she always looked. She hated those round blue eyes, the sweet, full lips, the face that could have been the model for every old master's Madonna.

Her breathing became choppy, and tears glittered in her eyes and poured down her cheeks in hot streams; she balled up her fists and squeezed her eyes shut, while the tears fell faster.

It never ends. God, it never ends. Why can't I just die?

Dying was all she wanted. Emptiness and an end to the pain she couldn't talk about, to the hellish unending memories, and that face in the mirror in the morning. She wanted the morning to come when she did not wake up at all. But the sun kept rising, and she rose with it—the light of day crept through even the blackest of blinds and tugged her eyes open. She hated morning more than any other time of the day, because morning was when she woke and remembered she was still alive.

She bit at her lip and stared at her face in the mirror with distaste.

Maybe I'll try again.

She looked at her wrists, at the two thin lines that ran lengthwise along the insides, and at the neat, tiny white puckers dotting the scars to either side. That should have worked, but it hadn't. The mailman, of all people—how had he known she was home, or sensed that something was wrong?

God, why hadn't she just locked the door?

She'd ended up on antidepressants and months of counseling with an inanely cheerful woman who had taken a liking to her, and as a result, had tried to make Sharra see that life was worth living. The woman had been certain that she could help, certain that Sharra's problems could be solved.

Her earnestness still made Sharra want to laugh.

The fact that the counselor had spent time trying to line her up with a couple of different young men . . .

Sharra couldn't laugh at that. She looked at the detestable person in the mirror, noting with clinical interest the sudden hunted expression in the eyes. Men. She tried to repress the little shiver that ran down her spine, failed.

She couldn't think of men without thinking of Jim, and his sweet, somewhat clumsy advances. She was drawn to him, in a way she hadn't been drawn to anyone in years. But she couldn't have him. And she couldn't tell him why—he wouldn't understand. She wasn't entirely sure that *she* understood.

Men, she thought bitterly. Nothing to laugh about there.

Chapter Three

Gali trudged along behind the other three exiles, over the crest of the rocky, bramble-covered hillside and down to the clearing on the far slope. She tucked her ripped cloak tightly around her and stopped, breathing hard. Her three companions stopped with her. Their weary faces were dirt-smudged and dark circles stained the flesh beneath their eyes; she wondered if she looked as weary, or as ill-used. A shadow lay across their path, and all of them stared at it warily. The Fangs of the Earth, twin whitestone pillars, towered over their heads from either side of the clearing. Disaster had already come, but even hollow-hearted and despairing, Gali could not see where further calamity would improve matters. She stared up at the Fangs of the Earth and shivered.

"This is where you were leading us?" she asked Mrestal, her voice accusing.

He nodded, and didn't meet her eyes. "Yes."

"We shouldn't be here," she said.

Mrestal stared at the Fangs with her. "The villagers are still after us." He dropped his pack just inside the clearing, and knelt beside it, rummaging. "Gali—" He turned to face her, put his hands on her shoulders, and stared into her eyes. She read fear in his face. "—it's bad enough we're tied to Terthal. But with Eryia dragging along with him, we have no choice. They might have let the three of us escape, glad to be rid of us, but not with her along. Her father will chase us into the jaws of hell to save face and keep his daughter from running off with an exiled thief."

Eryia glared at Mrestal and linked her arm through Terthal's. "I stay with my love." She flicked her ears back, and grimaced; her needle teeth gleamed in the sunlight.

Mrestal shrugged and gave Gali a disgusted look. "There, you see? For that, we must face death at the hands of the villagers."

Gali studied Eryia. Young and golden-eyed and fair, where Gali, Mrestal and Terthal were all dark-haired and ruddy, Eryia was obviously the daughter of great lords and highborn ladies. She had that legendary highborn stupidity, too, that would not see when it was condemning to death the very things it professed to love. So Eryia would stay with them—and her father and his many hunters would keep coming, and keep coming, and keep coming, until they got her back— and punished Terthal and probably Gali and Mrestal as well. And the only punishment which fit their crimes was death.

Gali had no choice in being where she was—Terthal was her half-brother, and worse, her pledge-kin; when he broke holy law trying to steal the Godheart, his sin became hers. Mrestal had a choice, but he loved Gali, and would not abandon her to share Terthal's fate alone.

Eryia, though—Gali glared at the other girl. Eryia was an idiot.

Mrestal removed a large green candle and several leather pouches of various sizes from his pack, and began emptying their contents onto the ground around him.

"Surely there is some other place we could hide," Gali protested. "The tales—"

"Are just that," Mrestal said. "Lies told to frighten the children into being good. No truer than the stories of the mehn who struck down the forests, or the tale of the Exile of the Folk. The Fangs are rock. They have a single secret, but I know it—and it isn't magic."

Mrestal lifted the candle in one hand, and used it to illuminate an enormous vermilion stone he held in the other. "There is power here—if you know where to look for it. But it isn't within the Fangs."

"Power? A rock and a candle give you greater magic than Vorstal and his hunters have to command, no doubt. And how will you use it?" Gali asked. "Will you strike down the entire village, oh mighty one?" Her voice sounded bitter even to her own ears.

Mrestal's face darkened with anger and embarrassment.

"It isn't that kind of power," he said. He paced off half the distance between the two stone pillars, then knelt and began digging in the dirt. It took him a few minutes, but eventually he gave an excited cry, and held up a flat disk of quarried slate bound around the edges by copper.

"This is the real secret of the Fangs. My grandfather left this here against some eventual need."

"Your grandfather?"

He frowned and turned his back to her. "Durkin Sdjado," he said.

Gali heard gasps from Terthal and Eryia—and, she realized, also from herself.

"Why have you never told me the mighty wizard Sdjado was your grandfather?"

"You never asked," Mrestal replied. "And I take no pleasure in the kinship—most people now think he was mad. It has never seemed either clever or profitable to claim the relationship."

Mrestal reached into another pouch and pulled out a small metal tripod with a wire net suspended beneath it. He placed the gemstone in this basket, lit the candle, and set the tripod over the flame.

He paused and in a soft, thoughtful voice, added, "If he really was a madman, of course, we're all going to die here."

He lowered the copper-banded stone ring over the tripod; it fit perfectly onto the tops of the three prongs. He brushed a bit of dirt from one side. The copper was badly tarnished, and in places eaten nearly away—Gali wondered if the stone ring could do what its maker had intended while in its current state. Mrestal seemed to have his doubts, too. He bit his lip and looked back over his shoulder—all four of them could hear dozens of angry men shouting to each other, their voices drawing nearer by the instant.

The candle flickered, illuminating the warm center of the gemstone.

Terthal said, "I don't think we should just sit here, waiting for them to catch us."

"No? Then by all means, run," Mrestal said. He glared at Gali's brother. "Losing you would be no loss."

The glow in the gem's heart spread outward; seemed suddenly to acquire a life of its own. The light swelled and coruscated, until it filled the entire clearing with a warm sphere of glowing crimson.

Gali looked beyond the edge of the clearing, beyond the pillars. The rolling hills around her, illuminated by the last glow of sunset, shimmered hazily, and new, ghostly shapes overlaid them, straight-edged cliffs that towered into the sky, marked off in neat, bewildering squares. A fountain began to tinkle, softly and steadily, where she sat. She could see the water leaping and dancing in front of her, but she couldn't touch it. It wasn't there—she could put her hand right through it without feeling any change . . . and yet it was there, too.

Strangest of all were two other pillars that sprang

into shadowy existence; they could have been twins of the Fangs of the Earth, except they were an ugly streaked black where the Fangs where white. The ghost pillars stood crosswise from the Fangs, so that they formed a perfect square around the clearing.

Mrestal watched, then sighed and sagged forward, relief marked clearly in every line of his body. "Now," he said, "we are safe."

He turned to Eryia, and gave her a smile more cutting than a thousand glares. "Your father and his men, if they enter here, will go right past us, blind as cavefish. Just don't move outside of the clearing."

"What have you done?" Gali asked, shivering. Between those ghostly, knife-edged cliffs, outside the clearing, monstrous things moved swiftly, growling and clamoring. Most of them paid no attention to the pillars, or the circle, but one dark shape stopped and stared for a long, terrible moment, either at her or through her. She froze, and willed it to go away. After a seeming eternity, it did.

Terthal looked at the ghost-shapes all around them, then back to Mrestal. "Just like that?" he asked. "You, who have trouble casting *fire—you* have protected us from the villagers?"

"It is not my work," Mrestal said. "I have only limited skill with my magic. This spell was something my grandfather discovered while he was experimenting here among the pillars, trying to learn what purpose they served. He told me about it—as a curiosity, perhaps, or possibly because he foresaw that I might someday need his spell. He called it his invisibility spell, and said it was damned worthless, because it only worked here." Mrestal shrugged. "So I brought us here, and I hoped."

Terthal snorted. "We're supposed to take your word that this spell of yours will protect us? Aside from the strange shadows it casts, it looks like nothing but red light to me." He turned to Gali and Eryia. "Are you going to trust in this?" he asked.

But the others were staring at Terthal, and beyond him.

Gali clapped her hand to her mouth to keep from screaming. Eryia's uncle and his foster son both passed through Terthal's body as though he were made of steam.

"It works," she whispered. "But not because we're invisible—" She wanted to scream, but she didn't. "We don't exist anymore. We're dead. Ghosts."

"Grandfather said the spell was unpleasant." Mrestal looked at his hands, then sighed. "We aren't dead, though. This spell only works as long as the candle burns. When that is gone we'll be dropped back into the reach of the real world—and if Eryia's family still remains, we'll be helpless against them."

Eryia laughed, and the sound of her laughter was sharp and brittle, devoid of real humor. "Pity your grandfather wasn't a better wizard," she said. "If this spell could work anywhere, Terthal could have used it to get the Godheart safely away, and none of us would be here."

Neither Gali nor Mrestal saw much humor in that, and although Terthal laughed, he turned away quickly and set about preparing his bedroll when no one else laughed with him.

There was an awkward moment of silence, then Gali spread out her own bedroll, and after a moment, Mrestal joined her in setting up their camp.

At intervals, the hunters passed like glowing spirits through the clearing, holding their lanterns aloft, sometimes moving right through the circle, passing between the stone pillars that marked the boundaries of the spell.

"They were here," one hunter said, kneeling among the four silent fugitives and pointing to tracks in the earth. "I can see how they arrived, but I cannot see how they left."

Another hunter snorted his disgust. "Simple and obvious, given a moment's thought. They walked backward in their tracks, then—though I wouldn't have thought any of them had the wit. They've found a way to double around us, I tell you, and are running for their lives back the way they came."

He stood up, through Eryia, and she whimpered and moved out of the way.

"I don't like this place," the first hunter said. "Perhaps they did turn back, but I see no doubled tracks, no missteps, no places where the heel of a footstep is dug in deeper than normal. I don't think they came back this way." He looked around him, and Gali could see that his eyes were white-rimmed. "I think the Fangs of the Earth swallowed them."

"Which would solve our problems." The first hunter looped his thumbs into his knife-belt and stared off into the distance. The massive ghost-monsters walked through him, babbling, but he was as unaware of them as they were of him. Gali watched the shapes meld and separate, and felt her stomach twist.

"Either way," the hunter added, "we've no need to stay around here. Let's follow the tracks back, and see if we can find a place where they branch off."

The hunters left, and the four exiles crouched together, eating a tiny, cold evening meal and sipping sparingly from their flasks. They were, Gali thought, a dismal lot. They all watched the candle, which had already burned through a quarter of its length.

"If it lasts until midday tomorrow," Mrestal said, "the last of the searchers may have given up. Since they think we have doubled back, and will likely assume we have made for the swamps, I think we should head for the next village, acquire provisions, then push west, into the mountains."

Terthal nodded his head in agreement. "I know a spot on the near side of the pass that is riddled with caverns," he said. "By the time they finish searching the swamps, we can be so thoroughly hidden that they'll never find us."

"For that matter, there are caverns around here," Mrestal said, "if we cared to hunt them out. This is poor land, though, and would make for uncertain survival in the long term."

"Whatever we decide for tomorrow, we should sleep now," Gali said quietly. "Whatever lies ahead will be a long and tiring ordeal."

The four of them bid each other quiet good nights, and glanced with worried eyes at the candle that burned beneath Mrestal's stone. Such a little candle, Gali thought. Such a small thing, to hold back a world and all the horrors in it.

Chapter Four

By the time Jim clocked out at noon, he had finished unpacking all the bargain books. His shoulders ached from slinging boxes. He was already tired, and that feeling of impending disaster, of the building storm, was back. He decided to hang around the mall, instead of going home and coming back at six.

He wandered down to Chick-Fil-A and got a sandwich, waffle fries, and a Mountain Dew for lunch, then headed for the center court, and sat down on the rim of the central fountain, right in front of the G. Galloway's, avoiding entirely the dreadful painted benches. Several of the birds that lived in the mall flitted between the tops of the browning trees. The fountain's tumbling waters murmured and chuckled, its voice a tranquil counterpoint to the insistent chirping of the birds. He lay his head back on the cool cement, and closed his eyes.

That simple act improved the mall's ambiance immensely. With his eyes closed, he couldn't see how awful the place looked—and once out of sight, it was out of mind, too. He rested contentedly, his stomach pleasantly full, his mind wonderfully blank.

He settled into a deep sleep.

Then something changed, and he jolted awake. The first thing he noticed was that the sky on the other side of the glass overhead was black.

Oh, God, I'm going to be late, he thought—and then he realized the mall was dark, too. Only the overhead fluorescents that were left on at night illuminated the central court—and everyone had gone home. He'd slept through the second half of his shift. He'd always dreaded the idea of doing something like that; now it had happened. He looked around, wondering how he was going to get out. And he wondered how everyone had managed to overlook him. The security people were supposed to notice obvious irregularities like tired employees sleeping on the edges of fountains.

Fountains . . .

The fountain beside him was making a funny noise.

It was still on—and that was weird. He was sure someone shut off the fountains at night, but if they missed this one, it might explain how they'd also overlooked him. But the noise he had noted wasn't just the regular fountain noise. Something wasn't right.

He watched the water. A shimmering curl of steam crawled along its surface, disturbed by the movement of the water itself. He realized the water in the fountain had begun to boil. The heat was stifling; several of the little mall sparrows had fallen into the water from their perches in the trees above. Now they floated next to him, motionless.

The bubbling grew fiercer. I ought to get out of here, he thought, but he didn't move.

A single red claw, tipped in black, reached slowly out of the fountain. It rested lightly on the ledge beside him—and two others crawled up over the edge and scraped the concrete next to it.

He supposed it was an indication of the creature's size that he thought of the talons as separate entities and not the fingers of a single hand, of a single creature. Not, at least, until the rest of the creature came up out of the water, splashing boiling water all around it. Those talons were attached to the thickest, most muscular forearm Jim had ever seen—and the arm was attached to a monster.

The beast shook its head vigorously, and spray shot across the mall in all directions. Steam rose from the monster's massive shoulders and broad, dagger-spined back as the fountain's waters evaporated from the heat of its body. Jim could have only described the expression on its face as a smile, though there existed nothing in that toothy visage that could be mistaken for friendliness.

Its teeth were huge—wicked, curved spikes, each as long as Jim's hand, and there were more of them than its mouth should have held.

Light from the overhead fluorescents glinted off the creature's hide—it was dun-brown and leathery, patterned in concentric circles with a hint of red and a flash of gold. Its markings and the shape of its head gave the creature the look of a large, furless cat—a bipedal, twelve foot tall, carnivorous hellcat.

Steam rising from the fountain obscured the creature's eyes. Jim fervently hoped this meant that the monster couldn't see him. He rolled off the side of the rim, slowly and silently, and flattened his body against the edge of the fountain, hoping the concrete lip hid him from view.

He lay there listening to the thunderous sound of his heartbeat; he panted and shivered, certain the noise of his breathing would lead the creature to him. The fountain kept up its bubbling, the heat stayed oppressive . . . but nothing else happened.

Maybe it didn't see me after all, he thought. He dared to hope. Perhaps he could crawl away and hide in a service corridor. Finally, Jim couldn't wait any longer. He had to know where the monster had gone. He peeked out from under the edge of the fountain. An enormous, glowing white eye, pupilless and indescribably malignant, stared back at him.

Jim made a strangled sound at the back of his throat and tried to become part of the wall.

The monster chuckled—or perhaps it was simply grinding the bones of its most recent victim between its teeth. Jim thought the noises would have been indistinguishable from one another.

He rolled to the side, jumped to his feet, and bolted, running as fast as he could to escape the beast. Then he looked over his shoulder, and the creature sprang, an impossible leap that stole away the lead Jim had gained in his mad dash. He looked back, and the thing leapt again, high into the air. He froze in terror, his heart pounding in his throat.

Jim, unable to move, stared helplessly at the monster—and the monster stared back, its open-mawed grin malicious and hungry. One of those enormous, clawed feet was going to land precisely where he was standing.

Jim yelled—

And woke himself up. God, what a nightmare.

Daymare. He sat bolt upright, his heart pounding. It was still daytime, thank heavens; sunlight poured through the skylights down onto the fountain . . . and him. That broiling sunshine was the source of the oppressive heat in his dream, he realized. The fountain made nothing but its usual noises. The water—was quite cool.

At first, groggy from sleep and dazed from the nightmare—it still seemed so real to him—he hadn't understood why people were staring at him, or why they were laughing; then he realized that he was sitting up with his left leg in the fountain. He lifted his foot and shook some of the water off. He was going to have to go home now, to change into a pair of pants that wasn't soaked down one side, and to put on dry shoes. He glanced at his watch, and grimaced. 4:30 P.M. already. He hadn't intended to fall asleep. Now he'd have to hurry, or he would be late.

He trotted through the mall toward the service entrance and his car, telling himself that people weren't staring at him or his soggy leg. People never noticed anyone but themselves—except these people all seemed to stare at his wet pants before turning away and grinning.

He couldn't believe he'd done such a damn stupid thing—sticking his leg in the fountain. He might as well have chunked his whole body in while he was at it. All over a stupid dream.

That dream, though . . .

He shivered despite the heat of the afternoon sun. That dream still left an edge of panic and a foul taste in the back of his throat; something more than the residue of sleep he knew from other, lesser nightmares. It felt real; even now that he was awake, that damned monster still hung on in his memory like someone he'd met and couldn't get rid of.

He usually dreamed in black and white; annoying textbook dreams about showing up at work naked, or going out with some strange, beautiful girl and having his tie fall into his soup. Now, it seemed that if he closed his eyes, the monster would still be there, waiting.

He hurried home, and slammed through the door into his dim, dingy, hot apartment. He was frustrated, and the sour stink of sweat clung to him—from the heat, from the drive home, (from the fear, his mind whispered). He didn't really have time for a shower, but he took a quick one anyway, then ran through the house scrambling for anything clean and dry and reasonably presentable. He had only two other pairs of work pants, and the ones that were clean—worn polyester Sans-A-Belt's, in a color that he thought of with distaste as dog-shit brown—matched neither of the clean button-down shirts he was able to find. He had his choice of pale blue or pale green, and chose the green—but then he couldn't find his only other tie and was stuck with the red one. It didn't match, but it was going to have to do.

He eyed his sweaters—with the tan crewneck on, he wouldn't have to have a tie, and his clothes would almost match. Of course, if he wore *that*, he'd melt into a pool of grease and teeth and hair three steps out of the apartment door. He eyed the red tie with dismay, and lifted up his collar and tied it in place. It wouldn't be the first time he'd gone into work looking like he'd dressed in the dark. He had been hoping to talk to Sharra, however—had even considered asking her out. He hated to go back looking so, well, frankly, so hopelessly bachelor-like when he talked to her.

He sighed, got ready to leave, and realized he didn't have his car keys. He ran back in, looked around frantically until he found them, and was already out the door when he patted his back pocket and remembered he'd left his wallet in the other pants. He hurried back in to get it, locked the door, and raced for the store as fast as the Nova would take him . . . which wasn't as fast as he needed.

He was late.

He walked into the store to find things in an uproar—continuing the mood of the day, he couldn't help but think. The power had gone out, and though it was back on, the computers weren't up yet, and Mrs. Talley, the nemesis of G. Galloway Books, had stopped in for a visit. The insane old woman came in once in a blue moon demanding new works by George Washington or General Robert E. Lee. Right now, she was railing at Ann because the store didn't carry a book her crystal-ball-wielding psychic told her would be on the shelves when she arrived. Jim hurried into the stockroom, signed in, then went out to relieve Ann.

"Excuse me, Mrs. Talley," he began, "but Ann has to go to dinner now. Is there something I can do for you?"

"There damn well ought to be something you can do for me, boy. You can start by firing that little snip of a girl," she shouted. Her heavily made-up face wrinkled into a dreadful scowl. "And then you can bring me the book I've traveled all this way to buy. I'm an old woman. I ought not have to put up with rudeness and nonsense and lies. I came in here to buy a book by none other than Frank-lin Del-ano Roos-evelt, boy. Sister Jeanne is privy to knowledge from beyond the grave, and she promised me he was putting out a book this month called *My Secrets to Power*, and I want that book!"

"Oh, Mrs. Talley," Jim said, keeping his voice even with the superficial calm he'd learned from years of dealing with screaming coaches and umpires, "I wish we could hook our ordering computer up to your psychic's crystal ball."

She glared at him. "Are you LAUGHING at me, BOY?!"

"No, ma'am," he told her with all the sincerity his heart could muster. "I would never laugh at you." He meant it, too. She pulled something like this every time she came to the store, and he didn't think it was the least bit funny. He'd like to tell her exactly what he thought of "Sister" Jeanne, the trailer psychic. If he thought for a moment she'd believe him when he told the poor old woman she was being fleeced by a con artist with a taste for eccentric old ladies, he would. Instead, he sighed and said, "I don't think we've ever heard of a single book your psychic has recommended, though."

"Then you aren't much of a bookstore, are you?"

"I guess not, ma'am."

Jim led her around, showed her the biography

section, pulled out a couple of different FDR books, then, when she showed no interest in those, aimed her in the direction of the latest Judith Krantz display, where she was sucked in by the solid wall of lurid purple covers. When she finally stomped out of the door, carrying only the Krantz, he leaned against the cash wrap for a moment and closed his eyes. On her way out the door, she'd still been screaming about the ineptitude of any store that couldn't keep up with titles by a major author like *Frank-lin Del-ano Rooooosevelt*.

After the moment he gave himself to steady his nerves, he took his place behind the cash wrap and smiled at the next woman in line. "I'm sorry we were delayed, folks," he said. "I'll try to get you through quickly."

Every customer in line gave him a sympathetic smile. They'd all seen the crazy old woman putting him through his paces, no doubt. It had happened before—sadly, it would happen again. Mrs. Talley was a fixture at G. Galloway—she only came in every three or four months, but her visits were always memorable.

Jim helped two customers he'd never seen before, then waited on Jennifer, one of his regulars. She handed him a copy of McCammon's *Boy's Life*, which he'd recommended to her the week before.

"You're gonna love this," Jim said. "It's the best book I've read in the last ten years."

"I hope so," Jennifer said. "You were right about *Death Qualified*, so I'm trusting you on this one."

She handed Jim her check. He flipped it over, stamped it on the back and said, "A check." He looked as stern as he could. "I need to see two IDs, a notarized birth certificate, a letter from your mom, a thumbprint, and a retina scan."

The customer behind her chuckled, and Jennifer

laughed. "Yeah, and Tuesday you asked me if I wanted fries with my order." She pulled out her driver's license and showed it to him. "It's the same as last time, and the time before that, and the time before that. Silly man."

"Not my idea. Chain policy." He wrote the information on her check and handed her license back.

She turned away from the register, and Jim, busy already with the next customer, wondered idly where Sharra was. She was fifteen minutes late getting back from her dinner break. When she did show up, she looked harried.

"Lines," she told him shortly when he made a polite inquiry about her absence. "Everywhere."

He nodded and gave her his best empathetic smile. "The mall is packed today."

"Some people have nothing better to do with their lives than shop." She put her bag down under the cash wrap and gave him a cold look. "I'll take the register now. You can go do—" she wrinkled her nose "—whatever it is you do." She made it sound like she suspected he mugged old ladies and kidnapped small children.

Jim sighed. So much for his best smile. Not much sense asking her out, either.

He thought about the spell book in the stockroom. It exercised a strange fascination over him. He didn't believe in magic—didn't believe in much of anything. But the book glowed brightly in his mind's eye; tempting, teasing . . . if ever there was a man who deserved a little magic . . .

Maybe I'll just try one of the little ones, he decided. One of the love spells.

He finished helping a customer on the phone, then let Sharra take over the register. He headed into the stockroom just long enough to look through the book, find a promising spell, and make a list of ingredients he'd need. He was pleased to find one spell that required nothing more than a candle, a bowl of water, and a handful of salt.

He went back out onto the floor, and shelved books and talked to customers until Ann came up to relieve him for a few minutes—then he ran to the McDaltey's Five and Dime right around the corner across from the tobacconists, and picked up his supplies. Less than five bucks total, and he'd gotten a big, fat candle, too. Love on the cheap, he thought with a sad smile.

He hurried back, stashed his paraphernalia, and shelved books again. Sooner than he would have thought possible, Jim glanced at his watch and realized it was already ten minutes until nine.

He went downstairs and turned off the overhead lights, then ran back upstairs to start clearing out the customers.

"Good evening, Kmart shoppers," he said, "our store is now closed. Anyone failing to make their purchases and exit the premises within the next ten minutes will be forced to stay and straighten the science fiction section with the rest of us."

Jim helped the last few customers upstairs find what they were looking for, then herded them down to the cash wrap and blocked the top of the stairs with the cart. He hurried down to help Sharra and Ann hustle the last few folks out of the store.

After they finished counting the money and closing down the registers, Jim walked Ann and Sharra out to their cars. "I want to get caught up on the bargain shipments before anything new comes in tomorrow," he said, turning back to the mall. The nice thing about that lie was that he was already done with the bargain shipments. When Sharra opened in the morning, she'd find everything he said he was going to do actually done. He added, "I'm tired of always being a hundred books behind. I'm going to work a couple more hours."

Back in the store, he locked the gate behind him and went into the stockroom. The book was down on Michael's shelf, in plain sight. He frowned—he was certain he'd put it back in his hiding place after he'd checked for ingredients. But maybe not. He looked at it closely. It was already open to the spell he'd chosen—"Simple Increase of Devotion."

Well, he'd obviously left it there. He was lucky that no one had seen it. That was awfully careless of him.

He studied the spell—the thick-and-thin script seemed to crawl across the page while he watched it, and the words blurred and swam.

Am I that tired? he wondered.

Maybe it was just the fluorescent lights. They sometimes made reading difficult, though usually only when the paper was bright white and the ink was dark black. Lukas Smalling had written his spells on creamy paper that had yellowed with time, and the ink, if it had ever been black, was black no more—the years had mellowed it to a rich, warm brown.

Jim sighed—he would manage to read the book, strange lighting or no. The longer he looked at his . . . no, not his, *the* grimoire, the more eager he became to give it a try. The rational part of his mind, the part that scoffed and turned up its nose at such superstitious nonsense, was firmly under the thumb of another part of him—a part he had never suspected existed.

With rising excitement, he stacked several boxes from the new Knopf shipment in the center of the floor. He looked at the loud green "New Release" sticker on each of the boxes, and read the title printed on the side. Ugh. It was P. J. Cletterman's new southern gothic, *Black River Secrets*, two twenty-five-copy boxes for the signing next week.

He sighed, and pulled out the red-and-white-checked cloth G. Galloway used on its card table when authors came to autograph. With his makeshift worktable suitably decorated, he brought out his bowl of water, poured a handful of salt out of the box, and set out his candle.

He carefully placed the book, open to the appropriate page, atop the stack of boxes. He lit the candle and ran to the corner to kill the lights.

In the flickering candlelight, the stockroom seemed a lot more . . . sinister. He suppressed a shudder, and took a long, steadying breath.

The spidery script crawled and twisted in front of his eyes—the majority of the spell wasn't in English, or any language he could even recognize, but for an instant he thought he understood the meaning of the foreign words he needed to say. In that brief moment, they didn't seem anything like a love spell. Then the feeling of familiarity faded, and the letters settled down on the page. He needed to hurry up. He didn't know if one candle burning would eventually set off the store smoke alarm—but he certainly didn't want to find out by alerting the fire department and mall security.

He read the entire page once, to familiarize himself with the text. He hoped he was just supposed to pronounce the parts that weren't in English phonetically. The fantasy stories he'd read in which the hero got himself in neck-deep shit for mispronouncing the name of an Elder God gave him a case of nerves that settled in on him like a bad toothache. But, nerves or no nerves, he wanted to try the spell.

His enthusiasm surprised him—at least, it surprised the skeptical part of him.

He read the introductory benediction. That was, mercifully, in English. Next came the main body of the spell.

He took a deep breath.

"KAL-IN-DO-nay! ME-shoo-MEH-mo!
  LUH-DEE-nag-GAY-lah, go-GAH-toe-mal-LOR-
  us!"

His skin crawled—without warning, he felt the air around him come alive. His pulse raced and his breath quickened. The spell was actually working; it was doing something.

The magic in the book was real.

Chapter Five

Gali woke suddenly, her heart pounding. She crawled out of her thin bedroll and stared into the red light that glowed all around them, and at the still ghost-cliffs, now empty of giant stalking monsters. Mrestal stirred beside her, and leaned on one elbow.

"What is it?" he asked.

"Something's wrong."

The red light from the gemstone flickered in a pattern that became increasingly regular. Gali, staring at the tripod, suddenly realized the white pillar directly in front of her was fading in and out of existence. She looked quickly at the black pillars to either side of her. Those were doing exactly the same thing—but when the white pillar became more solid-looking, the black pillars faded out, and as the black pillars returned, the white began to vanish.

Gali and Mrestal stood. Both Eryia and Terthal were also awake, and crawling out of their bedrolls to join them.

Eryia looked from face to face, eyes wide with fear. "What's happening?"

Gali gave her a furious look and snapped. "Do we look like we know?" Eryia flinched as though she'd been slapped, and Gali hung her head. "I'm sorry. I'm scared—I didn't mean to sound angry."

They all huddled together in fear, while two very

35

different worlds faded in and out around them. Their candle kept a safe sphere around them—but Gali wondered what good that little sphere of light and air would do if the world around them ceased to exist.

Then thunder crashed and shook the ground beneath Gali's feet. A brilliant white light flared—blinding light, but soon gone. Warm, sweet-scented air washed over her. Her sightless eyes reported swirls of rainbow colors that shimmered longer than the flash that blinded her. Then her vision returned, and for a moment she could see the warm, safe red glow of Mrestal's magical barrier . . . until their candle blew out, and they fell forward into the silence and the dark.

Chapter Six

As Jim said the first words of the spell, mist began to flow across the tablecloth. He froze. The enthusiastic, magic-seeking part of him was all in favor of continuing, but his rational self, which leaned toward self-preservation over experimentation, was lobbying like hell for a hasty retreat. He backed away from the table—

And the feeling of doom he'd felt earlier battered against him, fierce as Poe's raven croaking "nevermore." He knew nothing of magic, nothing of spells or what logic might exist to make them work, but he was certain, without knowing why, that leaving the spell unfinished would be in some way akin to punching a hole in a dam and then not plugging it shut.

The mist grew thicker. It crawled around his feet, and swirled to his knees, and, still rising, began to threaten to cover the book. Jim reluctantly started the second part of the spell. He scattered salt on the floor around him, then threw a pinch into the bowl of water, and intoned:

"FOR-SHORE-far-DO-may MY-to-mi-NO-mus;
gen-EE-gla-TO-gu-mus FAR-til-TRAN-ih-vay!"

The mist began to glow red. Sweat ran down his spine, and dripped from his forehead into his eyes. He thought he saw shapes in the flickering light—

ghostly pillars and rolling hills, and . . . something moving. He blinked to clear his eyes, but whatever he thought he'd seen had vanished. With grave misgivings, he chanted the last lines of the spell.

Nothing new happened. He breathed a sigh of relief, and read the English lines of completion, "My will is all will, my desire all desire—these things shall come to pass. So I will—so will it be!"

The air cracked around him, indoor thunder. The mist billowed up and swallowed him, clotting out the candlelight, blocking his eyes, his ears, filling his nose and mouth like damp cotton candy. The candle guttered out, and the instant it did, a brilliant disk of light erupted between Jim and his worktable, light that seared away all the mist in one blazing, blinding instant. Jim yelped and backed into a corner, as far away as he could get.

The light intensified, running through the colors of the spectrum and ending again in a pure, blinding white. At the base of the disk, Jim saw several tiny figures appear. They huddled on the floor; then the white light disappeared with a crack and the stink of ozone, leaving darkness. Jim's knees went weak, and he leaned against the shelving, breathing hard, waiting to see if something else was going to happen. A moment passed, and then another. The room remained silent and still and dark. Well, it wasn't precisely still— he heard something rustling in the Styrofoam peanuts scattered across the stockroom floor. Whatever it was hurried towards the stockroom's far corner. The thing that made the noise didn't come after him, though, and when he thought his legs would support him again, he felt his way quickly along the wall, and turned on the overhead lights.

He didn't know what he expected to see, but it bore no resemblance to what he found. The left half of the book boxes, his entire candle, and slightly more than half of the bowl had disappeared. The bowl was sliced off in a clean, perfectly straight line, as if someone with a Skil saw had sliced it in two . . . as if whoever it was had kept going when he hit the boxes full of books. And the books—

Jim shook his head, appalled by the scene in front of him. The books were destroyed, too. He pulled out a copy of P. J. Cletterman's southern gothic novel, *Black Water Secrets*. Something had bisected it, so that he was left with a triangular book that read:

P. J. Cletterm

Black

Wat

Se

The water moccasin on the cover was suddenly headless, too—which Jim considered an improvement. He didn't think much of P. J. Cletterman, who was big on pedophilia, incest, and infidelity—frequently all in a single chapter, and on at least one occasion, all in the same scene—and who, he suspected, was in need of psychiatric therapy . . . but Jim had a funny feeling, lousy books or not, that Knopf was going to raise its collective eyebrows when G. Galloway tried to return them.

As disturbing as the damaged book boxes were, they weren't the most worrisome thing Jim found. Where the other half of his makeshift table should have been, there was a pile of bluish, clay-rich dirt that took up space roughly equivalent to the missing box halves. He bent closer. A minuscule tripod sat in the dirt, with an extraordinarily tiny candle beneath it.

He bent down and picked up the tripod and the candle—and saw something he couldn't believe. All around the place where the tripod had been, there were miniature human footprints.

He stood and closed his eyes. No, there weren't,

he told himself. There were indentations that looked like miniature human footprints. They weren't, of course—they couldn't be. They were just indentations. He took slow, shuddery breaths and tried to calm himself down.

"Damn," he whispered. "Oh, damn." A huge pile of dirt, two expensive boxes of books destroyed, an awful mess in the stockroom . . . He rubbed his temples, pushed his glasses back into place, and ran his fingers through his hair. "I can kiss this job goodbye."

Then he straightened his shoulders and muttered, "No. Never apologize, never explain."

"Everything was just fine when I left," he told the walls. "I don't know what happened—and I'd be as interested in an explanation as anyone else would."

Most of that statement even had the benefit of being true.

He picked up the remaining half-bowl, the carton of Morton's Salt, and the grimoire—he didn't intend to have the police find any of *that*—and left the store as fast as he dared.

Chapter Seven

SATURDAY

Sharra woke from sweat-soaked, restless sleep, and bolted upright in her bed, shivering. Not even the heat of the room was sufficient to keep her warm against the old fear that had returned. "Spirits above and below protect me!" she whispered. She clutched the sheet and twisted it in her hands, and stared wildly around the room. "He's coming back."

The clock showed 12:40. She'd been asleep for no more than an hour, home for only two; in that length of time, somewhere nearby, one of *his* servants had figured out a way to open the gate that kept him safely imprisoned. She had hoped she would never feel that tug beneath her breastbone again, that fire that raced along her nerves and sang in her blood, that tingle of magic. *His* magic.

He would be coming for her soon. She closed her eyes, lost in her fear. She could never be safe again—sometime, anytime now, she would hear that familiar footstep behind her, or the jaunty whistling of an old tune, and she would be lost. He would possess her again, and once again, she would do whatever he wanted. When he vanished, he'd promised to come back for her—and she'd prayed to every god and devil whose name she could learn to make his words into lies.

He'd done a lot to her, but he'd never lied to her. She should have known that promise—that threat— was no lie either. He was free, or he soon would be.

Her nightmare.

Her master.

Her husband.

Chapter Eight

Gali fell—landed in the dirt—stood, lost her balance, fell again. She was suddenly lighter. She took a step and nearly launched herself into the air. Her eyes, adjusting to the darkness, showed her high cliff-shapes, not marked off in squares of black and white as those ghost-cliffs had been, and hundreds of caves and ledges where she and her companions could hide, if they could only reach them in time.

Mrestal, beside her, staggered and caught himself. "What's wrong with us?" he whispered.

"Well . . ." She frowned, and took a very careful, slow step. She didn't bound into the air this time, but actually stepped. "I feel lighter—almost as if I could fly if I tried."

"I almost did fly," Terthal said. "One step, and I popped into the air like a stone from a sling. And when I came down again . . . it was *slower*."

"Like floating," Eryia agreed. "It was rather amusing."

"It might be useful," Gali said. "Slow careful steps don't trip us or send us shooting into the air, but if we could leap without falling, we could reach those cliffs faster."

She took a deep breath, then jumped for the cliff as hard as she could. The results stunned her. She soared into the air like a bird, and shot up and up and still up before her path leveled out, then began to arc downward again. And when she landed, it was not on the ground but partway up the cliffs. Mrestal, stronger than she, sailed even higher, and ended up on the ledge above hers. Both Eryia and Terthal ran instead, but their running consisted of bounding leaps, a few instants of sailing through the air, then another moment of bounding near-flight.

They were not moving toward the cliffs, though— instead, they were charging toward a flat plain covered with thousands of carved white boulders.

Then the sun flashed on in the sky—nearer than her own sun, and whiter—

No. It was an artificial light of some sort, affixed to the top of the cavern far, far above.

No sooner had she recognized the light for what it was than she saw the creature that summoned it. It was one of the enormous demon-monsters that had haunted the world of black-and-white cliffs—but this was no ghostly presence. It was real—she could smell it, and hear it, and feel the world around her shiver when it walked.

The hills and the clearing were gone. The Fangs of the Earth, too, had disappeared. And that meant . . .

She grinned. That meant the hunters pursuing her were gone, too.

Impossible as it had seemed, she and her lover and her half-brother and the idiot girl he loved had escaped. They were free. They were going to live.

She frowned.

Maybe they were going to live. Some questions still remained—where were they . . . and what were they going to do next?

Chapter Nine

Jim couldn't sleep. Instead, he walked from one end of the tiny apartment to the other—back and forth and back and forth. He looked out the window at the beginning of each circuit, willing the darkness to end and the morning to come, as if by sheer force of will he could make the sun rise.

Once, Jim had loved the solitary pleasures of night, but darkness left him too many hours to think—and thought had become his enemy. He surrounded himself with friends when they were available, strangers when no friends were near . . . and when he was alone, he sought sleep as if it were a drug. Now, when he needed it desperately, sleep betrayed him, and left him at the mercy of his worst enemy. Himself.

Two o'clock in the morning, and the enemy was relentless.

Jim picked up the phone, then put it down. Who could he call at two in the morning—and if he could think of someone, could he hope that person might believe what he had to say? Magic. What sensible person could believe in magic? Even more ludicrous, that he had done magic? He didn't believe it himself, not deep in his bones; and yet he'd held the evidence in his hands.

He closed his eyes. There was one person he once could have called. Jim had had a best friend, once—

for years, in fact—the sort of best friend who had always stood by him; who created unassailable alibis so Jim's mother wouldn't find out about the stupider of his mistakes; who, only moderately talented himself, had thought Jim walked on water just because he could throw a baseball.

Willy Hadderand had been the sort of best friend a man could trust with his life.

Willy had come to see him in the hospital after the fight . . . after Jim knew the truth. Jim had been depressed—the doctors had let him know the arm was never going to be anything special again, that only through hard work and determination would he ever even *use* it again. Willy, worried, had tried to cheer him up, tried to reassure him that the world would go on without baseball. "You can do anything you want, Jim," he'd said. "This isn't the end of the world."

Jim would never forget his own words then. They'd been bitter, and vicious, and as soon as he said them, he would have given his life to have been able to take them back and leave them unuttered. "Easy for you to say," he'd snarled. "You never had a future to lose."

Willy's lips had thinned into a tight, bloodless line, and his nostrils had pinched in. The blood had drained out of his face, and he'd stood there, silent, for perhaps a minute—the longest and most horrible minute of Jim's life. Then he'd nodded once, sharply, and turned and stalked away. Jim had called after him—some inane apology—but Willy had kept walking, and he'd never looked back.

They hadn't spoken since, though early on, Jim had tried regularly to call. There had been, now, almost three years of silence.

I used to know the number, he thought. He still remembered it, but three years was a long time. It could easily have changed. He looked through the directory, down the short row of Hadderands. He located Hadderand, William J., III, thanked anyone who cared to listen that Willy hadn't moved out of town or gotten an unlisted number, and noted that the street address was different but the phone number wasn't. He picked up the phone again, and with shaking fingers punched it in.

The phone rang eleven times, and he let it ring. He would have let it ring a hundred if he had to. On the twelfth, however, a drowsy female voice said, "What?"

He almost hung up. Almost. Willy had been single and completely unattached three years ago. But things changed. He said, "I'm trying to reach William Hadderand. It's an emergency. Have I called the right number?" His voice shook when he said it, and he was sure he sounded insane, but the woman didn't even ask for identification.

She said, "Hang on. I'll get him." Her voice was soft and sexy—he hoped she was pretty. Willy deserved a pretty girl.

He waited a moment, listening to the rise and fall of urgent voices. Then Willy came on the line.

"Jesus, Norton, what happened? I thought she was doing okay!"

Norton? Then Jim remembered Willy had a brother named Norton. Evidently Jim had managed to call in the middle of some sort of family crisis, too. He said, "This-isn't-Norton-it's-Jim-please-don't-hang-up," so fast the words all ran together and came out sounding breathless and stupid and frightened. Well, that was fair enough. Jim was frightened.

There was a pause, as long as the one that day in the hospital room.

"Willy?" he croaked. "Are you there?"

Still no response, for long enough that he despaired, that his shoulders sagged and his eyes filled with tears and he started to hang up the phone. And then, "I'm here. What do you want?"

He stared at the ceiling and breathed a sigh of relief. He got another chance. Thank God he got another chance. "Something happened tonight . . . I didn't have anyone else to call. Willy, I'm sorry for what I said. You're my best friend—the only best friend I've ever had. Please forgive me."

"What do you want?" Willy's voice didn't sound angry, but didn't sound like he was willing to forgive and forget, either.

"Something really bad happened. I can't talk about it on the phone. Can you come over . . . please?"

"Now?" Willy's voice rose and quavered at the end of that single syllable. Jim had managed to shock him out of his anger. "My God, Jim, it's almost two-thirty in the morning! What kind of trouble are you in?"

"Bad trouble," Jim said softly.

Jim heard shuffling noises on the other end, a thump and a yelp—the sound, he would guess, of a man stubbing a toe on something—then Willy came back to the phone. "I'll be there in a minute. I just gotta get my pants on." Another thud. "And shoes. Where do you live?"

"Same place," Jim told him.

"Still?" A pause. "Damn. Okay. Give me—I guess ten minutes."

Jim hung up, then stared at the grimoire. The feeling of desperation left him the instant he hung up the phone; the book, as he stood there studying it, seemed no more ominous than his set of boxed Tolkiens or his Ellison collection in the corner. He was going to end up looking insane in front of Willy. The whole thing could have waited . . . it was no big deal. . . .

He picked up the phone and frantically redialed the number. The woman answered again.

"Is Willy still there?"

"No." If Willy's voice had mellowed toward the end of their conversation, his . . . wife's? . . . girlfriend's? . . .

had turned to ice. "He's already on his way to your place. He wouldn't say this, you creep, but I will. After what you did to him, and all the pain you caused him, you better not do anything to hurt him now. You understand me?"

Jim stared at the phone and winced. "Yeah. I understand."

"Why did you call again?"

Jim leaned against the wall and made up a probable lie. "I just wanted him to bring . . . something."

"I thought so." The voice grew colder. "I figured you were after . . . something." She gave the word a heavy, nasty emphasis. "He's bringing his checkbook. Creep." She hung up.

Jim sat in the chair and stared out the grimy, curtainless window at the street below. Willy had someone who loved him, and if the world were the sort of place it should have been, she would have liked Jim. She would have been a friend, too. Instead, she was an enemy—someone who rightly hated him because he'd hurt the man she loved.

He looked at the grimoire again. There was nothing in there to fix a broken friendship, or to repair a shattered past—but there might be something in it that he could use to prove to Willy he hadn't lost his mind, to earn back the trust that he'd once taken for granted. He turned out the light beside his chair and sat in darkness—listening to the faucet dripping in the bathroom, listening to the mice that rustled through his cereal boxes and trash.

He jumped when the car pulled up outside. He heard the door slam—a heavy door . . . no doubt some big American car. Willy had always preferred cars with some weight to them. It tended to keep them on the road better when he felt like taking a corner at speeds that defied gravity and physics.

The footsteps on the stairs proceeded cautiously,

with reason. The steep, rickety wooden stairway that led up to his apartment was unlighted. The rail was wobbly, several steps were almost rotted completely through, and the cracked concrete patio below made the possibility of falling a frightening one.

Jim turned his light back on and unlocked the deadbolt, the door lock, and the night chain. He opened the door before Willy had a chance to knock, and fixed his best attempt at a confident smile on his face. "Willy, thanks—" he said, and then Willy stepped into the light. Anything else Jim had thought to say died on his lips.

He wouldn't even have recognized his old friend if he'd run into him on the street. Willy wore an exe-. cutive haircut, and pleated gray wool pants with razor-sharp creases in them, a cream silk dress shirt—and what Jim had always called, at least to himself, an "execu-toned" body. The look came from time spent on Nautilus machines and tanning beds—it was a phony look that Jim had always associated with phony people, and would never have expected from his one-time best friend.

There was no hint that the person standing before him had just been roused out of bed at two-thirty in the morning, damned little even to indicate that this was a human and not a flawlessly dressed, carefully made-up department store mannequin. This new Willy was a far cry from the pony-tailed, skinny kid with the holes in his jeans who had stalked out of that hospital room.

Now, even more than before, he regretted asking Willy to come over. This was a stranger—and how could he ever explain to a stranger about magic, about the book he'd found, about the sense of doom that surrounded him?

Willy watched him with emotionless eyes. "Well? What's the emergency?"

Jim swallowed hard. "You've . . . uh . . . changed."

"Yes." Willy nodded stiffly. "Thanks to you." He stood just across the threshold, hands shoved into his pockets, waiting. Only the fact the Jim could hear Willy jingling change in his pocket betrayed the fact that Willy wasn't comfortable or calm either.

"Thanks to me?"

"You told me I'd never had a future—and when I thought about it, I realized you were right. I'd been satisfied being your friend, and watching you succeed . . . but I'd never thought about me. When I really considered what you said, I was determined to make you eat your words." He looked past Jim's shoulder, into the cruddy little room behind, and made a face. "From all appearances, life took care of that detail for me."

"I deserved that." Jim hung his head. "I should never have said what I said. And I should never have called you tonight, either. I didn't realize how . . . different . . . you were. I don't think you're going to be able to help me after all."

Willy snorted. "Ri-i-i-ight." He pulled his checkbook out of his pocket. "And how much money did you need?"

Jim's spine went rigid, and he felt the blood drain from his face. "None. I don't need any *money* at all." He started to close the door in Willy's face. "I'm sorry I got you out of bed—it was obviously a mistake on my part."

Willy jammed his foot in the door—he wore expensive slip-on shoes, too, Jim noted. They looked Italian. "Come on, Jim . . . you didn't know I was a stockbroker? That I've made a lot of money?"

"I didn't know and I didn't care. I don't think a . . . a stockbroker . . . will be able to help me at all."

"Karen was sure you just wanted money."

"Karen was wrong. I would have gotten a loan if I

needed cash," Jim said. "I need help. I should have known when you never returned my calls and never accepted my apology that I couldn't count on getting help from you." He tried to shove the door closed, but he used his right arm—not much strength in it— and Willy successfully shoved it back open.

He stood there, staring at Jim, "I'm sorry," Willy said, and for the first time, Jim saw someone he knew in the stranger's eyes. "I couldn't admit to you that you were right about me . . . and then it got too hard to call. I thought about it a lot, but the longer I waited, the more I just couldn't do it." Leaning against the door to keep it open, Willy asked, "Can I come in?"

Jim nodded, and slowly let go of the door.

Jim got both of them beers, and they sat at the rickety kitchen table. The book lay open on the table between them.

Willy picked it up, then frowned and flipped pages. He took a sip of his beer, flipped a few more pages, but slower, and finally closed the book and looked up at Jim. "Weird," he said.

Jim nodded. "It's what I called you about. It works."

Willy laughed and set his can on the table, but slowly stopped laughing as he realized Jim was serious. "I hope you're kidding. That isn't what you woke me up at two in the morning for—you're not *that* crazy."

Jim sighed, and tried to figure out how to word what he wanted to say so that Willy wouldn't think he'd gone nuts.

"I have this terrible feeling something is about to happen. Doom. The end of the world. Like that. And I tried a spell tonight in the bookstore . . . and something really bizarre happened." He set the tiny little tripod and candle in front of Willy and explained what he'd seen.

Willy wasn't laughing anymore. He glanced at the tiny artifacts, and said, "These are real cute, Jim . . .

but they sure aren't worth getting somebody up in the middle of the night over."

"When Sharra opens tomorrow and finds those books, she's going to call the police."

"Vandalism. Torn books and dirt on the floor. That is not a huge, terrifying mystery."

Jim needed Willy on his side. *If I did just a little spell,* he thought, *I could prove to him that this stuff is real . . . and scary. Then he'll understand why I need him to help me figure out what to do about the books, and what to do with the grimoire . . . and most of all, what to do about this feeling that the world is going to end—and it's all going to be my fault.*

He leafed through the grimoire's pages until he came across a spell for changing an object into gold. At least, he was pretty sure that was what the spell was supposed to do; the loopy writing, which hadn't bothered him too much when he was just glancing at it, had started to crawl and shimmy on the page again. But as best he could tell, page fifty-two promised to be a "Spell to Change Object Into Gold" and it didn't have any ingredient list at all. That, to him, was the clincher.

"Look," he said. "I'm going to show you what the book does."

"I thought you said it was dangerous."

"I did something wrong last time, and I picked too hard a spell. I'm going to do something easy this time."

He looked around the room, but didn't see any suitable object to transform. He settled on his almost-full beer can, because it was close. *Might as well drink my beer out of a gold can as an aluminum one,* he decided.

He set the can in front of him, and said, "Watch, okay?"

Willy shrugged, not amused, but at least a little curious.

Jim squinted, and started reading the spell. He did the English invocation, and then the magic words in the other language. As he read, the light over the kitchen table dimmed and flickered, and the room started to fill with fog.

Willy frowned, glanced under the table to see if Jim had something under there, looked back up, then stared over Jim's left shoulder and grew pale.

Unnerving reaction, Jim thought. He kept reading. He was almost to the end, when the beer can in front of him began to glow. Sweat trickled down the back of his neck, and the hair on his arms stood up. Magic didn't get any easier on the nerves with practice.

"Uh . . . Jim," Willy squeaked. He was still staring behind Jim's left shoulder, and his eyes were round and white-edged. "Jim, man . . . you've gotta stop!"

Willy was screwing up Jim's concentration. He stopped reading and frowned at his friend, and Willy scooted his chair back from the table. Jim noted sweat staining the silk shirt, saw the glazed expression on Willy's face.

"No," Willy said, in somebody else's voice. "Don't stop. Go right ahead."

He started to stand up, started to smile—but he was nothing like the person he'd been a moment before. His face didn't even look the same. The effect was so unnerving, so fearfully *real* that Jim forgot he was in the middle of a spell, and snapped, "Quit screwing around, Willy! You're distracting me!"

He heard a pop in the air right behind him, and Willy sat down again so quickly he looked like a marionette whose strings had just been cut. Jim finished the spell, and his can stopped glowing . . . and sat there, gleaming gold from pop top to base. He reached out to pick it up . . . and couldn't lift it.

The beer had turned into gold, too.

"Solid gold?" he whispered. He owned a tall-boy-sized lump of solid gold? "Wow," he murmured, and looked up at his friend again.

Willy looked like he was about to throw up. "Look . . . behind . . . you," he gasped. He was sitting in the chair, shaking, pale as a dead man, sweating bullets.

"Behind—?" Jim turned around—and screamed. A leathery cat-like face with fangs long as his hand and white, pupilless eyes grinned at him. The face was familiar—he'd seen it this afternoon. It was the face of his fear, the creature from his nightmare come to life.

"Haiiiiiiiiii!" he screamed, and scrambled backward, knocking over his chair and the table, dumping the book and the beer cans on the floor, and practically landing in Willy's lap.

Below, someone beat on Jim's floor with a broom handle and shouted, "Shaddup, y' moron, or I'll get out m' shotgun an' start shootin' holes in m' fuckin' ceilin'."

That horrible face leered at Jim, and the thing stood up straight . . . and kept standing—up, and up. Its head touched the ceiling, and it was still crouched over. Jim glanced down, stunned, hoping that perhaps it was floating. Its feet, though, rested on the ground.

"Oh my God." Jim backed up until the oven's door handle jabbed him in the rear end. He couldn't back any further . . . the door was next to the monster . . . and then the thing, whatever it was, grinned even more broadly, and started toward him. In the blink of an eye, Willy was backed into the corner with him.

"Why didn't you tell me what was happening?" Jim asked.

Willy shook his head, eyeing the approaching monster. "I tried, Jim. I tried. Didn't I tell you to stop?"

"Yeah. And then you told me not to stop. I thought you were screwing around."

"I never told you not to stop." Willy looked behind the two of them, and back to Jim. "There's no way out of here, is there?"

"If there were, I would be leading the retreat."

The monster stopped in front of the two of them, then reached out with a hand the size of a tennis racket, and dragged one claw through Willy from throat to pelvis.

Willy sagged against the stove, and Jim moaned.

The monster reached for Jim.

"Jim?" Willy wasn't dead yet, Jim thought.

The claw slipped into Jim's belly.

"Jim?"

Jim's mind circled and gibbered . . .

"It didn't hurt me, Jim," Willy's voice said, from somewhere far away.

. . . and Jim realized he felt neither pain nor pressure—that in fact he felt nothing at all but the cold metal of the stove jammed into his backside. He opened his eyes, and only then realized that he'd had them squeezed shut. The monster grinned in his face, its drool-dripping, tusk-lined smile big enough to swallow a basketball. The white-on-white-on-white eyes blinked, and the thing stood up straight. Its head disappeared through the ceiling.

The ceiling remained intact.

"It isn't real, is it?" Willy said softly. "You did this just to prove to me that the magic book worked."

"Uh, no," Jim said. "Not exactly. I turned my beer can into gold to prove that. I think all this proves is that I haven't learned how to do the magic right yet."

"I believe you." Willy straightened and very slowly reached a finger out to touch the monster's leathery leg. His hand went straight through it and out the other side. He pulled his hand back. "There's nothing there."

"Good." Jim pulled himself off the stove top and walked through the monster . . . and the thing whipped back down into a crouch and reached for him, talons ripping for his throat, fangs snapping over his head.

Jim howled and ran, and Willy followed him. The monster followed both of them.

"Outside," Jim yelled.

Willy followed; they clattered down the rickety stairs at full speed, without regard to their safety.

At the bottom of the stairs, they looked back. They could make out the portion of the monster that stood within the light of the house. The part outside the doorway was completely invisible, lost in the darkness.

Both of them stood panting on the concrete, staring up at the doorway. "It couldn't get us," Willy said at last.

"You hope." Jim couldn't get over the feeling that it was his cavalier stroll through the monster's body that had brought it back after him. He knew it hadn't ripped his head off so far—but it obviously wanted to badly. Jim's biggest problem was that he didn't know what sort of occurrence might permit the monster to get its wish.

Willy had evidently been thinking along those same lines, for he said, "You know . . . I don't think I'd use that book again if I were you."

Jim glanced at him sidelong. "Don't think so, huh?"

"Nope." Willy completely missed the sarcasm in his voice, for he continued, "That thing seemed solider when you first called it up or whatever you did to it. I'm sure it wasn't at all hazy, the way it is now."

Jim recalled the popping noise he'd heard behind him when he had first lost his concentration and said something other than the words of the spell. What if he'd gone all the way through it? Would the monster have ended up standing, solid and deadly real, in the middle of his kitchen? Would it have eaten him . . . and Willy, too? Jim certainly hadn't seen it when he was doing the spell. He would have kept going, straight through to the end. He'd been too busy watching the seductive glow of gold. Willy had seen the danger—

and had called out, before that bizarre little act he'd put on. If he hadn't, things might have ended quite differently. It seemed, as Jim stood there staring up at the white-eyed fiend that watched him from his home, that Willy might very possibly have saved his life.

Willy looked over at him and said, "Okay. So why don't you explain to me again about this problem of yours? I think I might not have been listening seriously enough the first time you told me."

Chapter Ten

The stockroom reeked of magic. Sharra stopped in the doorway, horrified by what she found. The taint was ancient, and evil . . . and worse, it was familiar. Two boxes of the latest Knopf release, special-ordered for an autographing, sat in the center of the aisle between the receiving table and the metal shelves of overstock; she could see that both boxes were badly damaged, and the damaged areas still glowed with the residue of the spell that had ripped them apart.

Dirt covered the floor—bluish dirt, covered with tiny impressions. She gnawed at the corner of her bottom lip and looked around to make sure she was alone; that was pointless, of course, because she was opening the store—no one would be in for at least another hour.

She knelt and studied the impressions in the dirt, then swore softly. She found boot tracks, thumb-print sized and unquestionably real. She'd seen such things before, long ago and in another place. Once the world had been overrun by the trouble-making, thieving miscreants who made those tracks, until some service-minded wizard had thrown them back to their own world and locked the gate behind them. *Ithnari*, she thought. The word meant "folk" in their language—but it should have meant "trouble."

In the years that followed their exile back to their

own world, the Ithnari had benefited from the forgetful nature of humans, and from a mixture of human wishful thinking and inexplicably good press. When the Ithnari inhabited Sharra's world, people knew them for what they were; they appeased the little vermin with gifts, and warded their houses against them, and wished them onto neighbors and enemies. The Ithnari had been gone long enough, though, that people had begun to think of the wee folk as "cute," and the bribes they extorted as payment for mythical good deeds. As though anyone could get honest work out of the tiny beasts.

Ithnari. Wee Folk. Elves. Sharra loathed them with a passion borne of bad experience and long memory.

They were back. She could feel them, hiding somewhere nearby. She wouldn't find them unless they wanted to be found; their limited magic was almost totally focused on the fine arts of hiding and stealing. If she could have, she would have fried them where they sat—they were abominable little rodents. An Ithnari had stolen the gold cabochon brooch her mother brought over from Caledonia when she sailed to America. The brooch had been the only thing Sharra had of her mother's.

She growled and snapped out of her reverie. The brooch was old, dead history, and the Ithnari, for all that Sharra hated them, were a minor problem. The trashed Knopf shipment, the clinging poison of that old magic, and the horrible feeling that her husband was somehow involved were the big issues.

If she left the books alone, the manager would call in the police. The police would certainly do a tiny bit of poking around—and she couldn't have that. Certain bits of her life would not bear close scrutiny, and they were bits that any idiot would stumble across in short order, if such a one came looking.

Which left her with the trashed books. She

rummaged through the top box until she came out
with one copy of *Black Water Secrets* that hadn't been
damaged by anything but the author's incompetence.
She closed her eyes, and put her hand against the cover
of the whole copy, and then touched it to each ruined
book, while she whispered an old spell—soft words
that built like tiny thunderheads in the enclosed space
of the stockroom, until her skin prickled with the
energy.

She linked the damaged books to the whole one,
so that, as long as they were in the store, they would
appear fine.

The spell was going to cause problems, of course.
People who would never think of touching obscure
Southern literary fiction were going to pick up the
books, because the magic that imbued them was going
to make them damned near irresistible. An unavoid-
able problem, that; people sensed magic and were
attracted to it. When the books went outside the range
of Sharra's little spell, they were going to lose the illusion of wholeness, and revert back to their damaged
state. She could imagine the trouble this was going
to cause in the days to come—but it was trouble that
couldn't possibly be linked to her.

She wished, briefly, that there was some way to
repair the books for real—such repair would elimi-
nate the possibility of uncomfortable questions—but
any creative change of an object's true form required
enormous energy and magical mastery, and she simply didn't have the skill or the power to do it.

As with everything else in life, she thought glumly,
destruction was easy, creation hard.

She put that single whole copy of the book on one
of the shelves, tucked in with other stock. Then she
unloaded all the other copies of *Black Water Secrets*
onto a stocking cart, and dragged the two damaged
boxes out to the dumpster in the back. She swept up

the floor, then went out and restocked the bestsellers, and put the money in the cash registers. She was straightening the magazines when Michael came in and pushed the gate back.

"Running a bit late, aren't you?" he commented. Usually she had everything ready when he came in.

She shrugged. "The, um, bestsellers were trashed."

He looked over at the neat pyramidal displays of the latest King and Koontz and Krantz novels—was there something magical about the letter K? she wondered—and said, "They look good now." Then he hurried to the upstairs stockroom to put away his lunch.

Sharra sighed, relieved. It had been close, but she'd made it. No signs of the bizarre disaster, no evidence that anything out of the ordinary had happened at all.

And that was the way she liked it.

Chapter Eleven

The elves spent the day sleeping and hiding, trying to keep from being discovered by the steady flow of giants that came in and out of the stone-floored room. As Gali watched them, she gradually pieced together a theory which made only too much sense. The giants must be the mehn of Ithnari legend, the fabled tall folk who were slow and stupid, sent by the gods to provide for the Folk and entertain them.

These didn't seem quite so slow or stupid, she thought, and they don't seem likely to offer much in the way of provision *or* entertainment. From her hiding place she'd tracked their movements during her watch, and noted with relief when they finally went away again.

When they were gone, Mrestal led the Ithnari out of their cavern hideout in search of food.

Gali had thought the giant's stone-floored room was huge—but it was the smallest and coziest place she found. Beyond it, the space opened out into an artificial cavern of unimaginable size. When her eyes adjusted to the scale of the place, she realized it was some form of library, and recognized the giant pillars and towers that lined the cliffs as books on shelves. She shook her head, stunned by this demonstration of the true size of the mehn.

Even in the giants' library, she could smell the

wonderful odors of food, but once she and the other three crawled beneath a metal rail, Mrestal murmured, "Oh, do you smell that?"

Gali did. It was indescribable, that wondrous scent—sweet and rich and slightly bitter at the same time, as intoxicating as summer beer.

All of the Ithnari circled, trying to pinpoint the source of the odor. Mrestal, the first to notice it, was also the first to locate it. He bounded across the gigantic passage to another cavern with a lower sky, a side room more like the giant's library than the soaring, impossibly high cliffs and towers of the tunnel that separated the two chambers.

They crawled beneath another of the metal railings, and stepped into this new hall, seeking the source of the wonderful smell. The room was overflowing with strange things, almost all of them wrapped and bundled so that the Ithnari couldn't tell what the packaging concealed.

"How can they live like this?" Eryia asked. "Everything is covered up, hidden under paper. How do they guess what to offer at market, when they can't see what they are bargaining for?"

Gali was about to answer that she couldn't understand it either, when Mrestal shouted to them.

"Over here!" he said. "I found it!"

They all ran to the sound of his voice, and found him lying on his back on one of the ledges between two of the high, metal cliffs. There was a pile of torn papers at the bottom of the canyon, directly beneath where he lay.

"This is what we smelled," he said. "And it *tastes* even better."

Gali jumped up beside him, and Eryia and Terthal were right behind her. Once she was on the ledge beside him, she could see that Mrestal was perched atop a large brown bench. It took her a moment to realize that it was the bench that was emitting the delicious aroma.

Mrestal reached beneath him with his belt knife, and carved a large splinter out of the substance he sat on. Inside, it was several different colors.

"Try this," he said. "It is truly wonderful."

Gali took the sliver from his hand and popped it into her mouth. An explosion of tastes filled her mouth; they were sweet, salty, rich and slightly bitter, all at the same time.

Mrestal gesture behind to him. Piles of the incredible stuff were ranked in neat rows behind him, wrapped in paper.

"This is more food than we could ever eat," he said. "I think we have found the Dreamlands."

"Oh, no," Gali said. "Not the Dreamlands. Even the Gods never ate this good."

Together they explored the wonders stacked on the different ledges. Gali sampled sweet breads studded with the bittersweet, gooey brown stuff they loved so well, and huge wheels of light, flaky daybread glazed in sugar; nuts, dried fruit, and staffs made of hardened sugar and painted in bright colors crowded the shelves.

Finally, Gali had eaten her fill. She sagged to the floor of the ledge, feeling full and content. She looked around her. The others, too, had stuffed themselves so full that they could barely move. They climbed slowly down the face of the cliff, stopping to rest a moment at each ledge. Not even Gali felt like jumping, and she'd eaten far less than the others. When they finally reached the floor of the chamber, they collected the packs they'd left on the ground.

"I'm thirsty," Terthal said.

"Just outside our library there was a fountain," Gali said. "We can go back."

She squeezed under the gate, and shouldered her

pack. Across the gleaming stone plain, another darkened doorway beckoned, filled with beautiful things that sparkled in the dim light. "I'm going to take a look," she yelled. "I'll catch up with you." She raced across and slipped beneath yet another metal barrier—this one tighter than the last, but not really a problem. Inside, she found enormous cases, the size of mountains, made of more glass than she had ever seen. The thought of so much glass, of what it must have cost, awed her—until she realized that the cases were full of gems—most of them bigger than any she'd ever seen before.

The white ones she considered boring, but she also found some glorious red stones, and a few green ones, and a huge blue one she fancied enormously. It was set in a crown of warm yellow gold, surrounded by more of those plain white stones. She frowned thoughtfully and leapt to the top of the counter. She could see locks on the backs of the cases—huge locks, with openings so large she would be able to slip her fingers right into the keyhole. She wondered if she'd be able to move the pins—then she wondered if she'd be able to reach the locks at all. Jumping up and down was all very nice, but without a ledge to land on, jumping wouldn't help her at all.

Ledge, she thought. I need a ledge.

She looked around in both directions. There was a ledge on wheels—bigger than a house, but just the right height for picking the lock . . . if she could move it.

Perhaps with the other three to help.

She bounced down from the top of the glass treasure case and ran to the gate. Her yells brought the other three in an instant, and in three blinks of an eye they had the rolling ledge lined up with the giant lock, and Gali discovered that she was, indeed, strong enough to move the pins. A moment later, they were trying on crowns—though most were unwearably small—and lovely gold-and-gemstone belts and wondering what anyone could possibly want with chains and ropes of silver or gold.

They loaded themselves down with treasure—Terthal rested a crown atop his head and tugged one up each leg to mid-calf, and Eryia, liking the look, copied it. Gali satisfied herself with the bluestone crown, which she braided into her hair to keep it from falling off until she found a way to re-size the headband, and a few colored-stone belts, wrapping each twice around her waist. They stuffed their packs full of treasure, too. The magic that brought them to this strange and wondrous place could send them back at any moment. But with the treasure they'd found, they could live like judges.

Eryia sighed and admired herself in a huge round mirror. "How can we stay here?" she asked. "I never want to go home again."

Mrestal nodded. "Me, either. The stories of the lands of mehns were false, but not for the reasons I ever suspected. They weren't grand enough."

Gali grinned slowly. "Perhaps there is a kernel of truth to the stories, though. Think of how, in the stories, Folk got the mehns to give them what they wanted."

The others tipped their heads and thought, and slowly, they smiled.

Gali ran her tongue along the needle points of her teeth. "We'll move in with the mehn that brought us here—we'll use the Old Ways to force it to do a magic that will keep us here," she said.

Mrestal laughed. "Ah, yes. Perhaps we can even force it to give us gifts, as the Folk of long ago were said to do with their mehns."

Gali leaned back on the padded surface of the ledge and closed her eyes. Mehns of old left out milk and bread, and a portion of the food from their table. They provided shelter for their Folk, food and clothing, jewels and other delights, and if they didn't, their Folk resorted to the Old Ways. Stealing, taunting, haunting, and cursing—the great loves of the Ithnari, and wonderful training tools for keeping one's mehn in line, from all accounts.

Gali smiled again. Long live the Old Ways.

She felt the earth beneath her shake, and lunged to her feet. "Listen." Mehns ran, their heavy footsteps making the world tremble as they charged nearer.

Mrestal glanced up, his expression worried. "You don't think they're coming here, do you?"

Gali looked at the lovely gemstones and beautiful belts they'd found and nodded. "Yes. I should have realized they would never leave a treasure house as unguarded as this place seemed to be. We've broken a silent warding."

"I sense no magic about this place at all," Terthal said. He sneered. "Aside from that mehn who brought us here, and the mehn this morning who spelled the books, I've sensed no magic about this place at all."

Gali hopped down from the cushioned ledge. "Perhaps if you're fortunate, Terthal, someday you'll learn that there are different kinds of magic. You sensed nothing when you tried to steal the Godheart, either. But you were caught then, too."

The mehns were close. They shouted at each other in voices that rattled glass.

Gali looked for a hiding place, and pressed herself flat into a depression in the wall closest to the huge metal gate. The others followed her lead—none too soon, for an instant later, the first of the mehn, a golden-haired female, peered in the gate. Two males charged up behind her. Gali could not get over how enormous they were, or how noisy. Or how blind. While she and her comrades huddled in the corner, almost in plain sight, the woman fumbled with the lock, slid the metal gate open, and walked right past the four of them. And the two males moved right behind her—looking left and right, but neither up nor down.

"Oh, God, look at this," the woman shouted. "Thieves have definitely been here. The back of the case—see, it's still open. And there are bare spots on that shelf—"

"They didn't take much," one of the males said. "Look at the stuff they left in the case they opened."

The woman crouched down. "God. There are two- and three-carat diamond rings on that shelf. I wonder what they did take."

The males leaned over the case and looked in. "What worries me is that whoever did it locked the gate behind himself. Makes it look like an inside job."

For a moment, all the mehns' backs were to the Ithnari. Gali ran around the door, flat out towards the library. Her companions stayed right behind her. They nearly flew across the broad, checkered plain—and when they reached their safe, dark shelf high above the ground and hidden in the dark, all of them burst out laughing.

"They never even came close to catching us!" Mrestal crowed.

Gali threw herself flat on the cold metal shelf and drummed her heels on its surface and laughed until she began to hiccup and little spots of light spun in front of her eyes. "The Dreamlands!" she howled. "It *is*—" *hic* "—the Dreamlands!"

Chapter Twelve

"It was amazing," Jim said. He shifted the phone to the other ear and sat in the doorway between the living room and the kitchen, facing the little window at the front of the apartment. "All the books were intact, no one said anything about the mess in the stockroom, nobody called the police—"

Willy sounded absolutely stunned by that—as stunned as Jim had felt when he first discovered what he couldn't help but consider "the miracle."

"I don't *know* how it happened. I looked at the books—they were fine. None missing, none damaged—I couldn't see any sign of the mess on the floor . . ." He reconsidered that, then frowned. "That isn't quite true. I just realized I saw some of that dirt swept under one of the shelves. Somebody cleaned up and—somehow—fixed things, but . . ." He frowned. "Sharra opened this morning. She's the only one who could have done it, but why would she have—and more importantly, how *could* she have?" He looked off into space, almost forgetting Willy on the phone.

The monster drifted near him, and tried to rip his insides out and, when that failed, to bite his head off. Jim shivered and closed his eyes. Damned thing. He completely missed what Willy said.

"What? Oh. Funny you should ask. It's still here." He glared at the nightmare beast, which had turned away and was sulking over in the corner next to the fridge. Then he looked down the hall to the nightstand beside his bed, and grinned. "There's a bright side to this, you know. The beer can is still here, too."

He laughed. "Yeah—that beer can is the first year of my college education." He listened, then started looking around for his car keys. "Tell you what. That sounds good, but instead of you coming over here, Willy, why don't I go over there? I could stand to get out of the house for a while...." He glanced at the monster again. Empty white eyes stared back at him, and the creature ran its rubbery purple tongue over the top row of its wicked, curved teeth. It looked hungry. "Great. I'll be right over. Where are you?"

He got the directions, finally managed to find his keys, and gave his live-in nightmare the finger before running out the door. As he pulled out, he heard his downstairs neighbors begin to scream, and before he could even get down the street, the whole family exploded out the door, still shrieking.

Jim winced. He suspected his neighbors would be packed and gone by the time he got home. He felt bad about that—it didn't seem fair that the thing he'd summoned up should go visiting people who had done nothing to deserve him. On the other hand, it was hard to regret that the jerk who pounded on Jim's floor with his broom handle and shouted profanities— and who frequently got drunk and screamed at his family at all hours of the day and night—would be gone.

The closer Jim got to Willy's place, the better he felt. It was good to be away from his troubles, if only for a while. He pulled into the driveway at the address Willy had given him, and was astonished to see how Willy's life had changed in just three years. His friend now lived in a good part of town, in a reno- vated Victorian with a manicured lawn.

Willy met Jim on the porch; he didn't invite Jim in right away—instead, he showed him around the perennial beds and vegetable garden he and Karen had put in. Willy named all the flowers, and frequently commented about one plant or another. "Karen especially likes dianthus varieties—" he said, "—because they always smell so nice," he said, and "Karen designed the border with the lavender and the rubrum lilies." He knew the long, technical names for most of them, and kept slipping into rapturous speeches about which plants did well together, and the beds they were going to put in next year in the backyard.

There was a moment of awkward silence as they came to the end of the garden tour.

Willy said, "Karen went out for the evening. I thought since she wasn't here, we could sit and talk—you know, just catch up. We sure didn't get much chance to do that last night."

"No, we didn't." Jim looked around wistfully. He was amazed by the homey domesticity of the place—if anyone had ever told him Willy would turn out to be a yard fanatic, Jim would have laughed in his face. He could remember when Willy's parents had to beg and bribe and threaten just to get him to mow the lawn. "I get the feeling Karen doesn't like me much."

Willy looked away, back over his yard and his house and his nice car—a relatively late-model BMW in rich gray—and sighed. "I had some hard things to say about you when she and I first got together. She didn't know me when my highest ambition in life was to own a complete set of *Spider-man*. She doesn't realize the ways you helped me—only the ways you hurt me. And she can't understand that I was wrong to just walk away like I did. She doesn't see cutting you off completely as having been the mistake it was."

"That's why she isn't here, isn't it?"

Willy stared at his feet. "That's why. She got mad

at me when I said you were coming over." He looked up at Jim and shrugged. "She'll come around eventually."

Jim followed him up the stairs and into the house. "I'd understand if she didn't. I was a lot more wrong than you were— Geez, Will, this place is great." He stopped in the doorway and stared.

Willy's smile was a bit sheepish. "Karen," he said.

Jim rolled his eyes. "I could have guessed. I remember your decorating scheme for your bedroom at your folks' house. Early American Trashdump." He walked around, admiring the glowing wood floors, the comfortable-looking furniture, the warm, inviting colors. The absent Karen was not big on knickknacks or ruffles—both definite points in her favor. Instead, she appeared to prefer furniture people could sit on and surfaces they could touch. He noticed a picture hanging above the couch and walked over for a closer look. It was a photo, Willy and an ordinary-looking girl with a good smile and straight, glossy brown hair cut shoulder-length, sitting together on a tree branch that hung out over a river. The two of them looked ridiculously happy. "That's her, huh?"

"Yep."

Jim glanced back to find Willy watching him with an expectant expression. "She's pretty," he said. "And she looks like a keeper to me. I think you're lucky to have such a nice wife."

Willy had looked pleased until Jim added that last comment. "We aren't married," he said. "I've asked her—a couple of times, actually. She—um. She had a bad experience. She says she doesn't want to get married yet."

Jim pursed his lips and studied his friend. Willy looked as unhappy about that fact as a human being could. "Is my being here going to cause trouble between you two?"

Willy settled into an armchair and propped one leg over its arm. "No." After a pause, he said, "Maybe. I guess." He closed his eyes and sighed, and leaned his head into the chair. "It shouldn't matter."

"Probably not, but I can see why it does. Maybe I ought to go."

"I love her, you know?" Willy didn't seem to have heard Jim. "There's never been anybody in my life before who made me think 'till death do us part' was a good idea." He leaned forward and picked up a wood pen that lay on the coffee table in front of him, and slid it through his fingers from end to end—again and again. "I want forever. But I want a chance to repair the mistakes I made, too. She needs to under-stand—to let me have the room I need to do that." He stared at the pen in his hands as if he didn't know how it got there, and put it down. He glanced up at Jim. "To answer your question, no, I don't think you should leave. I wish she'd stayed to meet you. Maybe she will next time."

Jim managed a weak smile. "It would be nice."

"Yeah." Willy slapped his hands on his thighs. "Enough of that. You try out the book again?"

Jim shook his head. "You've got to be kidding. My buddy, the ethereal creature from Hell, has been nib-bling on my head and ripping through my belly every time I turn around. I woke up this morning with him crouched on the bed on top of me, trying to rip my skull off with his bare hands. I don't know why he's a ghostly shape in my apartment and not a hot, toothy body breathing down my neck . . . but I don't want to find out it's because I've only used the book twice and it takes three times before he becomes completely real. You see what I'm saying?"

Willy sighed. "I guess so. Last night, using it again seemed like a bad idea, but now . . . well, now I'm not so sure. Think about it, Jim. It seems a shame—

you could have turned your kitchen table into gold, or your car or something. Kind of a pity all you got out of it was a gold beer can, especially when you still have the book."

Jim arched an eyebrow at him. "I look at it this way. I'm one gold beer can ahead—and I'm lucky the can was almost full. I could have tried the spell on an empty can . . . or a ball point pen."

He told Willy about the monster dropping in on the neighbors.

"That's terrible," Willy said, but he laughed.

Jim laughed with him. "Yeah, it is, but it couldn't have happened to nicer people. The husband is a drunk. The wife is this skinny little piece of trash who stomps around the neighborhood blaming other people's kids for the fights her snot-nosed rug rats start. Both of them yell 'lawyer' any time someone looks cross-eyed at them. We're talking slime-sucking pond scum." He imagined the monster dropping through the floor into the downstairs apartment, and suddenly a memory fell into place. "Willy . . . I didn't mention this last night but . . ."

"What?"

"I saw the monster once before. On Friday."

Willy looked impressed. "No shit? I've never seen anything like that in my life. Where did you see it?"

"You're going to think this is crazy, but it was in a dream I had at work. I fell asleep waiting for the second half of a split shift to start—and it attacked me by the fountain."

"Oh. A dream. So you didn't really see it."

Jim shook his head vehemently. "No, I really saw it. The monster in my dream was the monster in my house. It was the same creature—though I don't know how that can be."

Willy's smile was sickly. "I'll raise you one, Jim. I don't even *want* to know how that could be."

Chapter Thirteen

Sharra ran through every room, double-checking, making sure the house was locked—doors bolted, windows latched and pinned. Outside, darkness pooled in corners—hungry, watchful darkness. It swallowed normal night with malignant otherness, so that every whisper of breeze through trees was a whisper directed at her, threatening. Around each tree and shrub darker shadows lurked—and in them Sharra thought she made out shapes, the forms of men and monsters, the promise of long-staved-off but long-expected death.

She was being stupid, just stupid. The magic at the bookstore had not been directed at her. No one followed her. No one knew who or what she was. She was inside, safe, alone. The doors were solid oak, the window frames cored with metal. Her house—her old house—would keep her safe. She was frightened of nothing. She was reacting to the threat of a man long dead and gone, responding to her imagination's phantasms. Stupid.

She looked out into her yard, from the little pools of light the streetlamps threw into the broad and ugly stretches of featureless night, and as she looked, something ran across her back yard. Something small. Her skin crawled instinctively—but the reaction was absurd.

It was a cat, she thought. Or maybe a dog. Nothing more.

If she couldn't see out, she wouldn't see the movement; she wouldn't see the neighborhood pets on their way somewhere—and if she didn't see them, the cats and dogs couldn't frighten her. She lowered all her blinds and shut them, closed her curtains, turned on all the lights in every room. She hurried back and forth, and when she found a shadow, she banished it. She opened closet doors and aimed the light from lampshades inside, pulled up her bed's dust-ruffle, then sprawled on her stomach on the floor and, with her flashlight, checked each corner.

She threw open cupboard doors and checked under sinks; she looked behind the furniture. Back and forth through the house she hurried, trying to reassure herself that she was alone, that she was safe. Everywhere she looked, she found nothing. That should have been good enough, but the house was full of shadows. She didn't have enough lights to chase them all away—and she jumped at every creak the old house made, at every rattle or rumble from the world outside.

The grandfather clock in the hall ticked too loudly. She paced by it nervously, going from window to window and door to door, and at last, in exasperation she yanked the case door open and with a trembling hand stilled the pendulum.

There were shadows inside the clock case. With her pulse racing, she slammed the little door shut and hurried to the living room. It was bright in there—as bright as track lights and reading lamps could make it. Nevertheless, she turned on the television; some mindless sitcom came on—blaring noise, canned laughter, inane conversation that rolled out and filled her room. It was stupid . . . but the noise comforted her. She didn't look to see what show was on the television—the fact that human voices surrounded her was enough. She wasn't alone anymore, not with people talking and laughing and shouting at each other in her living room.

She took a deep breath, and smiled a shaky smile, and sat down in her rocking chair. She relaxed a little. There was nothing wrong, she told herself. Nothing after her. Everything was fine.

Fine.

Fine.

Fine.

Her thoughts kept time with the ticking of the grandfather clock in the hall.

Chapter Fourteen

SUNDAY

Gali slept nestled next to Mrestal, woke when he shifted restlessly. She felt magic again—at a distance, but flowing through something nearby. She'd been having a nightmare; she suspected the magic was responsible for it. The threads of magic wove cold and evil patterns through the night, warping and twisting the peaceful darkness.

She sat up, her pulse quickening, and woke Mrestal.

"By the Mighty Seven, that's foul," he whispered.

"And building," Gali said. "Getting ready to happen."

Mrestal sat up, pulled his legs to his chest and wrapped his arms around them. With his chin resting on his knees, he did a bit of magic of his own—a tiny little spell to trace the magic to its source.

Gali watched its progress with interest.

"I can't get past whatever is warping the spell to locate whoever is casting it," he said. "But the evil is easy enough to find."

Gali nodded. "The fountain."

"Not precisely. The fountain is nothing more than water. The source of the trouble is the two pillars in the center. You recall the pillars that appeared opposite the Fangs of the Earth when that first spell brought us here?"

"Yes."

"I would guess these are the same pillars. But where the power that flowed through the Fangs was, if not benevolent, at least neutral, the magic here is genuinely evil."

"Is the evil in the place, do you think?"

Mrestal said, "Possibly. Or possibly the evil is in whatever is trying to escape."

Chapter Fifteen

Jim's downstairs neighbors were gone, as he'd guessed they would be. The apartment directly behind his had been empty before. The one directly beneath that one had a light on, and a door propped open, and a truck backed up to the door. "Fred obviously went visiting while I was out," he muttered, and trudged up the rickety wooden steps. He was secretly pleased. The apartment building was thin-walled and crummy, but if three of the four apartments were empty, it really wouldn't matter.

Not that ol' Fred was a great roommate . . . but he did have some advantages Jim hadn't imagined when he'd accidentally summoned him up.

Of course, he had a couple of serious disadvantages, too.

Jim swallowed hard and opened his door. He halfway expected the monster to come charging at him from across the room—but it didn't. In fact, Jim didn't see Fred anywhere.

Maybe, he thought, the monster had moved itself down to an empty apartment. That would be nice. Jim walked back to the kitchen, turned on the light, and rummaged through the fridge for something to drink. He found a can of soda behind the Tabasco sauce, popped the top on it, locked up, turned off the lights, and ambled to the bedroom.

As his bedroom light came on, the monster rose up out of the floor, biting and clawing through Jim. When it tired of that, it leaned against his bedroom wall and watched him with those white eyes, and scratched itself, and laughed. Jim considered undressing—but he couldn't. He was going to have to sleep in his clothes.

The creature waited a moment longer, then crouched down until its face was level with his—and grinned at him, and mouthed something.

Jim frowned. It was trying to talk to him? He would have guessed speech to be far beyond its mental capacity. It mouthed the same pattern again. The damn thing was definitely trying to tell him something. The monster's mouth formed the same shape over and over, slowly and patiently. Jim had always been pretty decent at lip-reading, but humans didn't have huge tusks that interfered with the movement of their mouths.

It repeated its words again. Two words. No sound. Its tusks were right in the damned way.

He grabbed a handful of ball-point pens out of a water glass on the shelf above his bed and tucked two pens beneath his upper lip, pointing down, and two pens beneath his lower lip, pointing up. Then he imitated the movements of the monster's mouth.

Ill foo?

Ill you.

He got it suddenly, and stared at the monster, which he could not think of as Fred any longer. He felt his eyes grow wide. When they did, the monster gave him an ugly grin.

Kill you.

Jim's knees went weak. This was no mindless monster in his living room. It was intelligent, malignant. It had already gotten rid of the neighbors—Jim could expect no help. Now the beast watched him, with blank white eyes; hungry, patient eyes. Eyes that by their very lack of expression seemed to burn white-hot with anger, and hatred. The monster stared at Jim, waiting and watching, watching and waiting for the chance to kill.

To kill him—not just anyone, but *him*.

The monster had to go.

Chapter Sixteen

Sharra sealed the door with a drop of her own blood, pricked from her finger with a silver needle. The rest of her wards were already in place. In the workroom, safe behind doors of metal and walls of magic, neither Lukas nor his creatures could reach her . . . she hoped.

The grandfather clock tolled heavily, out in the hall. Tolled midnight—the empty hour. Funny how the sound of the television in the living room wasn't enough to cover the hollow, probing, throbbing sound of the gong. She closed her eyes and drew a long, shuddering breath, then forced her hands to unclench.

"Thinks he can get me," she whispered. "Thinks he can escape from hell, from death, from wherever he is and come back and win anyway." She dragged old, leather-bound notebooks out onto the worktable in the center of the room while she muttered, and rummaged on shelves for candlesticks and incense, for a knife and a silver rod, for a chalice and a small glass globe full of pale red powder. "Thinks he can make me die for him now—when, because of him, I've never been able to live."

She flipped through the pages of the largest of the books, pausing from time to time to study an entry. "No, Lukas. I don't know whether you're here, or whether you've only sent someone to watch me—but if you can hear me now, understand this—I don't care anymore. I haven't given up, and I'm not going to. You aren't going to get me. Not—hah! There it is!"

Her notes were very, very old, and the ink she'd written them in had faded in places. But the spell was as she'd remembered it. She'd figured it out shortly after Lukas had—vanished? She'd been sure he would be coming back any day, and she was going to be ready for him. It was a protection spell—more powerful than the wards she'd spun around her house, more secure than the shield she built around herself. The spell called a guardian. It could only work if Lukas really was returning; the spell was linked to the gate she'd pushed him through, the gate that had slammed shut behind him. If that rift between the worlds were still shut, her spell would do nothing.

The spell could not open the gate, but if it was already open, her guardian could pass through it.

If her spell worked, then the danger was real.

She could still hear the clock, ticking in the hallway. She had stopped that clock. The power that started it back up now hid in her house. She was in danger. She knew it. But this—this would prove the truth of the danger and end it at the same time.

"I've suffered long enough for you, Lukas. No more." She stared around the room defiantly. "You hear me, you bastard? You aren't going to win!"

The clock outside the room began to toll. She jumped, but it always tolled on the half-hour—a single, dreary *bong*. When it struck a second note, she wondered if perhaps she had lost track of the time because she had been working so hard. But then it tolled the third time, and her fingers clenched into fists—she'd not lost track of *that* much time. She counted the strokes, each one hammering its message into her soul.

"I'm . . .

. . . coming . . .

. . . back . . ."

She counted the strokes to ten . . . eleven . . . and then twelve, and closed her eyes, and felt the tears of anger and frustration pour down her cheeks.

The clock struck once more.

"Damn you, Lukas!" she hissed.

She started into the spell she'd created so long ago—the spell to summon a golene—and immediately she felt the snap of magic responding. She hated magic; she hated the way it twisted and coiled in her belly and the way it crawled through her mind, leaving a slimy trail in its wake that lingered for days. She hated touching it as she hated touching anything Lukas had touched, or feeling that she was following in his footsteps in any way. But along with the hatred, she also felt the thrill of handling raw power, the exhilaration of being in control on a deeper level than she could ever equal with anything else she did. She put her *self* into the spell, and felt the gate respond to her touch, and felt the many layers of reality shift and bend beneath her will.

Her creature stalked forward through cold mists and darkness, coming to her call. She could feel its ferocity and its strength and its loyalty. It was all she had hoped—a monster capable of withstanding the magical forces Lukas would surely bring to bear against her, and a creature that would fight for her, and die for her....

She sank deeper into the thrall of the magic. Her creature hurried nearer, growing and shifting as it approached the gate between the worlds, becoming more and more what she needed, bonding with her as it metamorphosed into the form she required, but keeping the special skills she needed.

It would look, to the unsuspecting, at least, like a

dog. The golene had been willing to mold itself to the shape she desired—and she'd done nothing to it that would decrease its effectiveness. It still had its knife-sharp retractable claws, along with an opposable thumb on each foreleg, hidden down in the tufts of fur. It had always had the ability to remain unseen unless it wanted to be seen—golenes, in their natural state, were capable of standing in the middle of crowds of their prey, completely unnoticed, until they picked out their targets. It was intelligent—more intelligent than any dog or wolf, probably more intelligent than any of the great apes. Not as smart as humans—but smart enough to make a formidable opponent.

"Yes," she whispered. "Come to me."

It reached the gate, and the fabric of reality shifted and parted, like curtains drawing apart, and the golene stepped partway through, into the powerpoint. So the gate was at least partially open. Sharra shivered, and for the briefest of instants, her concentration slipped.

It was then that Lukas struck. For one agonizing moment, other magic twisted through hers—evil that poisoned the careful neutrality of her own spell, and twisted the mind of the golene, shattering the bond of its carefully-crafted loyalty to her. Lukas's spell slashed across Sharra's mind, leaving searing pain in its wake. It ripped at the fabric of reality, and Lukas raced down the pathway of his spell toward her, clawed his way toward the open gate, toward his freedom, his hatred, his revenge.

Sharra had always considered the possibility that he might have some way of finding any point she opened between worlds, that he might be strong enough and fast enough to effect an escape. She knew he was a wizard, where she was nothing but a dabbler who'd been given good books and the time to practice. She had wasted neither the time nor the books, though;

she'd considered Lukas's likely moves, and prepared counters for them.

She picked up the silver rod and smashed open the little glass globe with it—the powder blew out in clouds and filled the air around her. Where it hit the flames of the candles it sparked. She felt the magic whither away from her, felt the gate shiver, snap closed, and harden—though it felt weaker than it had when she called the golene. Lukas had done it some damage, then, with his spell.

As bad, her golene was hers no more, and since it knew her and still shared some links with her, she must now count it an enemy instead of a friend. Another enemy—a deadly one. And it would start out near the powerpoint, since that was where it had been when she'd had to shatter her gate.

The powerpoint—the two pillars that sat on either side of the fountain in front of the G. Galloway—was going to become a very dangerous place for a while. She'd thought herself sensible to stay close to those pillars, to keep an eye on the magic they channeled and the gate they concealed . . . considering that her unlamented absent husband was trapped on the other side of them.

Sharra still remembered the day she'd rid herself of him. Lukas had locked her in her room, hadn't fed her in nearly six days. He'd thought her weak and nearly dead, and sought to finish the job, but she was suspicious. She spent those days resting and planning, marshaling her strength against him. She'd tricked him—pushed him unprepared into the gate. He was trapped on that side without his damned book—but then, somehow, the grimoire had disappeared. She now sensed the taint of its magic, though, and knew it had resurfaced. She even thought she knew where.

Jim Franklin looked enough like Lukas to make her stomach knot every time she saw him. He was bigger, and a lot healthier—and he didn't have the calculating look in his eye that she'd always seen in Lukas's. Still, the combination of his looks and his obvious interest in her were enough to frighten her. What frightened her even worse was the attraction she felt toward him. Every time she saw him, her breath came faster and her pulse raced. But she felt as though Lukas had reached out of his prison between the worlds and grabbed her by the throat.

Which, with every passing instant, he seemed more likely to do. She had no protector. Lukas could foul her spells. Her wards and shields were not preventing him from tampering with things in her home— even if he could not yet touch *her*, she was afraid it wouldn't be long until he found a way. He was closer. And with the golene released near the bookstore, her job of keeping an eye on the gate became harder.

She wondered what she had ever hoped to accomplish by watching it. Lukas was so much stronger than she that her odds of preventing his return were laughably small. She saw little point in trying—except that no one else in the world knew what he was, or what he was capable of . . . or what he intended.

She wished she weren't so alone.

Chapter Seventeen

The night had been a bad one for the Ithnari. Gali, all nerves and premonitions, had not slept at all. Early this morning, something had taken up a dreadful howling just outside the metal gate that closed off their home from the main corridor. After that, things had only gotten worse, and the other three had awakened as well.

Something was bashing itself against the metal grating that covered the door to their home, trying to get in. The four of them crept around corners and shelves until they managed to get a good look at the thing. Then they wished they hadn't.

It looked for all the world like one of the storybook dogs that populated the mythology books Gali had read as a child. It was covered with creamy golden fur that curled in soft waves from its long, floppy ears to its long, fluffy tail. Its eyes were soft and brown, its pink tongue lolled—Gali would have trusted the beast immediately. But it smelled like a hunter, and the same taint of evil magic that hung around the fountain clung to it as well.

"Hey!" One of the mehns who guarded the place at night ambled up to the creature. "Hey, fellah—did somebody lose you?"

The beast stood watching him, and Gali had a sick feeling that something terrible was going to happen.

She couldn't just stand there and watch. She charged out of her hiding place, screaming, "Run! Run!"

The man and the "dog" both stared at her for an instant—long enough that she could see the animal's soft brown eyes glow amber; long enough that she could see its lip curl up, exposing fangs half the length of her arm.

The man's response was different. He said, "What the—?" and walked toward the gate and her with a bewildered expression on his face. "Hey! You're wearing jewelry . . ."

He'd turned his back on the beast.

"Look out!" Gali shouted, and pointed at the dog.

It didn't matter. It probably wouldn't have mattered, no matter what she'd done. The creature attacked the man, who looked back too late to do anything but scream.

What happened next, Gali couldn't watch.

Chapter Eighteen

Jim floundered for the phone on the floor beside the bed, trying to find it without the inconvenience of opening his eyes first. His hand scrabbled over dirty clothes, books, more books . . . and finally, the phone.

He kept his eyes firmly shut and lifted the receiver. "Hello?"

"Jim . . . um . . . this is Michael . . . ah, Gilmore."

"Jesus, Michael, you sound awful." Jim rolled over and looked at his alarm clock. It was just past eight in the morning—a bit late for Michael to call if he needed Jim to open, but sometimes nasty bugs hit at inconvenient hours. Then he remembered it was Sunday. Eight o'clock was *really* early to call on a Sunday morning. "You need me to come in for you?"

"Uh . . . no. That's—oh, God, Jim. The mall isn't going to open today. Not at all."

Jim sat up in bed and rubbed his eyes. He couldn't imagine what could be big enough to convince the profit-minded ogres who managed Greentraile Mall to close for a day—one year they'd even tried to get all the stores to open on Thanksgiving Day.

"Really?" he asked, incredulous. "Why?"

"One of the morning crew found a night watchmen . . . in the shrubbery . . ."

Michael's voice trailed off, and Jim was afraid to ask. He didn't have to, though. Michael got his voice back and continued. "It was . . . brutal. The police are all over the mall, looking for evidence. They told us we should be able to open again . . . tomorrow . . . I guess." His voice was doubt-ridden. "They have a possible tie-in with a jewelry-store robbery that happened last night, too. The officer I talked to says he figures the watchman surprised the robber—but, my God, Jim, there was damn near nothing left of the guy. I can't imagine a robber doing . . . that."

"That's awful," Jim said, worried. "Go home and get some rest. If you want, I'll go in and open for you tomorrow—you were on the schedule, weren't you?"

"Yeah." He paused. "Thanks." Jim listened to the ragged breathing on the other end of the phone, and then Michael added, "I wish he hadn't been in front of the bookstore. If I hadn't gone in early to put together the Ingram order, I . . . I just wish I hadn't seen . . ."

"In front of the bookstore? I thought you said they found him in the shrubbery."

"They did. Most of him, anyway. In those plantings around the Phallic Fountain."

Jim hung up and flopped back on his pillow. Three words hung in Jim's mind. *Most of him*. They'd found *most* of the watchman. He thought about all the times he'd gone in early, or worked late—times he'd been alone except for whatever security was in the place . . . and that security was pretty thin. Terrible things could happen to people so fast, with no warning, and no reason. He hoped that Frank wasn't the watchman who'd been killed, and wished he had thought to ask Michael.

He suddenly realized he hadn't seen the nightmare monster since he woke up. He frowned—the thing had spent the better part of the night licking its lips and grinning at him, taking the occasional swipe at him and silently mouthing words Jim had decided he wasn't going to translate. He didn't know when he'd actually managed to drop off to sleep, but he hadn't enjoyed the process of getting there.

The more he thought about it, however, the more he did recall something. He didn't recall the time, but the monster had done something exceedingly strange in the middle of its vigil.

The memory crystallized—the monster had been glaring at him and drooling—same old shit, really, when it suddenly froze. Then its head snapped around and it lunged for the bedroom window, and stared out into the darkness for the longest time. Then, of course, it came back, and grinned at him, and leaned over to try to bite his head off—that had been just before Jim finally managed to fall asleep. Had the monster actually gone away then? That would be a wonderful state of affairs to wake up to in the morning.

His room was empty except for himself—the sort of change he could approve of—and sunlight crept through the blinds. He kicked off his sheets and reached for his glasses, then stumbled into the bathroom, bleary-eyed and aching. A couple of days without decent sleep started to hurt—and in spite of his stubborn refusal to let the insubstantial monster drive him from his apartment, he had to admit the thing scared him.

Then he found himself wondering if it might have gone to the mall.

He stood in the shower, letting the water pound on his back, convincing himself that the creature, even if it had gone someplace, couldn't have hurt anyone. It was no more dangerous than fog—if a lot uglier. He was feeling better by the time he got out of the shower, more awake, and free of the shadowy guilt that plagued him when he thought of the dead man in the mall.

At that moment, the thing lunged at him without

warning, charged at him through the shower curtain, emerging from the steam, claws out, tusked mouth agape. Jim jumped back, and the damned thing threw back its head and roared—only this time, Jim heard something when it did. Certainly not the full, ear-splitting roar he would bet it was capable of, but where it had been silent before, it was not now. The sound was hollow and tinny and far away—but not god-damned far enough away. And when its talons lashed through him, Jim felt . . . something. A change in air pressure, perhaps, or a sudden chill, or a tickle deep in his gut. Something.

Something, he thought, staring into its blank, evil eyes, was not good. Not good at all. He'd jumped back into the shower, shaking, which of course had been pointless because the thing had followed him in. It wasn't a very big shower, and with two of them in there, it was cozy enough to be positively obscene.

"Kill . . . you," the thing told him in its whispery ghost voice.

"Not if I get you first, buddy," Jim said, and walked into the monster, and through it. It took quite an effort of will, especially when he could actually feel its presence in the place where they both stood. But the creature seemed as discomfited by his walking through its body as Jim had been by all of its feints and sudden attacks, and Jim realized a little fact that had until that moment escaped his notice. The monster had only gone through him once—for all the times it had charged him, that time when it had come up through the floorboards, pretending to swallow him as it rose, had been the single time before this that their bodies had crossed.

It came out of the shower after him, and growled and slashed. Jim made a casual show of brushing his teeth, and backed straight through the thing as he did. He ignored the gooseflesh doing so gave him, and made sure he was standing as completely inside it as he could. The monster's expression changed from ferocity to a sort of queasiness, and without warning it backed through the wall and disappeared.

Well. That was nice for a change. Jim grinned at his reflection in the mirror, and started to shave.

As long as the monster didn't become any more solid than it currently was, Jim figured he'd found a nice, functional way to keep it in line. He smeared shaving cream on his face and began work on the right side of his neck.

He stopped partway through and raised a single eyebrow at himself. If the thing did become more substantial without him realizing it, of course, it was going to be a trick with a real short life.

The phone rang while he was patting his face dry, and he trotted into his bedroom—the closer of his two phones.

It was Willy.

"I just heard that your mall was going to be closed all day—the news about the guy who was killed there is all over the air," he told Jim. "The guy was named . . . hang on . . . I wrote it down just a minute ago . . . Shawn Sulma. You know him?"

Jim closed his eyes and tried to remember that name. He couldn't, and felt guilty for not knowing the dead guard, yet for being relieved that it wasn't Frank.

"Nope," he said. "I couldn't bet—but the name isn't familiar. Of course, I'm lousy at names, too."

"Yeah. I remember you asking girls out in high school and getting their names waa-a-ay wrong. You called Anne Parkes . . . Sylvia, I think. She wasn't all that happy with you."

"She never would go out with me after that. Of course, since she never went out with me before that, either, I don't know if that was the problem. She might have just hated me." He closed his eyes, remembering stupid old embarrassments as if they'd just happened, and added, "And thank you so much for bringing it up."

"People value old friendships precisely because it's only with old friends that they share a history." Willy chuckled. "Meaning they know each other's old jokes and can bullshit about things that drive their significant others crazy. Hey! Speaking of significant others—since you have the day off, and since it's the weekend, you want to get together? I'll bring Karen, and you bring whoever you're dating, and we can have a picnic or something. It will give Karen a chance to find out she likes you."

"I'm not sure about a picnic, but I'd love to get out of the house. My monster has started making noises, and I can sort of feel something where he's standing now."

There was a long silence on the other end of the phone. "Um . . . Jim," Willy said at last, "that sounds bad. Very bad. Did you do . . . you know . . . anything to . . . um, exacerbate the problem?"

Willy had suddenly switched into jargon. Jim wondered if Karen had just walked into the room where he was on the phone. Jim could understand why Willy wouldn't want to talk about Jim's monsters in front of her. "Is Karen in there?" he asked.

"Yeah," Willy said.

"Right. Well, about the monster—I didn't do anything," Jim said. "At least, I don't think I did. When I went to sleep last night, the thing was strictly a silent movie, and today it has sound and Sensurround. My new roommate has not been improved by these upgrades."

"Yow," his friend said thoughtfully. "I bet not. Tell you what. I want to come over and see the . . . upgrades . . . and maybe we can do the picnic thing afterwards. You think?"

Jim sighed. *Do the picnic thing.* He rolled his eyes and tried to pretend such yuppie words had not rolled out of the mouth of his old friend. As for the picnic itself . . . he didn't have anybody to ask out—except maybe Sharra. "I'll see what I can do on the 'picnic thing'—" he said, making sure his voice gave those last words special emphasis, "—but you check with Karen now to see if she's willing to have me over. As for you dropping by to see my visitor—sure. Come on. Maybe you can come up with an idea on how I can get rid of the damned thing. Like hold an exorcism or something."

Willy laughed, then covered the mouthpiece on his phone, and held an extended, muffled conversation with Karen; when he came back on the line, he said, "Karen said fine."

Jim thought that had been a mighty long conversation to boil down to fine, but he let it lie. "If she's sure—" He sighed. "Okay. I'll see if Sharra can come, then."

Jim hung up the phone and closed his eyes. Sharra was not the easiest person in the world to talk to at the very best of times. Every time she looked at him, her eyes filled with a "deer-caught-in-headlights" expression that unnerved Jim. She looked at him a lot, but when he tried to make jokes with her, she'd find an excuse to slip off and do something else—always a legitimate excuse, but he suspected if she wanted to, she could have found equally legitimate excuses for staying nearby. And she didn't.

He'd never actually asked her out—she'd never given him any reason to think she might accept. But he was sort of in a bind. It was bad enough that he didn't have much of a job compared to either Willy or Karen, who apparently was an up-and-coming junior executive for a branch office of a big corporation. It would be worse if he also didn't have anyone who was willing to be seen in public with him.

He'd memorized Sharra's home number one of the many times he promised himself he'd call her up. He always wanted to, but he'd never quite dared before. This time, his fingers dialed it while the rest of him made excuses. He shifted from foot to foot, and fidgeted, while the phone rang . . . and rang . . . and rang.

Six . . . seven . . .

He knew he ought to hang up. If she wasn't home, he couldn't make her come to the phone—

Eight . . .

—and if she was, it was pretty obvious that she didn't want to pick up . . .

And then she did pick up after all.

"He—" *sniff* "Hello?"

He heard another sniffle, and the quaver in her voice. His heart thudded heavily. "Sharra? It's Jim Franklin. Are you all right?"

sniff "Jim?" He felt the change in her voice instantly. She'd been crying—he would have bet anything she had—but as soon as she heard him on the line, an edge of wariness, even suspicion, overrode the sorrow.

God, that hurt. He'd never done *anything* to her. Not a thing. "It sounds like I've called you at a bad time," he said. "I'm sorry. I'll talk to you later."

"What did you want?" The wariness was still there, mingled with curiosity.

"It doesn't matter, Sharra," he said softly, all of a sudden certain that he didn't want to expose his hopes to her ridicule. "It really doesn't."

The sigh on the other end of the phone sounded ordinary enough—simple exasperation, and curiosity winning out over wariness. "You've never called me before, so it must have been something."

He didn't want to tell her, but in the clutch, he just couldn't think of an innocuous lie fast enough. "I just wanted to ask you if you'd like to go on a picnic with me and an old friend of mine and his girlfriend. It wasn't anything important."

The other end of the line became dead air for the longest time. Then he heard a wistful little voice say, "A picnic?"

His pulse raced. She actually sounded like she was considering it. "Sure. You know, tablecloth on the grass, tasty food in wicker hampers, a couple of bottles of nice wine . . . maybe even a game of volleyball after." He was reaching on that last, but it sounded good to him.

"I . . . really could stand to get out of the house . . . for a while," she told him. Some of the wariness was back in her voice, but she sounded just a bit hopeful to him, too.

"So could I," he said fervently. "And Willy is a great guy. I haven't met Karen," he said, "but I've seen what she did with their place. She's an amazing gardener."

Sharra laughed. "I think that's a plus in a person."

"It sure seemed like one to me." Jim took a slow, steadying breath. "Would you like to go then?"

There was another long stretch of silence from her end. Then, "Yes. I would."

"Willy and Karen wanted to leave about twelve. I'll pack things for both of us—"

"If you don't mind, I'd like to do that," she said.

He was startled. "Really?"

She chuckled. It was a sound he'd never heard from her in all the time he'd known her. He liked it. "That sounds like such a mundane activity. I think I'd enjoy it."

He wondered what about her life had been so odd that preparing a meal sounded like fun—but he didn't ask.

"Great," he said. "Then I'll pick you up around noon."

"Fine."

He paused. "Um, Sharra . . . where do you live?"

"You don't know?" This tidbit of information sounded like it left her stunned.

"Uh . . . no," he said. "Should I? You live in a famous local landmark or something?"

"No . . . I just supposed you *would* know, that's all." She gave him the directions to her house, and he realized, scribbling on the pad, that the wariness was no longer apparent when she talked to him.

He hung up wondering why in the world she would think he would know where she lived.

Chapter Nineteen

Sharra hung up the phone, leaned against the wall, and shoved her hands into the pockets of her jeans. How peculiar. Jim's timing was bizarre, certainly—if he were in some way tied to Lukas, as she had halfway suspected. If he were not, of course, then his timing was as obvious as the fact that he knew they would both have the day off.

"I would have bet my last dollar he knew where I lived, though," she muttered. He'd sounded so sincere when he said he didn't know, so surprised that she had expected him to.

The paranoia said Lukas had always been a marvelous dissembler; he'd sucked her into his web with his bashful ways—but the part of her that wanted to believe pointed out that there had always been an edge to Lukas, even when she'd first met him. A faint and enticing air of danger. She'd never felt anything like that around Jim.

She walked into the kitchen to begin putting together a picnic lunch for the two of them. She'd been deadly serious about getting out of her house for a while. She'd spent the night in the workroom. All night long the clock had struck thirteen every hour on the hour, but come morning, Lukas—or his creature, if such it was—had tired of the game. She had slept some, but not much, and had come out in the morning to hear the television blaring the news of the murder at the mall, and she'd been vigorously sick. Then she'd cried. She wouldn't take all the blame—it had been Lukas who'd twisted the golene into something other than the devoted protector she'd summoned.

But she couldn't overlook the fact that if she had not attempted to summon a protector, a man would not now be dead. She wanted to be away from her life and her fears for a while—and being with other people was the only safety she'd ever really known, illusory though she suspected that safety to be.

She had another motive, too. If she spent an afternoon in Jim's company, under the watchful eyes of two strangers, she might be able to discern any ties he had to Lukas, if they existed. And if he were innocent of that foul taint, which she found herself hoping that he was, perhaps she could discover that, too.

Chapter Twenty

Gali crouched at the top of the shelf, as close to the huge metal gate as she could manage, and watched the killer dog. It sat quietly, its tongue hanging out, its brown eyes gentle and happy, with its back pressed against another storefront, studying the mehns who were working around the dead one. The dog was out from underfoot, and it kept very still—and Gali knew the mehns didn't know it was there. She knew this because every time she glanced away from it to see what the mehns were doing, it vanished, and only the fact that she knew without doubt that it sat there allowed her to relocate its shape once her eyes had lost it. The mehns didn't know it existed, and didn't suspect they were being watched.

She wondered about telling them—but they didn't know she existed, either, and from the reaction the first dead mehn had to her, she wasn't sure she wanted them to.

For another thing, the dog seemed to have forgotten her presence. She didn't want to remind it, for if the beast were dangerous to the mehns, it was certainly a hundred times more dangerous to a creature her size. Since all it was doing was watching, she felt no obligation to reveal herself.

She closed her eyes and leaned back against a book. She was so tired—none of the Ithnari had managed to sleep after the horrible killing, and she didn't think she would be able to relax yet. But it felt so good just to close her eyes....

She woke to silence. The mehns were gone. So was the dog.

She sat up with a yelp, and heard a chuckle behind her. "You looked like you needed a nap, so I let you sleep."

"The dog!" she said.

"It was gone when I came out here. I suspect it left when the mehns opened doors to the outside and set it free."

She shivered and rubbed her arms nervously. "I hope so, but we can't know that. It can disappear, Mrestal. It could be anywhere, and we wouldn't even know until it galloped out of nowhere and swallowed us."

"What do you mean it can disappear?" He frowned and looked out onto the broad stone plain.

"I snuck back out here when the mehns came, and looked for it until I saw it—and I watched it until I fell asleep. Every time I looked away from it, I couldn't see it when I looked back—even though I knew it was there. I had to keep looking at the same spot until I could convince my mind that the creature really was there—and then I could make out the shape of it, and after that, I could actually see it. But it might as well have been invisible until that moment."

Mrestal paled.

"What's the matter?" Gali asked him.

"Terthal and Eryia went out looking for food. They wanted to see if they could find something more, well, lasting than that sweet stuff we ate yesterday."

"Then they're out there now?" Gali bounded down from the shelf and hurried to the gate. She looked out into the silent, cavernous passageways that ran for leagues in either direction. "Which way did they go?"

Mrestal joined her by the gate. "Off the way we hadn't been before, I believe."

"Do you think they'll be all right?"

"Well . . ." Mrestal bit his lip. "I'm sure they'll be cautious."

"Terthal? Eryia?" Gali wrinkled her nose and sighed. "I can't really see either of them being cautious. Or even sensible."

A breeze brushed her skin and, instinctively, she sniffed the air and cocked her ears, swiveling them after the movement.

"What?" Mrestal whispered.

"Didn't you feel that breeze? And the smell—ugh! Like swamp rot."

Mrestal shrugged and sniffed the air. "It's faint," he said at last.

"Excuse me, then. *Faint* swamp rot. That makes it better?"

Mrestal pinched her bottom and she elbowed him.

"Be serious, love. What if there's something out there?"

Mrestal slipped an arm around her. "You're tired and jumpy. This is a huge place—it's going to have drafts. And if you think about it, you'll recognize the smell; it's coming from the fountain. They didn't get all the blood up, and I'd almost bet they didn't find all the pieces, either. Carrion never smells good." He settled onto a book and tucked his knees up to his chin. "I can feel the magic from these Fangs of the Earth better now, too. It's stronger than it was—but that doesn't have anything to do with that dog-thing. Still, do you want to find some weapons and make sure Terthal and Eryia are safe?"

Gali tipped one ear forward and tilted her head to one side, staring at him. "Weapons? What would we do with them? That dog killed a mehn; it would get less than a good nibble from the two of us, and not have to work very hard to do it—and weapons would probably only make us taste better. Seasoning, as it were. If the dog is still out there, and if it comes after us, our only real hope will be flight." She sighed. "But yes, I do think we ought to go looking for my idiot brother and his truelove."

Mrestal sighed. "The sensible thing to do is just to wait until the two of them get back, then figure out a way for all of us to leave this place safely."

Gali nodded. "Yes. That's *sensible*. Unfortunately, I'm responsible for Terthal. He's family, and pledge-kin as well. By extension, that makes me responsible for Eryia, too, I suppose. So the sensible thing isn't going to be an option."

"If you're going looking for them, I'll go with you."

Gali wrapped her arms around her lover's neck. "And what, heart of mine, is sensible about that?"

He licked the inside of her ear with his rough, warm tongue and she giggled. "I'm the only one allowed to taste you," he said. "I have to make sure nothing else tries."

She ran her tongue lightly along the needle-like tips of her teeth and grinned. Behind the safety of the metal gate, she could still think of the land of mehns as the promised land. She could think of gemstones for the taking and cavernlike shelves with food stacked higher than her head. She could consider the possibility of love, especially love with Mrestal, whose clan didn't approve of her, and who had forbidden them to marry. It was so easy to drift into the bright and shining pictures of the future—and so easy to push away the grim, uncertain present.

"We ought to go." She looked out through the bars again. Somewhere in the distance, she heard high-pitched peals of laughter—Terthal and Eryia. So they weren't in trouble, after all.

Mrestal smiled. "Why don't we go see what those two idiots have found?"

Gali was still cautious enough to keep an eye on the surrounding terrain, an ear cocked, and her nose straining to catch any scent that might warn her of danger. But Eryia and Terthal—mostly Eryia—were making enough noise to rouse a city. A person listening to them would have doubted they'd ever so much as successfully stolen sweetmeats from their mother.

"And you wonder why he got caught," Mrestal said, shaking his head.

"Not really," Gali said. "But I didn't wonder before, either. Terthal spent his whole life wanting to have fun. I took after our mother and my father, and became both practical and skilled. He took after his father, though, and has no more sense than that poor man had."

They bounded along the checkered stone plain at a steady pace, slowing as they moved into areas of dappled shadow, cast by the sun through the trees. They stopped at the corner where one vast plain intersected with another, and peeked around it. Everything looked fine—and more importantly, it smelled fine, and Gali's tiny spell-casting detected no magical creatures at all ahead of them.

They kept following the racket their associates were making, and discovered Terthal and Eryia in a storefront filled from top to bottom with the most incredible and gruesome things. Gali's brother and his highborn lover had discovered the mechanism that caused two noisy, boxy contraptions to careen along a complex track. They rode atop the leading boxes as they wound around a bizarre miniature countryside complete with ugly, boxy buildings, crude representations of trees, and a convoluted series of tunnels and bridges. Both Terthal and Eryia had turned this into a clever sport, leaping into the air every time their metal steeds roared under the bridges, and landing atop them again as the contraptions rattled out the other side. It looked insane to

Gali—but then, everything in the store looked equally insane.

She strolled across the cloth-covered floor, liking the springy way it felt beneath her feet, and the way it prevented her footsteps from making any noise. But she found little else to like in her surroundings. Silent, still animals with garishly colored fur hung from the ceiling and lurked on shelves along the walls. Multitudes of stuffed lizards lined the floor, frozen in fierce postures. She found weapons displayed everywhere—giant bows and arrows and crossbows and knives and shields, as well as other weapons she would have guessed to be crossbows, too, from the triggers and grips, but which lacked any discernible method of firing their projectiles. She guessed the place to be part armory and part trophy room, and she wondered what sort of people would frequent such a place. The eyes of the beasts all around her seemed to follow her, and the sensation unnerved her.

Terthal yelled, "They're all . . . dead and stuffed! We checked first!"

And Eryia added, while careening around the tracks and leaping over bridges, "My father had trophies like those . . . in his hunting room! Not so big . . . but then, everything is bigger here anyway!"

Gali nodded, and wandered deeper into the cavern, past giant, brightly colored boxes and all sorts of little things with wheels—until she came around a corner, and discovered dozens . . . no, tens of dozens . . . of women her own height staring at her from behind clear little walls. All of them had lovely hair that curled down to their waists, and sometimes even to their feet—shining locks of gold or red or rich brown or silky black. They wore the glittering robes and gaudy jewels of royalty—though even from a distance, Gali could tell the jewels were of poor quality.

In an alien way, the women were rather pretty, Gali

thought—though they didn't seem to have enough jaw
to support any sort of decent teeth. Their faces wore
blank-eyed stares and stiff, false smiles, however, and they
were all tied down in painful-looking positions. She could
see no sign of breath or life in any of them. The few men
among them looked even worse. Gali yelped softly and
felt around for magic, but could find no sign of it.

"Mrestal!" she shouted.

Mrestal joined her at a run—and slammed to a stop
when he caught a look at what she'd discovered. "Oh,"
he whispered. "By Togmire's Horns! What sort of trophies are they? They look dead, don't they? Do you
suppose the mehns stuffed them?"

"Or dried them."

Mrestal shivered. "Or starved them. Look how skinny
they are."

Gali nodded slowly. "Or froze them inside those horrible pink coffins. Maybe the coffins use some sort
of magic I can't detect. See the wizard's runes and
sigils scrawled across them?" She pointed to the broad
white slashes and swirls that marked the outside of
each coffin.

"If we can get them out and break the spell, they
might survive. Otherwise why would the wizards have
tied them down?" She jumped onto a shelf and inched
forward, holding her breath, afraid something would
suddenly grab her and imprison her as well. "Perhaps
we could set them free."

Mrestal nodded, and whistled shrilly to the other
two Ithnari.

The noise of the contraption wound down and died,
and Terthal and Eryia trotted around the corner, questioning expressions on their faces. But their uncertainty
became horror; golden-haired Eryia saw the rows upon
rows of captive golden-haired women and screamed.
Terthal's eyes went round, and he staggered back a
half step.

"We're liberating them," Gali said.

Terthal nodded grimly. Eryia, her hands clasped to her throat, was frozen in place, her expression almost as stiff as that worn by the unfortunate women. "Oh, how *could* they?" she whispered.

While she stayed on the ground, Terthal joined Mrestal and Gali on the first shelf. The three Ithnari crept cautiously to the nearest coffin, drew knifes and ripped into the clear stuff that served as the casket's lid—Gali was astonished at how easily it tore. And the coffin was flimsy, too—increasing her certainty that the women were trapped by some arcane form of magic. But then she came to the first of the captive's bonds, and began to revise her opinion. The woman had been strapped in place with heavy strips of metal coated with a soft, brightly colored material. Gali suspected the captors had applied the coating to prevent their prisoner from bruising. The fiends had been thorough, too—straps bound the woman's ankles, her waist, her wrists . . . and even her neck.

Gali imagined herself in the stranger's place and was sick over the side of the shelf. After the worst of the sickness passed, she pressed her cheek against the cool metal of the ledge, and tried to prepare herself to deal with the horrors that awaited.

She looked up as she felt the first wash of a magical healing spell, to discover Mrestal attempting to revive the woman.

Terthal walked over and crouched next to her while Mrestal tried all his healing magics. "What sort of monsters could *do* this to people?" he wondered softly.

Gali didn't know. She simply couldn't imagine.

Then she saw something that made her lightheaded. "Oh, no! Look," she gasped, and pointed to the woman's neck. "They've slit her throat."

Mrestal stopped his spellcasting and looked closer. "They've done worse than that," he whispered.

"They've cut her whole head off, then stuck it back on again."

Gali looked from one man to the other, and angry tears began to roll down her cheeks. She got up and walked from coffin to coffin, checking for scars. "Every one of them, Terthal. They've sacrificed every one of them in the same terrible way."

Terthal shook his head. "There's no hope, then."

Eryia, below, had been listening. At Terthal's verdict, she dropped to the floor and began to sob.

"We can't leave them here like this." Gali was shaken. The horror she'd witnessed the night before seemed nothing compared to this perverted wholesale massacre. "The monsters that take pleasure from looking at these poor creatures and thinking of their suffering cannot be permitted to just . . . just keep them . . . and . . . and *display* them this way."

Mrestal looked pale and fierce. Sweat beaded on his forehead, but his jaw jutted and his voice was firm. "Yes," he said. "We have to do something."

Gali put her hands on her hips and said, "We can build a funeral pyre and send their souls on to the gods as they deserve."

Terthal said, "But their gods aren't our gods."

Gali cocked her head at him and raised her eyebrows. "We don't know who their gods are—and they can't tell us. Any gods are better than none, I think." She wiped tears from her cheeks with an angry swipe of the back of her hand and said, "I'd prefer the gods of strangers to the wizards who killed me."

Mrestal had begun shoving coffins over the side—and Eryia, to Gali's amazement, had quit shuddering and was dragging them to a clear spot in the floor and starting to build a pyre.

Mrestal helped Gali hand down the body of the woman they'd removed from her coffin—the corpse was slick and cold, and while the skin of her legs and face still felt fairly normal, her arms and her upper torso had become as hard as armor. Gali felt sick touching the pitiful corpse, but she forced herself to; the atrocities that had been visited on the poor woman's corpse were no fault of her own. Gali shoved the coffins down, too—they were horribly light, which lent credence to Mrestal's starvation theory. Terthal jumped off the shelf and carried the single loose body to the pyre—Eryia didn't want to touch the dead woman, and in all honesty, Gali couldn't blame her. Then he helped his love carry and stack the hideous pink coffins.

Gali cleared until her back ached, climbed up a level, and found even more horror waiting. "Oh, Mrestal," she screamed. "They have children up here!"

The place was a charnel house—atrocities stacked on atrocities. Grimly she set in, throwing the children's coffins down, too. Never in her life had she imagined herself capable of such courage; never would she have thought she had it in her to be an avenger, a bringer of justice.

But looking at the nightmarish stack of poor frozen women and girls and men, she thought, I can be brave. I can be fierce. And if I ever discover the perverted monster who did all of this, I'll find a way to get revenge for all these people. Somehow.

Then they were at the end of it. All the victims in their pink coffins waited in a giant pyre on the floor. More nightmares lurked further down the shelves, but Gali was exhausted, and her three fellow liberators were no better.

"What about the bigger ones?" Eryia asked, pointing to more corpses on shelves at the end of the aisle.

"We'll make our stand with these tonight," Gali said. "Maybe it will frighten whoever did this enough that they will cease their evil. And if not . . ." She pursed her lips and frowned. "We'll come back for the rest of them."

All four Ithnari joined on the ground and stood together, well back from the piled boxes. Mrestal closed his eyes, and did the little magic that lit the spark—and the coffins began to burn. Smoke curled around them, and tongues of flame engulfed the mountain of bodies. Gali began to pray loudly, a request for her gods to welcome these strangers, alien though they were, into the Ithnari Dreamlands. Terthal joined her in her prayer, and Eryia began a song to comfort the spirits of the dead. The flames licked higher, and smoke rolled out. Then the ground underneath the pyre began to burn. Gali looked at the springy stuff under her feet and nervously began backing up. Mrestal still had his eyes closed, concentrating on the fire—but suddenly it seemed to be going quite well enough without further help from him. Gali grabbed his arm and dragged him back, and as soon as she did, he opened his eyes and saw their danger.

The fire began to spread outside the ring of the pyre. Other things caught, and more smoke billowed—and suddenly a thousand demons began to scream overhead, and rain poured from the roof of the perverted temple to the mehn god of the dead.

"Get out!" Mrestal shouted.

All four of them ran for the metal gate.

And stopped.

The dog sat just outside, on the cool safe surface of the stone plain, watching them—a wide grin on its face, its tail wagging gently.

Chapter Twenty-one

"Hey! Willy! C'mon in." Jim was digging through two bags of clean but unfolded laundry, trying to find an appropriate shirt and a pair of jeans that weren't too tight or too scruffy, and any two socks that matched.

Willy paused before he walked in—considering that the monster was lurking right by the door, waiting, Jim could understand Willy's reluctance—but he came in anyway, ducking just out of reach as the creature swiped at him.

"No," Jim said. "Don't duck. If he knows you're afraid of him, he'll keep coming after you."

Which, in fact, the creature did. It slashed out again, and this time its claws went right through Willy's belly.

"I *am* afraid of him," Willy said. His eyes widened as the monster crouched down to eye level and told him, "Kill you," in its washed-out voice.

Jim shook his head vigorously. "Watch." He stepped toward the monster, who saw him coming and nervously backed up a step.

"He's backing away from *you*?"

"You bet. Through you, buddy," Jim snarled. He charged, and managed to slide right into the monster's incorporeal middle. The monster shrieked—a tissue-paper whisper that still grated along his nerves—and vanished through the floorboards. "See?" he asked.

Willy looked green. "That's disgusting."

"It works. And it's better than having the damned thing trying to chew my head off all the time."

"I can see that," Willy said. "I guess. I still think you ought to figure out which spell in that book of yours would get rid of him, and use it. Where did ol' ugly go, by the way?"

Jim shrugged. "Downstairs, probably. Doesn't matter. All the other places are empty now."

Willy settled into one of the chairs that wasn't too rickety, checking first, Jim noted, to make sure he wasn't going to get anything on his pants. "All of them? I'll bet your landlady is thrilled. I suspect keeping a monster in your apartment is in violation of your lease."

Jim laughed. "Yeah, but you'd be amazed at how it improves the neighborhood."

Willy grinned, but then his expression became serious again. "It worries me that he seems to be getting more real, Jim. You're dealing with having him around right now, but what happens if one of these days you wake up and he's solid and pissed and hungry?"

Jim cracked his knuckles and stared off into space. "To be honest with you, I'm about ready to pack my bags and join my ex-neighbors anyway. I don't dare try another spell. I keep doing them wrong. Both times I've tried something I thought was simple, and both times, something terrible has happened." He looked over at the tiny tripod sitting next to his phone and frowned. "I still haven't figured out what I've done— but until I figure out where I'm going wrong, I don't intend to take a chance on any more magic."

Willy sighed and stuck his hands into his pockets. "You've done things right, too. I mean, come on . . . a solid gold beer can—that sucker would sell for enough to buy you out of this dump forever. Have you had anyone appraise it for you yet?"

Jim frowned. "I didn't get a solid gold beer can. I

got a solid gold beer can *and* a monster in my house. Personally, I consider that rather an important distinction. When I did the spell to make Sharra like me more, I vaporized half a Knopf shipment . . . and had something appear out of the middle of thin air—rats, or maybe mice . . ." His mind reminded him of the very human little footprints he'd found in the dirt, and he closed his eyes and leaned back in his chair.

"Well, yeah. You've definitely made some mistakes. But hey—Sharra's going out with you, isn't she?"

Jim's eyes snapped open. All the pleasure he'd taken from the moment when she agreed to go out with him dissipated like fog on a hell-hot day. She had accepted his invitation to the picnic; what if she'd only done it because of that damned spell? What if it wasn't because she wanted to spend an afternoon with him at all? He'd tarnished their date for himself because he could no longer be sure of her reasons for accepting.

He considered canceling. "Dammit," he muttered. He pulled his glasses off and cleaned the lenses on his shirttail while he thought. No, he wouldn't stand her up. There was at least a chance her going out with him had nothing to do with his stupid magic spell. If he got a chance to talk with her alone, he'd come clean—confess what he'd tried to do. Besides, he really did want to know how she'd managed to cover up his disaster with the Knopf books—and why she'd bothered. If he was lucky, she'd just laugh and shrug it off, and that would be the end of it.

The phone rang.

Jim jumped up to get it, and Willy said, "Hey—you mind if I take a look at your beer can again?"

Jim pointed him back to the bedroom and said, "Be my guest." He picked up the phone, anticipating bad news.

"Jim? It's Sharra."

Jim sagged against the wall. Bad news. "You have to cancel, don't you? Look, I understand—" He was thinking that at least her call answered the question of whether or not his spell had affected her.

But she interrupted with a puzzled laugh. "No. I don't have to cancel. I just realized I didn't know whether you liked tomatoes on your sandwiches or not, and I know some people hate them."

She wasn't going to cancel. "Oh." He felt ridiculous. Nothing like letting his insecurities all hang out. "I'm sorry to assume like that," he told her. "Things have been—" The monster came up through the floor and stalked back toward the bedroom and Willy. "—a little odd around here lately. I like everything. Really. Whatever you're putting together for you, just do the same thing for me. I don't need anything special."

"Okay. What about drinks? Iced tea suit you?"

Out of the corner of his eye, Jim saw Willy bolt into the bathroom, all hunched over and clutching his stomach. "Oh, God! Hang on a minute, Sharra. Willy, are you all right?" He stared down the hall—he didn't see any blood on the floor.

Willy turned on the bathroom exhaust fan. It roared like a freight train, and precluded any chance that Willy could hear a word he'd said. He sighed.

"Sharra?"

"I'm here. Is anything wrong?"

"I don't know. Willy—that's the guy we're going on the picnic with—is over here, and he just . . . um—" The indelicacy of hinting at Willy's possible intestinal problem presented itself, and Jim decided on the vague approach. "Um, he just looked like he wasn't feeling too good."

"I hope he's all right." Sharra's voice was solicitous, but with the tiniest edge of suspicion.

Jim said, "I hope so, too." He meant it. He doubted Sharra would go out with him if he suddenly told her Willy and Karen weren't going to be there. She'd figure that he'd been lying from the start; that he'd never intended to have anyone else along to begin with.

Thunder rumbled in the bathroom, and Willy shouted something Jim couldn't make out. He froze with the phone dangling from his hand, staring down the hall, bewildered. Thunder? In his bathroom?

From very far away, he heard Sharra ask, "What in the world was that?"

The noises had stopped, "Um—" He tried to remember anything ever sounding exactly like thunder in his bathroom, but came up blank. Then Willy yowled, and Jim said, "Hang on!" and dropped the phone on the floor. He ran for the bathroom door, preparing to kick it in, when Willy staggered out, looking waxy and sick. "What happened?" Jim asked.

Willy shook his head, bewildered, and stared at Jim as if he'd never seen him before. "Your . . . plumbing . . ." He pushed past Jim and staggered into the living room. "It's loud."

"That wasn't my plumbing." Jim frowned. "What's the matter with you?"

"Don't—ah, don't feel too good." He collapsed on a chair and his head lolled back. His skin was the most horrible shade of gray, and his shirt was soaked through with sweat.

Jim walked over and picked up the phone. "Sharra, Willy looks really sick. I'm going to have to drive him and his car home or maybe to the hospital, and then figure out some way to get back here. I don't think the picnic looks like a possibility. I'm really sorry."

Jim heard a short, quick intake of breath on the other end of the line, and then Sharra said, "Give me his address and I'll pick you up and give you a ride home."

"You don't need to do that," Jim protested.

"I want to. Besides, I already have this lunch nearly packed. You can't expect me to eat it all myself."

Jim gave her the address, thanked her and hung up quickly. "Willy, give me your keys," he said.

Willy's eyes were only partly closed, and rolled back in his head. He didn't answer. Jim shook him, and he *still* didn't answer. If it hadn't been for the groaning, Jim would have thought he was dead. Jim fished through Willy's pockets for his keys, then picked him up. With Willy draped across his shoulders, Jim hurried out the door and down the rickety steps to Willy's car.

Willy started coming around as Jim backed out of the drive. Jim was relieved—he'd been trying to figure the fastest route to the emergency room instead of Willy's house. His old friend still didn't look any too good, though.

"How are you feeling now?" Jim asked him. Willy was staring out the car window at the passing terrain with an intensity Jim had previously only seen displayed by dogs riding shotgun in pickup trucks.

"Fine. I'm fine." Willy's voice came out deeper than usual. It had an oily sound, and was oddly accented. "Where are we going?"

"I'm taking you home. Karen can put you to bed and figure out what's wrong with you—or whatever else needs doing. We'll cancel the picnic today. I think that will be the best thing we can do."

"Karen . . . ? Cancel the picnic?" Willy nodded slowly, never taking his eyes off the world that rolled past the car windows. "Yes. That is best."

"Right." Jim glanced over at his friend. Willy didn't sound like himself, though his color was improving by the minute. "So why don't you tell me what happened in my bathroom. I've never heard the pipes make that noise before. That sounded more like a storm than the toilet flushing. Did the monster do something to you?"

"No. And . . . you . . . didn't have a storm in your bathroom." Willy looked at Jim with the spookiest expression on his face. His voice was flat, emotionless; he sounded most unlike himself. "It was the plumbing."

"Come on, Willy! I know better than that."

"Plumbing," Willy insisted. He lay his head against the leather headrest and closed his eyes.

Jim pulled into Willy's drive and honked the horn.

He was already out of the car and around to the passenger side helping Willy out when the brown-haired girl from the pictures came to the door, then ran down the steps when she saw Willy hadn't driven himself home. Jim pulled his friend to a standing position and tucked a shoulder under Willy's arm, and nodded at Karen. "I'm Jim Franklin."

The woman looked at him as if he was something disgusting that had washed up on the beach, and said, "Karen. What happened to him?"

"I would guess a sudden intestinal bug, but he hasn't been very helpful with answers," Jim told her. "He ran into my bathroom while I was on the phone—I saw him holding his stomach and running bent over. When he came out he was pale and sweaty, and he's still obviously not quite back to his old self."

"Hah." Karen wrapped an arm around Willy's waist to take over from Jim, but when she did, Willy pulled away from both of them.

"I can stand." Willy looked from one to the other of them, then turned his back on both and stalked into his house.

Karen gave Jim a glare that would have melted asbestos, and he winced. "I didn't do anything to him," he protested. "Honest to God." He handed Willy's keys to her, and she snatched them out of his hand and said, "I suppose you need a ride home."

"No." Jim was suddenly and profoundly grateful for

Sharra's offer. He hadn't been expecting a warm reception when he brought Willy back less than intact . . . but Karen's greeting had outstripped his worst expectations. "A friend is going to pick me up."

"Good," Karen said, and turned to walk back into the house.

Not even going to invite me in, Jim thought. *I guess I can be glad the picnic isn't going to happen.*

A horn was tapped lightly at the end of the drive, and Jim turned to see Sharra smiling at him from the inside of her new black Prelude. He waved once, then glanced behind him to see Karen studying the woman with an expression of surprise.

She obviously didn't think anyone like Sharra would have anything to do with someone like me, he thought. He couldn't be smug—Sharra really didn't have anything to do with him. But he could take a bit of satisfaction from the fact that Karen didn't know that.

Sharra gave him a shy smile when he got into the car. "Where to? Your house?"

Jim thought of his apartment, complete with rickety stairs, run-down, depressing interior, thundering plumbing and screaming monster, and thought again. "I'd . . . rather not. My place is kind of messy. Would you like to go ahead on the picnic now?"

She gave him a strange, sidelong glance, then sighed. "Sure, why not?"

Sharra picked a public park not too far from her own neighborhood. She and Jim carried the basket and blanket down to a grassy glade on the bank of the stream, and spread the picnic out beneath the cool shade of two ancient willow oaks. Jim had been to the park before, and knew a bit of the history. "These trees are over two hundred years old," he told her. "They were here during the Civil War, and even before that."

Sharra looked up at the trees and smiled an odd, quirky little smile. "I know." She sighed, and her eyes got a faraway look. "This has been one of my favorite places for . . . well, a long time."

"Really?" Jim was pleased. "I've always loved it, too. There are some nice walks down along the stream. Maybe later . . ."

"Maybe." She unwrapped her sandwich and bit it. "Eat," she told him.

The meal she'd fixed was delicious; she'd gone to a lot of trouble to make it special. He ate in nervous silence, though. She seemed relaxed and happy, but she watched him with a surreptitious intensity that made every bite he took an ordeal. Even if she hadn't been studying him when she thought he wasn't looking, he would have had a hard time concentrating on the food. He wanted to ask her about the mess she'd found in the stock room, and he wanted to tell her about the stupid thing he'd tried to do. The net effect of it all was that, when he finished eating, he could not have described a single bite of food he put into his mouth.

Except he did notice she'd put tomatoes on the sandwiches.

He choked down the last of his dessert—it was sweet, his mind informed him. Singularly useless information.

"You liked?"

He nodded. "Good. Everything was good." That seemed lukewarm. "Terrific," he added.

"Something's bothering you," she said at the same moment that he said, "Sharra, there's something I wanted to tell you—ask you."

She laughed. She had the most perfect laugh he'd ever heard—warm and throaty and sexy and honest. "I thought so. But which is it? Ask, or tell?"

He sighed heavily and stared out at the tannin-stained water that slipped silently past. "Both. Did you find anything odd in the stock room yesterday morning?"

"Odd?" Her eyes grew serious. "I *thought* you were the one who knew how that mess had gotten there. Want to tell me what happened?"

"No," he said frankly, "but I will anyway, because I feel I owe you an explanation. And an apology."

"You owe me an apology for leaving a mess in the stockroom?"

Jim shook his head. "Sharra, I owe you for a lot worse than that." He studied the backs of his hands—the little brown hairs that ran from his wrists in a thin triangle to the knuckles of his little fingers, the fingernails bitten to the quick, the tiny scrapes and scratches and papercuts on his fingers. He kept his eyes down, and continued. "I found a book in with one of the hurts assortments we got in a couple of days ago—a funny book, all hand-written, that claimed to be a journal. It was written by a guy named Lukas Smalling in the mid-seventeen-hundreds, but it wasn't a journal. It was full of magic spells—"

He thought he heard Sharra gasp, but when he looked up, she was examining a blade of grass and casually listening, so he decided he must have imagined the gasp. He continued. "—and one of them was a magic spell to convince a person who didn't much care for you to like you." He was watching her when he said that, and she looked up—their eyes met for an instant, and he caught a guarded, almost hunted expression before she looked away. He cleared his throat. "I wanted you to like me . . . so after work, I stayed late, and tried out the spell." She'd looked back; she was watching him steadily now.

"You tried it?"

He nodded. He could feel the heat in his face; he knew she was thinking he was a lunatic, but he didn't want to lie to her. "Honest to God, Sharra, I didn't think it was going to really do anything—and I sure didn't think it was going to do what it did!"

"It did something?" She frowned a little, and looked out over the water. "What did it do?"

He frowned. "I'm not entirely sure. It ate half the Knopf shipment. . . ."

"I wondered how that had happened."

"Yeah. I figured. I wanted to ask you about—"

She cut him off. "Later. What else did the spell do?"

"Well . . . it dumped a lot of dirt on the floor, and some little . . . um . . . Look, Sharra, some of what I have to say is going to sound completely nuts."

"I doubt it."

"Wanna bet? I found tiny footprints in the dirt, and these miniature artifacts, and though I can't be sure— and though I'd love to think I just scared up a couple of mice—I think I created some tiny people."

Sharra was shaking her head vehemently. "You didn't create them. The creation and transmutation of matter are impossible through magic, as is any attempt to control the emotions of another person."

Jim sat back and stared at her.

She cocked her head to one side and watched him with a steady gaze. "What?"

"You didn't take that the way I thought you would."

"You were expecting screaming and hysterics?"

"I was expecting you to tell me I was full of shit."

Sharra smiled slowly—it was a sad, tired smile. "I know a fair amount about magic. At one time, it was an all-consuming study for me; now it is something I wish I'd never heard of . . . but that is neither here nor there." She looked out over the stream, and watched a young family playing ball in the grass just beyond the other bank. "So you wiped out a bunch of terrible books and crossed paths with the Ithnari. What else?" She didn't look at him when she asked, but he sensed that the question wasn't asked casually.

"I was afraid I'd made you like me against your will."

She shook her head. "Couldn't happen. I liked you anyway, but you remind me of someone I used to know—someone who hurt me a lot." She propped an elbow on one knee and rested her chin in a cupped hand. "I admit I've been avoiding you—I was afraid you'd turn out to be like that other person."

Jim's heart lightened. She'd already liked him? But to have her compare him to another guy—that was always bad news. "So?

"So . . ." She pulled her legs in tightly and rested her chin on her knees. "You aren't like the other person I once knew. *You* tell people the truth. I can finally believe that."

Her smile, when she looked at Jim, was warm, and her lips trembled. The world brightened around him, brightened with a hope he hadn't felt in years—hadn't felt, in fact, since the day his future had died. His life had started over; he had a second chance at happiness. He leaned over and kissed her.

She scrambled away from him so fast she fell in the grass, kept rolling, and jumped to her feet. "Don't," she whispered. "Please, don't ever do that again." Her voice shook, and she was pale as death.

He read terror in her eyes—a deep, ugly fear that ignited rage deep inside him. He'd done nothing to cause that fear, but someone had. And he was betting that someone was the man he reminded her of.

If I ever meet that guy, he thought, I'll rip his heart out.

But, for the moment at least, Jim had blown his chance to spend the day with Sharra. She was gathering up her blanket and her containers; she'd wiped the fear from her face, but only blankness replaced it, and that hurt Jim as much as the fear had. He wanted to make things better for her. He wanted to make her world right.

Next time, he thought. If there *is* a next time.

And then he thought—Please, God, let there *be* a next time.

They didn't talk much on the ride home—and Jim didn't bother inviting Sharra in. She wouldn't have come even if he had asked . . . and at the moment, considering his new roommate, he didn't dare ask. She dropped him off and waved distantly, and he trudged up to his lousy apartment, attacked the monster as soon as he went into the living room, and headed back to his bedroom.

Something was different.

He studied the mess—it was hard to pinpoint one specific wrong in such a sea of disarray, but he figured out what the problem was after a moment—and when he did, the hair on the back of his neck prickled. The book was gone!

He saw Willy again, with his hands clutched to his belly, running for the bathroom. What if Willy had been holding the book under his shirt? He'd become fascinated by the book.

Jim considered the thunderclap in the bathroom, and compared it to the noise he'd heard the first time he'd tried a spell. The sounds had been identical. So Willy had not been able to resist the temptation. He'd done a spell.

And the spell had done something unexpected.

Had Willy taken the book home with him?

Jim didn't think so. When he'd carried Willy outside, he hadn't felt a book. The grimoire was probably still in the house, then. He started looking in the bathroom—and found it right away. It had fallen between the sink and the toilet.

Jim tried to figure out the consequences of Willy's action.

The monster hadn't been made more real. Willy didn't leave carrying a gold baseball bat. The toilet hadn't been transformed into solid gold, either.

Willy had been sick at first . . . but even that had passed quickly. So what had he done?

Jim was going to have to find out.

Chapter Twenty-two

Sharra crouched in the corner of her workroom with the doors locked. She wrapped her arms around herself and rocked back and forth, fighting her tears.

I don't want to die, she thought. I don't want to die now.

Jim's kiss lingered in her memory—all warmth and gentleness and tenderness . . . and caring. She'd been without that sort of caring in her life for so long.

I could love him, she thought. He isn't anything like Lukas, except for the way he looks. I could love him, and he would love me back; I wouldn't have to be alone anymore.

She slammed her head against the wall once, then again, and once more.

Dammit. I wouldn't have to be alone anymore.

But that couldn't happen. Couldn't.

If she loved, she died—died an ugly, painful, horrible death; the moment she was no longer a virgin, she would wither away; turn to bone and the bone to dust in her lover's arms. That ill-gotten bastard Lukas had made it so, with a smile on his face, and with laughter in his voice. And even if she'd successfully shoved him into the cage he'd planned for her, she hadn't beaten him, hadn't banished him.

His rage was still fresh in her mind; his curse hung over every breath she took, as it had hung over every breath she had taken since she'd turned the tables on him.

I'll never be free of him until he's dead, she told herself.

She would never be free of him at all. She couldn't kill him. She had neither the magic nor the ferocity. And that was not her prophesied fate. Sharra was to be Lukas's sacrifice—his "lamb upon the altar," as he'd called her.

Despair wrapped itself around her like a cold, wet blanket—and in the end, she opened her arms and embraced it.

Chapter Twenty-three

The dog waited, grinning at the four Ithnari, while behind them the pyre stacked high with its grotesque burdens crackled and blazed. The unceasing din of the howling demons, the roar of flames, the hiss of water that poured out of the ceiling high above, the pungent reek of smoke and burning bodies created a wall of sound and scent so dense it stunned Gali.

She pulled the neck of her tunic up over her nose, covered her ears with her hands and looked out onto the cool, smooth promise of the stone plain. The dog had made itself visible to them on purpose, she thought. It wanted them to know it was there, and to know it hunted them. "We need weapons," she shouted over the cacophony.

"Fire!" Mrestal ran back toward the worst of the conflagration, and returned bearing a flaming brand. "Get one, and we'll go. Surely that monster won't attack us if we're armed with fire."

Gali, Terthal, and Eryia found their own torches; then Mrestal led them through the metal gate and out onto the plain. Once they were free of the temple of the dead, Gali heard more of that demon-screaming, though it came from a distance, and was drawing nearer; she guessed more demons were on their way to the feast of souls. She hoped that, when they arrived, they wouldn't consider her worthwhile prey.

She and the others carried their burning brands high and marched along the corridor in full sight of the dog—and it watched their single file march past and grinned, with its tongue lolling out and its tail thumping slowly on the ground.

"Keep it in sight," Mrestal said. "Don't look away from it. And don't run unless it comes after us—it might not chase us if we move slowly."

They walked sideways to keep it in their sight, all the while waving their little torches in the air. Smoke roiled out of the burning temple of death and began to fill the corridor. It stung Gali's eyes, and made it difficult for her to watch the dog. Her torch was already burning down; she didn't think it would last much longer. The Ithnari's safe domain was around the corner and down the corridor, still far away. The dog was behind them, unmoving, unbothered by the smoke and the noise, watching out of liquid brown eyes, panting.

And then it wasn't.

For an instant, her mind didn't register the fact that it was gone. When it did, sheer dread at the doom that undoubtedly closed on her froze her to the ground for one seemingly infinite instant. Then she screamed, "Look out!" and took off. Her giant, bounding steps catapulted her down the corridor and around the corner. The brand flew out of her hand; she didn't care. She was certain that tiny flaming stick couldn't save her—the demon-dog was after her. She couldn't hear it, could see nothing of it when she glanced back. Still, she knew it was coming—coming fast.

She panicked, forgetting their plan. It wasn't likely that all four of them had lost sight of the beast, but Gali didn't care. She couldn't see it, and the possibility that Mrestal or one of the others could still see the monster had no control over her fear. She bolted for safety. And when she ran, so did her friends. They scattered across as well as down the corridor as they fled, lessening the odds that the monster could get all of them at once.

Gali peeked over her shoulder—still she saw nothing, though now she heard the dog, breath panting and claws scrabbling on the smooth tile floor. It was gaining on them.

Then it appeared, right behind Eyria and Terthal, who ran close to each other. The demon-dog extended its claws and bounded into the air; the talons splayed out like knives, aiming for Terthal. He twisted, lunged—barely evaded the nightmare beast; while it landed and immediately shot up into the air again, this time aiming for Eryia.

She was neither as quick nor as agile as Terthal; the dog, with its second pounce, hit its target. Eryia screamed and the beast stopped running, tossed her into the air with one foot, and caught her in its teeth. Her scream died with horrible finality. Gali kept running, as did Mrestal. Terthal, though, turned back and charged, his brand clutched in one fist—though the flame had gone out and the tip was nothing but a faintly glowing ember.

Gali screamed, "No, Terthal! Run!" but her half-brother paid no more attention to her than he ever had. He charged and leapt, bounded straight up at the thing's muzzle, and jammed his stick into its near eye. It howled and dropped Eryia—but even from well down the corridor, Gali could see there was no hope of saving the other girl. The dog had bitten her nearly in two; Eryia was dead.

The dog howled again and lunged after Terthal, who darted out of reach, then ran between the monster's legs, scooped up Eryia in his arms, and started for the bookstore gate.

Mrestal was safe behind the metal bars; Gali squeezed through and joined him. Then they both watched the desperate race between Terthal with dead Eryia in his arms and the enraged, one-eyed demon-dog.

"Closer," Mrestal muttered. "Just get closer, Terthal, and gods, don't get caught."

Gali expected with each of Terthal's steps to see the dog swallow him up, yet her brother made the gate with enough of a lead to climb in to safety. "Hurry!" Gali shouted at him, and held a hand through to pull him in, but he didn't take it. Instead, he tried to shove Eryia's body through the bars—but she hung limply and caught on the crosspiece, and he didn't get her through on his first attempt.

Gali heard screaming, and realized it was coming from her own throat. "Drop her! Get inside," she pleaded. "Hurry, Terthal! Gods, hurry!"

Mrestal did the little magic he knew, and spelled a flame at the dog's face; it struck, and burned, and the beast backed away for an instant—but only that. Then the flame went out—snuffed by a magic stronger than Mrestal's. The dog came after Terthal again, and Mrestal's fire didn't even slow it a second time.

Terthal gave Eryia's body a second shove, and this time she toppled through onto the floor of the bookstore. But even as her body fell to the floor, the demon-dog caught Terthal, and its claws ripped through him.

No matter how long she lived, Gali would never be able to wipe her brother's scream from her memory.

The short, fine hairs on the back of her neck stood up, and she shuddered and backed deeper into the store. The dog tossed her half-brother into the air as it had Eryia, and caught him, and he howled again. Again it tossed him, and again he screamed.

"NO!" Mrestal shouted.

Gali looked up—Mrestal had jumped up on the shelf far above. His face was pale with fear, and tight with fury. Gali felt him draw power to himself, the angry, hungry, evil magical energy that coiled in the two Fangs of the Earth that flanked the fountain. She felt the shape of his spell, the rage and the desperation of it, and shoved a fist into her mouth to keep herself from crying out. Mrestal couldn't save Terthal—she knew that, and so did he. Terthal had thrown his life away. Mrestal could only do what he could do. Mrestal released his spell, and as Gali stared, unable to turn away, Terthal's body began to swell and thicken. Then, she heard a quick series of wet, sticky pops and sharp cracks, and he melted into nothing.

Mrestal sobbed and dropped to the surface of the shelf. Gali jumped up to his side, then quickly looked away. He'd paid a hellish price for his spell—the skin on the palms of his hands was burned nearly off; they were red and raw and blistered, with black, crackled skin at the centers of the wounds.

He rolled on his side and pulled his injured hands in toward his chest—he groaned, and beads of sweat poured from his face. "I couldn't let that thing torture him, Gali," he whispered. "I'm sorry I couldn't save him."

Gali sat beside him and stroked his hair. Her tears for Terthal were a long way off—she was angry at her half-brother for his death, as angry as she had been for his life. "I spent twenty-three years trying to save him," she said bitterly. "What I couldn't manage in a lifetime, you shouldn't expect to succeed at in a single moment."

She stared down at Eryia's body—poor mangled, broken thing. She couldn't look out into the corridor; the dog sat out there, grinning and licking his bloody jaws and waiting.

She'd hated Terthal for the burden that he'd been on her life. She'd hated him because he'd never used the enormous talents he had; he'd never done anything in his life unless it was easy, unless it amused him, unless it was dishonest or for personal profit.

She'd hated him because she could not help him; because he was not the person he could have been.

She'd hated him because she loved him and she'd failed him.

He was dead, and her heart insisted he would have lived if she had been better at teaching him, or if she had tried harder . . . if she had somehow been better, or more of what he needed.

The cold, harsh emptiness of her failure ate into her gut, and she clenched her fists and stared down at Mrestal—who'd at least managed to do something. He'd kept the monster from torturing her brother, at great cost to himself—the magics that took lives demanded a high and painful price. Mrestal's hands would never be the same again. The flesh would heal, but the pain would eat its way into his soul, and it would never leave.

So her failure of Terthal had in the end been a failure of Mrestal, too.

She turned away from her love, and looked down again at Eryia. Another failure—Eryia should have been safely at home with her parents. Instead, Gali would have to find a burial place here, in this land of smooth stone plains and cold stone cliffs that towered up to covered skies. There were few places to bury Eryia in this cold, hard world of stone—little loose earth, and few stones small enough that she and Mrestal could raise a cairn over their fallen comrade's body. Some of the old Ithnari still burned the bodies of their dead. She did not know what Eryia would have wished, but she did not wish to brave the corridor and the wide stone plain, to carry Eryia's body to the little patch of dirt beside the fountain.

Later, she would decide how to bury Eryia and how to see her brother's soul safely to the heavens.

For the moment, however, she remembered a large roll of cloth in the little room upstairs. She picked up Eryia and carried her back. She would wrap her in the cloth until she had time to deal with Mrestal's wounds—until she had time to think of what to do next.

Chapter Twenty-four

MONDAY

Jim was glad he was opening with Kerri. She knew the ropes, and would do the actual opening, which would let him get his display done before customers filled the place. He hurried across the parking lot, slipped in through the back door and tucked the grimoire onto the returns shelf at the very back of the stockroom. A part of him hated giving up that book—another part of him thought he ought to burn it.

But he was certain that getting rid of the damned spell book would simplify his life. It was just too much trouble—and too much of a temptation—to have at home. He tried not to think about the magic he was giving up—tried especially hard not to think about what another solid gold beer can or two would do for his bank account, his college fund, and his future. He kept reminding himself that another gold beer can might mean another monster in his living room. He could do without.

Sharra was going to be in as soon as the store opened—and Jim didn't know if he could face her. He didn't have anything pleasant to think about, so he tried not to think at all. Instead, he immersed himself in his work. He had to design the front display window this month; he had to come up with a clever way to entice people into shelling out their hard-earned

cash on the useless tie-ins and merchandising gim-
micks for the new Batman movie. He stacked the
Batman IV novelizations into big, dramatic black piles
in the display window, and tried to come up with an
idea. He would have to have something cool to move
the books, because from all accounts Jim had gotten,
the movie had only been fair, and was not going to
move the merchandise for him.

While he was contemplating his design, Kerri rolled
her cart over to the fiction section, which was right
next to the display window, and restocked *Black Water
Secrets*, which against the staff's expectations was
moving like greased pigs down a chute, though
according to the computer this was only happening
in their store. Jim wondered if some local cult had
ordered mass lobotomies for all its members this
month. At least the author would be thrilled when
he came in to sign on Saturday.

While Kerri was filling in the holes on the shelves,
Franklin Ray, the night security guard, came up to
the gate and motioned for Jim to come over.

"What's up, Frank?"

The guard leaned toward Jim and his voice dropped
to a conspiratorial whisper. "You hear about what happened last night? They broke into Kay-Bee Toy, and
started a fire. That reporter that came around this
morning said he was going to call the story the Great
Barbie Massacre."

Jim's eyes narrowed. Frank was a nice enough guy,
though from everything he'd seen, the deputy was more
than a little paranoid—the sort of guy who loved those
conspiracy theories about JFK and the Mafia and the
Communists and aliens from outer space.

"I heard about the fire when I was driving in." Jim
didn't see how anyone could have *not* heard about the
fire. Even if it hadn't been all over the radio, he would
have known as soon as he got to the mall. Workmen

were cleaning and nailing up big sheets of plywood to cover the storefront until it could be renovated.

"The morning DJ's tried to tie the arson, the murder, and the jewelry theft into one big, messy crime," Jim said, shaking his head and edging back toward his book display. "Sounds kind of unlikely, don't you think?"

"It fits," Frank answered. "All three of 'em were 'locked door' crimes—none of the gates showed any signs of tampering, the back exits remained locked and bolted, and almost all of the employees of all three stores have iron-clad alibis."

Jim shook his head—it looked like Frank was the "unidentified source within the sheriff's department" that the DJ's had quoted. "That seems kind of thin," he said. "What possible link can there be between a small-time jewelry heist, a murder, and a fire in a toy store?"

"That's what I'm tryin' to tell you," Frank said. "It's some kind of a cult thing."

"A cult, or *occult*?" Jim asked.

"Exactly," Frank replied. "It's both. I don't know want kind of voodoo was going on in that toy store, but them Barbies were stacked like logs in the fireplace; those were Satanic goings on at that Kay-Bee. Take my word on it."

Jim looked at Frank to see if he was serious. Apparently he was. He snorted, disgusted. "Oh, for Pete's sake—a Satanic ritual? With Barbie dolls? Come on, Frank. We're talking setting fire to kid toys here. More likely somebody needed a break on his income tax." He turned away from Frank and stacked a few more books on the display.

"This is serious! You can't just look at the fire— you have to look at the deeper meaning."

Jim rolled his eyes. Deeper meaning. Some nut torched a toy store and before you could blink, more than just the deputy would be stalking around with protest signs and muttering about "Satanists"—and calling for the removal of gaming materials from all the area bookstores. It never failed. "The world is full of nuts, but that doesn't mean the cases are related," he said, and made a pointed gesture out of turning away from the gate to work on the display. Over his shoulder, he said, "Maybe all the Barbie and Ken dolls had an orgy, and in the heat of the moment they spontaneously combusted."

Frank said, "You think what you will, but mark my words—when this is all over, you'll see I was right." He stalked off into the mall.

Jim sighed and put the incident out of his mind.

He covered the side and back slatwall with the movie novelization, then unloaded the *Complete Frank Miller Batman*, a marvelous book, into the chrome-and-glass display. He was hoping the Miller would move the other stuff—it was his one sure thing. He hung black plastic bats from the ceiling and made sure he had a few of them flying upside down, just to see if anyone would notice. Then he opened the gate and went out into the mall to see how the display looked from the hallway.

Pretty good, he thought. But it was missing something.

It was missing his personal touch, he decided after a moment. As it stood, the display could have been the work of anyone in the store . . . except for the upside-down bats which, except for Scott, none of the other booksellers would have thought of. But upside-down bats were not up to the standards his regular customers expected from him.

Let's see, he thought. Maybe I could do another top ten list. Top Ten Reasons to Skip the Movie and Buy the Book? Nah. That would just get him into trouble. Top Ten Batman Slogans . . . Top Ten Batcurses . . . Top Ten Reasons Why It's Tough Being Batman, maybe?

That last one had possibilities. His previous top-ten-list display—Top Ten Ways to Find Out if Your Date Is Human—had gotten rave reviews and sold bucket-loads of the crummy how-to-get-a-date book he'd had to move.

He went into the upstairs stockroom, pulled out a yellow legal pad, plopped onto the rickety folding chair at the card table, and began to sketch out his ideas. The first one came easily.

> 10) The Todd MacFarlane/Batman Year Two Batcape keeps leaping out of the closet under its own power and trying to take over my job.

He liked that. He and Scott, the other SF guy in the store, had made more than one joke about Todd MacFarlane and the incredible expanding Batcape—it covered two-page-spreads and crept out of its boxes into the next frame all the time. It was the kudzu of the superhero accessories world.

So he'd keep number ten.

Next.

> 9) People keep asking me to explain *Crisis on Infinite Earths*.

He grinned. Nobody had that storyline straight. Lots of customers wouldn't get the joke, but the ones who would were sure to like it. And it was pretty far down on the list, so the people who *didn't* get it would still keep reading.

He closed his eyes and thought hard. He came up with the next three right in a row.

> 8) Alfred met a health food guru; now it's bean sprouts for Batman.
> 7) Social Services is on my back for dressing a young boy up in green tights and a

yellow cape and keeping him out until all
hours of the morning.
6) Robin hooked the Bat-computer up to the
Nintendo and caused a city-wide black-
out when he reached the end of level
three on Super Mario Brothers.

He wasn't sure about number six, but he loved
number seven. And he figured even folks who weren't
Batman fans would get those jokes.

He had trouble coming up with an idea for the next
one. He got up and paced from one end of the stockroom to the other. At the far end, he sniffed—something smelled pretty rank back there. He frowned, and
started looking around for the source of the smell . . .
but then he got a few more ideas. He ran over and
wrote them down.

5) I keep getting obscene phone calls on
the red phone.
4) Second movie did poorly at the box
office—Michelle Pfeiffer doesn't call me
anymore.
3) Can't get the seams straight in my Bat-
tights.

He had a hard time concentrating on his list. That
bad smell in the room wasn't overwhelming, but once
he'd noticed it, it nagged at him. He pushed it out
of his mind and scribbled down a possible entry for
number two.

2) Robin got a speeding ticket; they
doubled the insurance rates on the
Batmobile.

It seemed a little weak to him, but it would have
to do—he wanted to get the display done. He shifted
on the hard metal seat, rested his chin in one hand,

and stared off into space. Something rustled behind him. He turned and looked into the shelves—they were dark, full of shadows and nooks and crannies. If a mouse were in there, Jim would never find it.

Bet that's where the stink is coming from, though, he thought. There's probably a dead mouse in the stockroom somewhere.

He considered the possibilities of dead mice in Batman's life, or dead mice in Batman's lunchbox, or anything else to do with dead mice . . . but the dead mouse avenue turned into a dead end. He shook his head—dumb joke—and closed his eyes, and tugged on the elastic of his Jockey shorts. And got his idea. He wrote:

1) Too much starch in the Bat-shorts.

He smiled and read his list over once. He'd have to stop by Office Max on his lunch break. He had to pick up a big sheet of poster paper or maybe even a Bienfang foam board for the sign. Maybe he could get Ann or Kerri to do the writing—his own he might be able to pass off as bat-scratchings, in keeping with the theme, but it would be better if people could read what he'd written. He thought the list would make some customers laugh . . . and probably sell them a few books while they were at it.

The more they buy, the less we have when returns hit.

Something rustled behind him again, but this time he didn't turn. A small hand mirror lay next to a hairbrush on the table, and with a slow, casual movement, Jim picked it up and aimed it over his shoulder, looking for movement behind him.

At first he saw nothing. But the rustling continued, and he fine-tuned his aim, until he did see something.

The problem was, he didn't believe what he saw.

Two tiny faces stared back at him. They were not mouse faces—but they weren't human, either. He saw slanted eyes, pointed ears, pointed teeth. The creatures' bodies were humanoid—two arms, two legs—and the creatures wore clothes. They were only about a foot tall, he guessed. He saw one male and one female, and if he'd had to supply them with a name, he would have called them elves. They looked the way he imagined elves would look—well, not elves like Tolkien had written about, but a lot like the little people who'd played such a big part in Irish legends.

They were, at most, two feet behind him.

He thought, I could swing around and grab them—if I'm quick, and if I don't telegraph my intentions.

He watched them watching him. They weren't paying any attention to the mirror—their eyes were focused on the back of his head.

They pointed, and whispered—that was a part of the noise he'd heard—and gestured in his direction. They appeared to be arguing about him.

I wonder what they are?

To some extent, he knew what they were. They were the creatures he'd accidentally summoned with his magic spell—he was certain of that. He had not wanted to believe they were real, but even if he'd been able to ignore the import of the footprints and the artifacts, there was no way to ignore the two miniature people behind him.

He wondered if they were dangerous.

Their argument was heating up. For just an instant, they took their eyes off him, the better to glare at each other.

He dropped the mirror, spun and grabbed, all in a single smooth motion. One hand wrapped around the middle of each of them and tightened, and he picked them up. They yelled—tinny little squeaks.

They were heavy—easily four times as heavy as he'd expected them to be.

And they fought.

The male bit him on the hand. Needle teeth sank into the tender flesh between his forefinger and thumb, and with a howl of pain, he dropped that one. The other one scratched and kicked. Before it thought to bite him, too, he shifted his grip to the back of its little tunic, then watched it squirm.

"Put me down, you!" the creature yelled. She was rather pretty, he thought. He dangled her in front of his face and sucked on the bleeding wound her companion had given him. Her long brown hair fell to her hips in two thick braids, her eyes were large and slanted, heavily lashed and of an interesting copper color, and her sharp features were . . . well . . . elfin.

Except for the teeth, which Jim considered, after his experience with them, purely demonic.

Her friend had been kicking Jim in the ankle, trying to get him to drop her. When that didn't work, he jumped—and Jim's mouth fell open. The little man leaped up even with Jim's face in a single jump—damn near six feet straight up. Jim had never seen a feat like that in his life.

The girl glared at him and swung around, trying to get loose. She was nowhere near as large as a housecat, but she weighed as much as one—maybe fourteen or fifteen pounds, and she had the same sort of dense, wiry muscularity. She got a piece of him with one hand, and he yelped. She had the same claws as a cat, too. His wrist bled, little red droplets spattering the floor. He wondered absently if his tetanus shot was up to date.

"Look, dammit," Jim said, "I'm not going to hurt you. I'm just curious. What are you, and where did you come from? If you'll let me, I'll help you . . . if you need help. Do you need help?"

Neither of the little creatures said anything. The girl kept fighting, trying to scratch him again and twisting around as if to bite him, though with her held out at arm's length, she wasn't having any luck.

The tiny man, however, began climbing Jim's leg. Jim tried to shake him off, but couldn't. He worried about those teeth—his polyester work pants weren't anywhere near as sturdy as blue jeans, and the claws digging through his pants leg were like tiny knives. Worse, Jim worried that a bite in the right spot would ruin more than his day. He told the girl, "I'd put you down, but I don't think I could catch you again. Quit trying to shred me, will you? I just . . . want . . . to *talk* to you."

She glared at him in anger and disgust. "I suppose you expect us to believe the words of a murderer. You will not stuff and mount *me* in sacrifice to your perverted gods of death." She fought harder, scratching and kicking at Jim's fingers.

She had an accent. He couldn't place it; it was foreign, but not of any nationality he'd ever heard. He'd almost expected an Irish accent—but there was nothing of the mellifluous Irish in her sharp, snappish little syllables.

Jim was confused. "Stuffed and mounted? What do you mean?" He brushed her friend back to the ground with one careful swat—the climber had stopped precisely where Jim had been afraid he might.

"Don't pretend you are innocent," she snapped. "We found the shrine to your death-god, and burned the Ithnari corpses your people entombed in the wizard's pink coffins." She went limp and still in his hand, and her eyes unfocused. In a faraway voice, she said, "And now, I will burn you."

A tiny flicker of flame burst against the back of Jim's fist, and he reflexively dropped the little woman. Too late, he realized that he hadn't imagined the slight thickening in the air—it was a small and subtle thing next to the thunderclap he got when he used the grimoire, but he had recognized it nonetheless.

He scrambled after the fleeing elves—he couldn't help thinking of them as elves—trying to snatch them out of the air as they bounded around the stock room.

"Don't leave! I have to talk to you. It was some magic I did that brought you here, I guess—though I sure didn't mean to. But if you know anything about the weird stuff that's been happening, I wish you'd tell me."

He grabbed for one of the little people, and managed to catch the man and reverse his grip before the little monster could bite him again. When the woman saw that Jim had captured her companion, she clenched her fists and leaped straight at him. Jim saw it coming, so he didn't quite get the wind knocked out of him when she punched him in the stomach. And them something clicked in his brain, and he figured out what the girl had been talking about.

"Pink coffins," he said, laughing. "Oh, that's good."

The one in his hand was trying to twist around far enough to bite Jim on the hand. "You think it is *funny*!" he shouted. "Gali, burn him again!"

Jim had been expecting that—had, in fact, already felt the pressure starting to build. Fortunately, the little woman apparently had to stand still and concentrate to make her magic work. Jim scooped her off the floor with his free hand, and shook her to break her focus.

"Listen to me," he said. "Those things you burned were not—are not—whatever it is that you are. They were just toys, plastic dolls for children to play with. They were never alive to begin with."

The girl shrieked, "Liar! We saw them! We lifted their bodies down from the shelves." Her face contorted with hatred and her voice rose to a painful shrill that probably had every dog in five miles writhing. "Your people—your *fiends*—dismembered them and put them back together again. Stuffed them. Chained them in coffins so you could walk past and gloat and mock and stare at them in death."

"Christ!" Jim stared at the elves. "Haven't you ever seen toys?"

"I've seen liars. I'm looking at one now."

"Damn." Jim shook his head. "Look, you two—I can prove to you there's nothing evil about Barbie dolls." He looked off in the distance and frowned. "Pernicious, maybe . . . but not evil."

She swallowed hard. "Terthal . . . Eryia . . . what if they died for nothing?"

The elf-woman was beginning to consider that he might be telling the truth. Good.

Her companion said, "Not for nothing. Never did they die for nothing. Our cause was noble. We must act as our natures direct us, for good or for ill."

"In other words," Jim said, "no good deed goes unpunished." One last thing fell into place for him, and he paused, uncomfortable with his next question. "Your dead friends—" he began, "—they wouldn't happen to be up here, would they?"

The female winced, and the male answered, "One of them is. The other—is no more."

The female elf hung her head, and tears glistened down her cheeks. The male looked away, and Jim saw him swallow hard. Suddenly he felt awkward holding the two of them like they were pet hamsters or something. Seeing their grief made them more human, more real.

"Look," he said, "I know this isn't dignified, and if you promise you won't run off, I can put you down . . . but stuff has been going on that I just don't understand, and the two of you are at least a part of it."

"You *are* the one who brought us here, aren't you?" the male said.

Jim nodded. "Yeah. I don't know how to send you back, though—and even if I knew how, I couldn't right now. I'm having some . . . ah . . . *problems* with the book I used." He thought "problems" was a pretty mild description of the difficulties he was facing when he used the grimoire, but he didn't go into details. "So . . . can I let you down? Will you promise not to run away? Then I'll go and get what I need to prove that the dolls weren't killed."

Both elves nodded.

He sighed and settled them both onto the card table . . . and as he did, the door behind him opened. Both creatures shot across the room to the shelves in a single leap, and were gone. Jim jumped and swore, and Kerri poked her head in and said, "I need some help downstairs. We just opened the gate, and Sharra and I already have lines." She sniffed. "Jeez, Jim—what is that *smell*? You forget to take a bath?"

Jim wanted to deck Kerri for scaring off his elves, and he didn't think her comment was very funny, but he said, as patiently as he could manage, "A mouse must have died back under the air conditioner or something."

Kerri stared at his arm. "Why are you bleeding?" she asked him.

He looked at his wrist, streaked with lines of bright red and still dripping slowly onto the floor, and at the little circle of bloody pinpricks on his hand, and said, "Uh . . . I cut myself on . . . um . . . one of the shelves."

"No shit. Looks like workman's comp to me. You ought to leave all the blood all over your hand like that and show Michael when he comes in. That'll give him a real thrill."

Jim imagined that Michael would be simply enthralled by the idea of a workman's compensation case. Michael hated paperwork—and workman's comp was paperwork on top of paperwork. Then Jim imagined a doctor looking at the bite wound and asking him what made it. He decided he wouldn't go down-stairs all bloody. "I didn't realize what a mess I was," he said. "I'll be down in just a minute."

The upstairs bathroom had bandages and soap. He used both while he hoped that the elves—for lack of a better word—didn't have rabies, and headed down-stairs, his Batman Top Ten list clutched in his unwounded hand.

He just hoped the two creatures would give him another chance to talk to them, so he could find out what they knew. His gut told him they were involved in more than building a funeral pyre for Barbie dolls—and uncomfortably, he realized that he was beginning to think like Frank, the security guard.

Sometimes even the paranoid were right.

Chapter Twenty-five

Sharra couldn't look at Jim. His kiss was still fresh in her memory, as was the hurt in his eyes at her rejection. She pretended nothing in the world existed but her register and her line of customers, pretended she couldn't hear Jim's deep, cheerful voice beside her at the next register—pretended she couldn't feel the warmth of his body inches from hers.

The enormous mob of people consisted primarily of women who'd seen the new celebrity diet-and-exercise book touted on Oprah and Sally Jesse Raphael, customers who, in locust-like fashion, had reduced the two large piles to two small ones in about an hour. Sharra sighed. Those piles weren't going to last much longer, and the customers were still coming. She was going to have to start taking special orders soon—going to have to start telling people that the book was no longer on hand, and that there would be a wait.

Mixed in with the wanna-be-skinny crowd were the irate and befuddled customers who had bought the copies of *Black Water Secrets* that she had magicked. They were all trying to return the half they still owned, and Sharra was having a hard time looking them in the eye.

No one knew what to do about forty-three people, each trying to return the remaining half of a book they claimed was whole when they bought it, but not when they got it home, and Knopf was saying they wouldn't take the damaged copies in return because it was obviously an attempt by the religious right to destroy copies of Cletterman's controversial new novel without having to pay for them. Sharra was afraid the chain was going to have to absorb the loss, mark the books down, and sell them as a curiosity. Which was going to give a totally new meaning to the word remainder, she thought with a sick smile.

A customer handed her the next-to-last copy of the celebrity diet book. She turned it over to scan in the ISBN, and glowered at the glossy photo of the woman on the cover and thought that any character actress who lost two hundred pounds, started fitting into size 3 jeans, and became a leading lady—and then had the nerve to write a book about the experience—ought to be shot on sight.

God, but it was busy! Three of them should have been able to take care of the registers and cover the floors and assist customers *and* restock on a regular day—but this wasn't going to be a regular day.

She wished bookstores had some way of telling which of those celebrity books were going to take off and which ones were going to die an ugly death—of course, she imagined publishers wished they could predict the same thing.

Well, there it was—fifty-five copies of the same blasted book in just over an hour, and G. Galloway was out.

And the woman in front of her, who looked a lot like the "before" picture of the celebrity, was desperate for the book. Nearly in tears, in fact.

"Let me run upstairs to the stockroom and see if we have a copy or two still tucked away back there," Sharra offered. She would have bet money they didn't, but it wouldn't hurt Sharra to check, and she could always call around to the other stores to see if she could find someplace that would put a copy on hold for the lady if the search came up empty.

As a last resort, there was special-ordering, but Sharra could tell this lady wanted the book *today*.

"I'll be right back," she told the other folks in line, and trotted out of the cash wrap, up the stairs, and back through the Sci-Fi and Reference sections. If they had any extra copies of the book, they would be shoved in the upstairs overstock.

A feeling of evil washed over her as she stepped into the stockroom; hit her as hard as a fist to her gut. She backed up into the closed door and her hand fumbled for the knob. The light was on . . . nothing hid in the shadows . . . nothing moved. . . .

But she felt a presence. She sensed the taint of Lukas's magic, and something more. Something that burned like cold fire along the little silvery scar across the palm of her left hand—a pain that pulsed in time with the racing of her heart. The magic tied to that scar had been quiescent for more than two hundred years; in that time, she'd forgotten both the pain and the meaning of the pain. Now she remembered.

And with memory came the curse itself.

The nightmare from her furthest past floated up through the floor, a trick she hadn't known its kind could do. A trail of spittle streaked one corner of the creature's mouth, and its pupilless white eyes registered her presence through means other than sight. Its thick lips curled into an evil smile, and it said, "Mine," in a voice so soft Sharra could almost have thought the word came from her imagination. But the word gave truth to the vision—the monster remembered her, as she remembered it.

The two of them were, in a sense, blood-siblings, sharing the immortality with which Lukas had cursed them. They shared the scar, shared their magic-bound blood, shared their pain . . . and their hatred of each other. Only blood could free them from their bond—blood and magic—and Lukas had intended the blood that freed the monster to be Sharra's, had intended the monster to be the survivor. The thing had been Lukas's summoned demon, the monstrosity he called the ghell; he intended to make the monster somehow help him bind the world Sharra knew with another, more deadly world—Lukas had intended to use the magic of that ephemeral, alternate world to make himself master of this one.

So she and the hell-spawn were bound; if the ghell killed her without Lukas's magical intervention, it would die as well . . . but maybe, she realized, it wanted to die. She'd wanted to die often enough. The ghell lunged at her, fangs bared and claws splayed, its white eyes glowing in the fluorescent light. She scrabbled one-handed at the doorknob behind her, trying to get the door opened in time, to get out of the way; but her hand, suddenly slick with sweat, slipped off the smooth metal—and then the monster was on her, biting and clawing . . . and then it was through her.

Her stomach knotted in the instant she and the ghell occupied the same space; when it had passed through her, she stood, sick and light-headed, trembling against the door.

She'd screamed out loud. She realized that when she heard Jim shouting at her from down at the cash wrap, wanting to know if she was okay—he would be pounding on the stockroom door any second. She couldn't face him; wherever the ghell was, Lukas would not be far behind, and her fate—her doom—would be following after. She didn't want Jim hurt, and if he tried to help her, he'd get hurt.

"I'm fine," she shouted, though she could hear the shakiness in her voice well enough. She opened the door just a crack. "I . . . slipped. I'm a mess. Give me a second to clean up, and I'll be right back out."

The ghell charged her as she walked toward the bathroom, though it stopped short of running through her a second time. She felt damp and cold where its claws passed through her belly, a dreadful chill—but she remained unharmed. The ghell saw this too, saw that it wasn't able to hurt her, and by the time she got to the bathroom, it gave up, and sank down through the floor.

Sharra closed the door behind her and leaned against the wall, shaking. Tears welled up in her eyes, and she fought them back. She'd get through the day—she would manage somehow. When she got home, she'd go over her books one more time to see if she could figure out some way to beat Lukas. She hadn't come up with a certainty in over two hundred years; she wasn't likely to live long enough to find what she needed. But she'd keep at it until she couldn't anymore.

She got herself under control, and when she did, noticed that something in the bathroom smelled bad.

No . . . worse than bad. Something smelled dead.

She looked around the restroom—it was a typical tiny staff bathroom, with a toilet, a cheap sink, a roll of paper towels, book posters pinned to all the walls, and a freestanding cheap metal shelf unit shoved into the corner with all sorts of allegedly useful junk which somehow never seemed to get used jammed into every bit of available space. The smell seemed to be coming from the shelf unit.

Sharra looked over the top shelf . . . nothing.

Over the middle three shelves . . . nothing.

The bottom shelf had several rolls of the world's cheapest toilet paper shoved to the front. Sharra saw an odd bundle shoved between two of them, and pulled the rolls out onto the floor.

Something had been carefully rolled up in the toilet paper. The resulting bundle looked like a miniature mummy. Sharra found the end of the paper and tugged, and the bundle unwrapped itself.

A tiny, dead face stared up at Sharra from glazed eyes. Someone had woven gem-covered rings into the dead girl's golden braids; a diamond bracelet wrapped around her mangled waist; more human rings banded both her legs at mid-thigh and calf. She wore clothes of an ancient design—leather knee breeches sewn fur-side-out, underblouse and long tunic, boots with tops that wrapped instead of tying.

Sharra knew what the girl was, if not who she was. She was Ithnari.

She might have believed she'd run across the descendant of some long-ago Ithnari trapped on this side—but the timing was too much of a coincidence for that to be possible. Jim had mentioned "little people." This had to be one of the Ithnari that had come through a gate when he'd accidentally opened it, and he'd somehow pulled them through. *All the way through.* The worlds were moving together.

Time was shorter even than she'd feared.

She rose, leaving the dead Ithnari where she lay.

Omen piled upon omen, and disaster upon disaster. Sharra wondered if she might ask to get off early—she imagined telling Michael when he came in that she had to go home to find a last-minute way to save the world.

She stepped into the main stockroom, heard rustling and whispers from behind the returns shelf—the other Ithnari, no doubt—and walked past the ghell, which snarled at her. She thanked Providence *that* had not yet fully escaped through the gate. It would, of course; the instant its world came fully into line with hers, it would become both fully real and deadly.

When that might happen, she couldn't know. She wished she could be far away and safe when it did.

She could tell Jim had been looking for her when she walked down the stairs; from his expression she could also tell some of the wrongness of the last few minutes still showed on her face. And the customer who'd been waiting for Sharra was as obviously shocked as Jim was.

"Sharra . . . are you all right?" Jim's voice was uncharacteristically hoarse.

She nodded. "I'm fine. Really." She turned to the customer. "I'm so sorry . . . we don't have the book." She hurried the rest of the way down the stairs and said, "I'll be happy to call around the other local stores to see if one of them has a copy of the book they'll hold, or I could see if I can transfer a copy in from one of the other G. Galloway's—they can't have all sold out this fast. . . ."

Odd, wrong movement caught her eye—something skulked at the entryway of the store that shouldn't have been there. She glanced over the customer's shoulder, into the deep, intelligent brown eyes of a golden retriever. The dog stared at her, then walked past people who seemed not to see it at all, right into the center of the store; it jumped up on a dump table of bargain books and sat down . . . and wagged its tail and flexed its blood-caked talons . . . and grinned at her, *right at her*, and she saw fangs twice as long as any she had ever seen in the mouth of any normal dog. . . .

The golene had found her.

As the world turned dark around the edges and the sound of the sea began to roar in her ears, she had just an instant to reflect that she wasn't taking things as well as she'd thought, before she collapsed to the floor in a heap.

Chapter Twenty-six

Gali saw the dog saunter into the bookstore, sniff the air, and tread slowly and carefully between customers until it came to a low table covered with books. It jumped up on that, and one of the mehn saw it when it did—she fainted, a reaction Gali could understand. The dog didn't attack the fallen woman, though—it jumped down and strolled right past the resulting commotion, straight up the stairs and back to the door to the upstairs stockroom. To Gali's horror, it then raised up on its hind legs, opened the door for itself, and trotted inside.

Gali shivered and woke Mrestal, who'd been sleeping beside her. The two of them had found a nice spot in the middle of one of the ceiling displays, and had spent the morning after they escaped the mehn that captured them watching people. They'd considered themselves safe; she could see now that she and Mrestal had been lying to themselves.

The dog was hunting her and Mrestal, perhaps, or homing in on the smell of Eryia. Even if it had been hunting her, Gali didn't think it had seen her. That gave her, at least briefly, a survival edge. She wondered how she and Mrestal could best take advantage of that edge while they still had it.

Mrestal said, "It's really in there?"

Gali nodded. "We're going to have to find another

home tonight." She froze as a browser stopped directly in front of the display in which she and Mrestal hid; he looked from her to Mrestal, and his eyes flicked over the rest of the display—but after an instant, he nodded and began digging through the shelves in front of him. In a lower voice, Gali continued. "What about the mehn who caught us today? He said he wanted to help us. Why don't we let him?"

"Do you think he means it?"

"If he's lying, we can surely make his life miserable enough that he'll repent the lie." Gali grinned slowly, and twitched her ears.

Mrestal stretched across several volumes and yawned. "I would do much for a night's uninterrupted sleep. Almost anything, really." He shook his head sadly. "But what can we do about Eryia? We have to find a way to bury her soon—I wouldn't dare burn her, after seeing what the last pyre did, and we can't get her to earth—with the dog locked in here, we can't reach her and carry her safely to the gate, whereas if the dog is locked *outside* the gate, we can't get her to the dirt by the fountain."

"We'll have to leave her," Gali said. "The shame will mark us, but there's no honor in giving one's life to bury a dead friend. Especially not if, even after we die, Eryia remains unburied."

"Leave her lying near the ground in that stinking room?"

"We'll find a place for her—something better than the place we found." Gali recalled seeing something that might work. If they found a way to get past the dog, perhaps they could move her.

It would take some thought—as would what they intended to do next.

Then something interesting happened. *Their* mehn—the one who'd brought them to the new world—came running up the stairs, retrieved a large, grimy blue bag out of the storage room, and ran back down the stairs again—and then he and the female mehn who had fainted left. The dog, with a thoughtful expression on its furry face, trotted after the two of them.

When it was out of earshot, Mrestal said, "We could stay here now."

"No." Gali shook her head vigorously. "The dog may come back. It may not follow them wherever they're going. No. We need to get out of here."

Mrestal sighed. "Yes. You're right. Do you have any idea how we can leave safely?"

Gali thought for a moment, then smiled and nodded.

Chapter Twenty-seven

Jim looked up from the computer screen. His shift was almost over, and he was dead on his feet. It had been a very, very long day. He'd taken Sharra home after she fainted, gotten back only to discover that his monster had followed him to work. He now realized that the monster was bound to the book, would go wherever the book went. So he'd had to sneak the book out of the store on his lunch break and take it back to his apartment before the damned monster started charging out of the stockroom after customers. He had missed his lunch because he had to pick up a Barbie doll at Sears, and when he came *back*, he had to deal with a list of desperate and crazy people who wanted an assortment of books he hoped he would never see as long as he lived. Finally, he finished his display—and, he thought, discovered that elves were real.

People who complained about their tough days just didn't know anything, he decided.

"Okay, Mrs. Wilson, that's all I need. The book should be here in a week to ten days. We'll give you a call when it comes in." He managed a smile for her. She'd taught him in second grade—she didn't look a day older than she had then . . . he still guessed her age at just under a hundred.

"Thanks, Jimmy. I'll see you next week."

Jimmy. He shook his head and grinned. Mrs. Wilson was all right. Jim finished typing in the order, and printed it out, then put it in the stack to be called in the next morning. He was finally caught up with all of his paperwork, and was about to retreat upstairs to make one last run through his section when Kerri came over from the cash wrap.

"Jim! There's a lady on line one who wants to talk to you—and she really sounds pissed."

Jim raised an eyebrow. "Pissed? At me? Did she ask for me specifically? Or just for whoever was in charge? Because Michael just got here."

"She definitely wanted you."

Pissed and asking for him. Uh-oh. He couldn't think of anyone who might be mad at him . . . except maybe Sharra, and she didn't have any reason to be. He'd been so worried about her when he drove her home that he'd hovered, and she'd gotten annoyed with him, but—

He sighed. "Okay. I'll take it in the stockroom."

He hurried back to Michael's office. It couldn't be Sharra, either, he thought. Kerri would have recognized her voice. Jim took a deep breath and picked up the phone, shifting to his best "I-know-it's-all-my-fault-but-I-promise-I'll-make-it-right-again" voice.

"G. Galloway Books, Jim speaking. How may I help you?"

"I think you've already *helped* enough," said a complete stranger's voice on the other end of the line. "You've destroyed my life. But I'll get even. I just wanted you to know I'll find a way to get you for this."

Jim's mouth hung open. The woman's voice sounded familiar in the same way any Southern woman's would. No more than that. The caller seemed certain of his identity, but he had absolutely no idea who she was or what she was talking about.

"This is Jim *Franklin.* At G. Galloway *Books,*" he

told her, hoping with that clarification for an "oh, my God, I got the wrong number"—but he didn't get one. Damn. Whoever she was, she must have really meant him. He closed his eyes and said, "I'm sorry. I'll be more than happy to fix whatever's the matter, if you'll just tell me what happened. Could I get your name, please?"

"You don't even know who this *is*?" she screamed. "If you're going to totally screw up my life, you should at least have the common courtesy to recognize me when I call you. To think that I said you were only a creep. You slime. You damned . . . *pervert*! You'd have to get a personality upgrade to be a creep!"

At the word "creep" something clicked in Jim's mind and suddenly he knew who it was—Willy's girlfriend. The word wasn't what tipped him off, though. It was the *way* she said "creep." She gave it a weird, rising inflection that somehow made it seem worse than any four-letter word he knew.

"Listen, um . . ." Oh, God, he'd forgotten her name. "I'm at work right now. Would you mind calling me at home?"

"Yes," she snarled. "I'd mind."

"I'm not supposed to take personal calls—"

"You can take this one," she responded. "Willy just kicked me out of our house and threw my stuff on the lawn. We were doing fine until the night you called. We've never even had an argument. He hasn't seen you in what, three years? The two of you get together three times, and the next thing I know, he says he never wants to see me again. There's gotta be *some* reason—maybe he's sleeping with you."

Jim flushed, trying to keep his temper in check. He failed. He had felt really bad for her until she said that—but that was more than he'd take from anyone. Sleeping with Willy? The blood drained to Jim's feet and cold rage swallowed him. He spoke slowly and put as much ice as he could into each word. "Listen, dammit. Maybe he's tired of sleeping with you. Maybe he's found a girl he likes better—*maybe* he decided he liked *celibacy* better. Listening to you right now, that wouldn't be too hard to believe. But *I* don't have to take this, from you or anyone else. The best thing about modern communication," he said, fuming, "is that it's voluntary." Jim slammed the phone down hard enough to ring *his* ears, and glared at the phone.

His gut felt like it was on fire. His hands were shaking and his knuckles were white.

"I *do* hope that wasn't a customer," Michael said.

Jim jumped and turned. "Jesus, you scared me," Jim said. "I didn't hear you come in."

"Not surprising," the manager replied. "In the future, if you must take personal calls, make *some* effort to keep your voice down. The last part of that . . . discussion . . . carried out to the floor, and I'm afraid it offended several customers."

Jim nodded. "I'm sorry. I really am. It won't happen again." He was, in fact, more sorry than he'd thought he would be. He was thinking about Willy's girlfriend, and Willy—and wondering what could have possibly happened to split them up. He'd seen love once or twice before, and that had been love-with-a-capital-L that Willy was carrying around. Now, just a couple days later, he threw the girl and her stuff out of the house? He wondered if it had anything to do with the book.

Michael nodded. "I would appreciate it." He studied Jim for a moment, then shook his head and gestured at the clock. "Time, man. You're off. Go home and get some rest. You look like you need it."

Jim thanked him and, still pondering the strangeness of the phone call, went to the upstairs stockroom to sign out and get his backpack.

Kerri was up there, too, getting ready to leave. She

arched an eyebrow and studied him. "Not a happy call, I hear."

"Not," Jim agreed. He didn't feel like discussing it beyond that one word.

Kerri waited long enough to see if he'd take the opening she'd given him, and when he didn't, nodded. "Well, tomorrow is another day."

Jim sighed. "Trite, but true." He picked up his backpack and turned to leave. "If it's like this one, I think I'll take a raincheck."

Behind him, Kerri gasped. "Oh, my gawwwwd! It must have died in my *purse!*"

He dropped his backpack on the card table and gave Kerri a questioning look.

"The thing we smelled earlier. I think it's a huge rat!" she said. "It weighs a ton." Mingled disgust and horror stretched her face in comical ways. She held her purse out at arm's length and turned her face away from it.

Jim tried hard not to laugh. "Died right in your purse, huh?" He held out a hand. "I'll get rid of it for you." He sighed. "I've had experience with this sort of thing." He had, too. His apartment became, at times, the Great Rodent Dying Ground.

He carried the leather handbag into the bathroom and pulled a paper towel off the roll by the sink, wrapped it around his hand, and opened the top of the bag, ready to reach in and be the hero. The stink was bad—but he'd encountered worse. He peeked in— no sense pulling out something embarrassing along with the rat—and his amusement died a cold, sharp death.

The dead thing in the purse was no rodent. It wasn't an it, even. *She* was another little person like the two he'd discovered that morning, but her body had been mangled by something that had tried to make a lunch of her, and nearly torn her tiny body in half.

He picked the dead elf up, feeling the weight of

responsibility for her life; he'd somehow brought her into his world, and something in his world had killed her. He wrapped her in the paper towel, wondering for just an instant at the magnificent collection of gemstones adorning her body, and pondered what to do with her. He couldn't flush her down the toilet as he would have a mouse, nor could he just dump her in the trash—she deserved, he thought, some sort of burial . . . some sort of dignity.

He was going to have to take her home. Gently, he wrapped her in several more paper towels, then carried both Kerri's purse and the dead girl out into the main stockroom.

"Here," he said. "I'm afraid some of the stuff inside might be kind of messed up."

"Oh . . . gross." Kerri closed her eyes and looked a little pale. "What was it?"

"Just a . . . big mouse." Jim lied badly. He knew it—but Kerri wasn't in the mood to question his find, or thankfully, to ask to take a look at the body. "Something . . . got it," he added, and watched Kerri swallow convulsively.

She nodded. "Thanks for taking care of it for me. Why are you carrying it with you?"

Jim took a deep breath. "It was too big to put down the toilet, and, um, I didn't want to leave it in the bathroom because, uh . . . I didn't know if the janitor would empty that can tonight. It's going to smell pretty bad by morning. So I figured I'd take it home and . . . um, dump it there."

He unzipped his backpack and dropped the body in, then retrieved the Barbie doll from the top shelf, tossed it in, too, and zipped the bag shut. He hadn't seen the elves since Kerri had barged in on them this morning—he'd just have to show them that Barbie was fake tomorrow.

He had been planned on going home, showering

and changing, then running by Sharra's to see if she was feeling any better. He wasn't sure she'd welcome him—she'd made it pretty clear by the time he got her home that she didn't want him hanging around—but during their picnic he'd asked her a whole lot of questions, and he'd only just realized that she hadn't bothered to answer any of them.

He gave that fact some thought during his drive home, and decided Sharra was either on the run from the law, or trapped in a relationship with a real asshole, or else had some sort of god-awful fatal disease that was also transmissible. Nothing that promised any hope for a future for the two of them, in any case.

He pulled into his driveway and groaned—he could see the monster lurking by the front window. Hoping the thing had not somehow become fully real while he was at work, Jim swung his backpack onto his shoulder, and was momentarily startled by how heavy it was. The corpse weighed more than he'd realized.

But his mind quickly went back to the problem of Sharra. It's just my luck to fall in love with a girl with problems, he thought.

That thought stopped him cold. Was he really in *love* with her? Maybe it was just infatuation, in which case he could walk away; God knew he didn't need to take on anyone else's problems, not ever again. He was done with brave deeds and noble gestures, through with heroism and saving people from each other or the harsh world or their own stupid selves. The world had no room in it for knights on white horses—not anymore.

"Enlightened self-interest," he muttered, walking toward the stairs. "That's my creed."

And if the question came up, that was what he would tell Sharra, too. He was sorry he'd kissed her, he didn't mean anything by it, he was going to bow gracefully out of her life and wish her the best of luck in the future.

He nodded firmly and fumbled with the lock on his door. That was certainly the best way to handle this.

He wouldn't even bother with the shower-and-shave-and-change routine first. He'd go over just the way he was, and make sure she hadn't suffered any permanent damage from her fainting spell at work, and he'd give her the news he figured she'd really want to hear . . . as soon as he'd found a shoebox and buried the elf-girl.

Practical, efficient, and looking out for himself—*that* was Jim Franklin, he decided, feeling better.

He dug around through the mess in his closet until he found the shoebox he'd been certain was in there. He didn't usually save them, but he'd had to pick up another pair of work shoes just the week before—the floors at G. Galloway were hell on cheap shoes. He wondered where he ought to bury the little elf; since he no longer had neighbors, he could probably put her in the weedy yard back of the apartments, but that seemed tacky. The place down by the creek where he'd had his picnic with Sharra would make a good spot.

He hated the very idea of what he had to do next. He went back out to the kitchen to get the corpse, dreading having to handle it again.

His backpack sat where he'd dropped it, on the counter . . . already open.

He looked in. The little corpse was gone.

Jim spun around and stared at the monster hulking in front of the window. Oh, shit, he thought. If it could eat the elf, it could do something to me, too. But did it eat the elf?

What else could have taken it?

Nothing else, he decided. He started sidling toward the door, moving slowly and keeping the monster in sight. The thing seemed to be paying him no attention at all, but he was sure it knew what he was doing.

Holding his breath, shaking inside, he moved to ten feet from the door, then eight feet, then six feet—

And the monster turned and leapt in a single smooth motion, straight for the door, fangs bared, claws spread. It landed less than a foot in front of him, and Jim yelled and turned and fled; he raced down the narrow hall trying to decide if his bedroom door would hold against the thing long enough for him to break out the window and jump to the ground below. The jump might kill him, he thought, slamming the door in the monster's face, jamming one foot at the base of it, and reaching behind him to drag his bed against it—the jump *might* kill him. He wedged the bed under the doorknob, surprised the damned thing wasn't battering against it on the other side. He figured that before it thought of beating the door down, he ought to wedge his dresser against the bed.

He turned—and the monster grinned at him.

Jim shrieked and backed into the wall—and the monster, still grinning, charged at him and said, "Kill you," and slashed at his gut.

The claws ripped through Jim's belly . . .

Painlessly?

Jim's eyes narrowed, and he stared up at the monster. It was in the room, but it hadn't come through the door. It had come through the wall. It *wasn't* solid.

It grinned at him and said, "Kill you," again, and Jim saw red.

"Kill me?" he yelled. "Kill me, will you? Well, I don't think so. Kill *you*! THROUGH you, you bastard!"

He charged the monster, trying to jump right into his middle. This time it was the fanged nightmare that backed up, yelling. The monster dematerialized through the bed and the door, and vanished into the hall beyond. Jim shoved the bed out of the way, yanked the door open, and raced after it, mayhem in his heart.

The monster, which had slowed to a walk, heard him coming, and ran away.

Jim caught up with it, ran into it again—and the monster, with a howl, slipped down through the floor.

Behind him, Jim heard clapping.

He turned and found the two elves from the bookstore sitting on his kitchen table, applauding. Of the dead third elf, there was no sign.

He stared from one to the other and frowned. "You got here in my backpack, didn't you?"

They grinned and nodded, but said nothing.

"Where's the other one?"

The two of them pointed outside and toward the back of the apartment. Jim could see nothing in that direction from his apartment—it shared a wall with the other apartment, the one whose main view was of the weedy, disreputable back yard.

Jim walked out on the rickety landing and looked back.

The back yard was on fire. The weeds were blazing merrily, and black smoke poured from the yard—he could see a circular outline in the center of the fire that burned brighter than the rest of the conflagration, and with flames of a green hue instead of the raging orange. He suspected the blaze had started there; but wherever it had started, it was, in the August-baked weeds, spreading in record time.

Jim bounded down the steps to the hose the four apartments shared for car-washing—he turned on the water and began spraying it low to the ground and right in front of himself, beating down the closest flames and working in and from side to side in a methodical pattern.

He got the fire under control, beat it back to that still merrily blazing center, and put out all of it but the bright green flames in the middle. The burning center, though, proved intractable. While it wasn't a gasoline fire, he wondered if it was, perhaps, something chemical. The water from the garden hose didn't even make it sputter.

Jim frowned. When he looked closely at that little circle of flame, he could make out a familiar shape at the heart of it. There lay the third elf . . . and there, too, lay the answer to how the fire had started. Jim looked back at his landing. Both elves stood there, watching him fighting the fire.

He yelled, "How do I put this out!"

Neither answered him.

"Dammit, I have to know. How do I put this out? The apartment will burn down if it spreads that far!"

They looked at each other, then one of them jumped from the landing to the ground below, and bounded to his side. "You can not put it out," the male told him, while he watched Jim futilely playing water over the green flames. "It will go out of its own accord when Eryia's spirit has ascended to the Dreamlands."

"Great," Jim muttered. "With my luck, she'll go to Hell."

Apparently, Eryia did go to elf-heaven—but she took her own sweet time doing it. By the time Jim got into the house, the clock had already rolled past the magic 10 P.M. phone-calling hour—he couldn't possibly call Sharra, and he decided he was too tired to call Willy to find out what had happened between him and his girlfriend. He took a quick shower instead, and grabbed a bite to eat.

Then he glowered at his two guests.

"Aren't you going to feed us?" the girl asked.

Jim glared at her and shook his head.

"You aren't going to feed us?" The male looked startled, then sly. "We could make your life miserable."

"Like you haven't been already? I just spent four

hours in my back yard putting out a fire you two started."

"We could do worse."

The monster started to come into the kitchen, but Jim growled at him and said, "Through you, bud," and the nightmare reconsidered, and drifted down through the floor to the apartment below.

Both elves looked at each other, then at Jim. "The ghell is an evil creature," the girl offered at last.

"No shit." Jim slapped peanut butter on two additional slices of bread, smeared jelly over them, and jammed the slices together. "You called it a 'gal'?"

"Ghell. It is one of the lesser creatures from the demon-world. I'm surprised you are able to frighten it."

Jim snorted. "Yeah. And the first time it turns solid will be the last time I get to frighten it . . . because then it's going to eat me."

The male nodded. "Probably. That's part of what ghells do—they eat the bodies and the souls of their victims—but they do magical favors for people who can control them. They're very wicked."

"Eat the body *and* the soul, huh? Thanks so much for telling me. I just love knowing that. Tell you what—" He stopped talking long enough to take a huge bite out of his sandwich, then continued, talking around the food. "Since you're so full of fascinating information, why don't you tell me what you are, and *who* you are, so I know at least as much about you as the ghell. If you do, I'll give you something to eat. Deal?"

Mrestal said, "First, you were going to prove that these 'Barbies' which we cremated were never alive."

Jim nodded and reached behind him, getting the backpack off of the counter. He pulled out the doll. The two elves backed away, and Gali looked as though she were going to be sick.

"It's nothing to be afraid of," Jim said. He loosened

the wire ties that secured the doll to its box, then held it out toward the elves. "It's just plastic."

"This proves nothing," Gali said. "It is the same as the ones that we liberated from undeath in the crypt of the death-god."

Jim grabbed the Barbie's head with one hand and her legs with the other, and pulled the head from the doll. The elves gasped, and Gali looked even more disgusted.

"Murderer," she said softly.

Jim said, "It's not what you think," and held out the hollow head of the doll for the elves to see.

It took them a few seconds to gather the courage to glance inside the severed head, but when they finally did, both of the Ithnari gasped, astonished.

Gali whispered, "There is nothing inside its head."

Jim grinned. "That's a large part of the appeal, I suspect."

Jim took out a pocket knife and sawed one of the Barbie's legs in half. The undifferentiated pink circle of soft plastic with its hard core of white bore no resemblance to anything that had ever lived. Finally the elves believed; then and only then were they ready to discuss the things that had been happening at the mall.

An hour later, they finished talking, and Jim rocked back on the legs of his chair and stared at the ceiling. "The candy bars at McDaltey's, the jewelry at Bob's Jewel Shop, the fire at Kay-Bee, *and* the fire here— you guys are a regular crime wave."

Mrestal sighed. "I can't believe we thought the Barbies were real."

Jim wrinkled his nose and said, "Don't feel bad. You'd be amazed at the women who think that Barbie's real."

"Then the Barbie, it's a sort of religious symbol? Like an idol?"

Jim grinned. "Exactly like." He leaned forward again,

and the front two legs of his chair dropped to the floor with a thump. He stopped smiling and said, "Gali, do you have any idea where that dog came from?"

"It came through the magic gates. It was summoned."

Jim sighed. "I hope I'm not the person who brought it here."

"I would think you'd know if you had. It takes a powerful magician to manipulate the gates—that isn't something done by accident."

"I accidentally brought you through the gates."

"Accidentally. How could you possibly do that?"

Jim rolled his eyes. "If I knew how it happened, I wouldn't have done it. I accidentally brought the ghell here, too."

The Ithnari both shook their heads. "Tell us how you did these spells."

So Jim told them about the book, and the magic words, and the things that didn't go the way he'd expected.

"Where is this book?" Mrestal said.

Jim brought it out, and spread it on the kitchen table. The two elves—or rather, Ithnari—sat cross-legged, turning the pages and reading. Finally, Mrestal looked up.

"Show me one of the spells you did."

Jim looked through the book, struggled with the loopy, squirming letters, and found the love spell he'd tried to use on Sharra. The two Ithnari glanced over it, and Mrestal said, "Jim, this isn't a love spell. It's one of several spells in this book designed to break the first seal on the gate."

Jim shook his head. "Right there, it says, 'Simple Increase of Devotion.' You see? In the header?"

Mrestal said, "There is a simple illusion spell over the pages of this book. Didn't you check that first?"

"How would I check a thing like that? I don't know anything about magic."

Mrestal paled. "And you used some unknown magician's spellbook anyway? You deserve to be eaten by a ghell!"

"How was I supposed to know it was real? The bookstore is full of crap like this, and none of it works."

Gali leaned back on her elbows and crossed her legs at the ankles. She grinned at him, and her pointed little teeth gleamed in the yellow light of the single bulb. "It wasn't like this then, was it? The first of the spells in this book was designed to open the gate between the worlds. Lukas Smalling, the wizard who created the spells, designed it so."

"But that book is more than two hundred years old," Jim said. "I don't think I need to worry about old Lukas anymore."

Mrestal stuck his hand into the peanut butter and got himself a huge gob of it. He settled on the tabletop next to Gali and the two of them took turns taking fingerfuls of peanut butter and licking their fingertips with evident glee. Mrestal said, "You *might* have to worry about him. Inside the gate, locked between the worlds, time doesn't pass. And a magician with the ability to create these spells and use you to work them is a magician with enough power to be a threat, even now."

"Fine. Maybe he's a threat." Jim was getting sleepy— it had been one hell of a long, weird day. "But if he's still a threat, what is he threatening?"

Mrestal looked at the book again. "The second spell is the one that brings Lukas's servant to him."

Jim winced. "The ghell?"

"I'd figure that would be his sort of servant."

"And the others?"

"The third spell is supposed to bring Lukas himself. The fourth . . ." The Ithnari shivered and his eyes darkened. "The fourth will bring the demons of a hundred planes to do Lukas's bidding."

"Oh." Jim looked at the book, thinking about the demons of a hundred planes, and trying to compare them to the single demon in his living room. His stomach turned itself into a very tight pretzel at the image that conjured. "And what sort of bidding do you think he might have in mind?"

Mrestal looked up. "Nobody knows that but Lukas."

Chapter Twenty-eight

TUESDAY

Sharra wasn't sick.

She *was* terrified.

She'd been sleeping in—she wasn't due to be at work until noon—when something set off her housewards. She sprang out of bed, pulling her pitiful excuse for a magical shield around herself like a tattered bathrobe. She could never understand why her spells didn't get any stronger. She had all of Lukas's reference library to study, as well as his notebooks, but she never seemed to advance.

She crept down the hall, her heart pounding. The clock began to strike, and Sharra jumped. It tolled thirteen, slowly, the once-musical notes dulled and transmuted into the thudding of a huge, evil heart—thirteen ugly, cursed pulses that reminded her she was not alone and not safe in her own home—though the actual time according to the clock was 10:24.

She crept from window to window and door to door, checking her wards, feeling for the signature of whatever—or whomever—had set them off. She found nothing. Whatever the danger had been, it had merely brushed past them on its way to somewhere else. Her heart slowed down to a normal rate, and she caught her breath and sagged onto her couch and laid her head on the overstuffed armrest.

Not yet, then.

In spite of the lowered blinds, she could tell the weather outside was beautiful—slivers of sunlight streamed through the gaps around their edges and scattered bright patterns like gold coins across the faded rugs and old wood floors. Though the windows were closed and the doors shut and locked, she could hear birds singing outside her window—the simple song of a cardinal, the chattering of finches, the virtuosity of one mockingbird who'd made the telephone pole in front of her drive his post, from whence to deliver his incredible librettos. She could hear the rhythmic creak of the next-door neighbors' swing set, and knew that Lise was out hanging her laundry on the line, while her four-year-old daughter May was busy flying through the air on her private plane, her flying horse, her beloved swing. The sounds played counterpoint to Sharra's sterile, lonely life, and left her wistful and hurting.

Sharra heard the garbage truck rumbling down the street, and remembered she hadn't put her trash out. She thought of the simple, underrated freedom she'd known only days before, to run out her door lugging a bag, waving; she'd do no such thing now. Her trash would wait—if there were still a world in three days, she'd carry it out then.

She wouldn't step out her door now—not for anyone. Not until the trouble that was coming was over.

She could feel Lukas in the air around her, in every breath she took. She was no more able to describe the feeling, even to herself, than a hound dog would have been able to give words to the act of finding a rabbit trail in wet dirt and leaf-mold—but she was no less sure of her senses than that hound dog would have been.

Lukas was near, searching for her, hunting her with every bit of magical skill and human cleverness at his disposal. When he found her, the world would end—at very least for her. If his magic worked as he hoped, and as she feared, the world would end for almost everyone.

She needed help. She couldn't beat Lukas alone. She might, she thought, have a few days to gather help, to convince people of the danger—though she watched the readers of the New Age section at G. Galloway's closely, as she had, for the preceding two hundred years, kept a close watch on the local occult groups and covens, hoping to find a worthy assistant, or even a teacher. There wasn't a one who was even her equal at magic—there never had been. She imagined she could enlist the assistance of the coveners and New Agers she knew—they were, for the most part, good, caring people—but when Lukas struck, she'd be throwing them into a magical meat grinder, and dead they would be of no use to her.

And she thought of Jim. She'd feared he was the reincarnation of Lukas the first time she'd seen him, and there still hung about him that taint of wrongness—anger misdirected, guilt and blame mixed badly and aged poorly, self-pity—all things she had felt in Lukas, had felt driving Lukas.

Those elements were in Jim, but Jim had other qualities that had never brushed against Lukas's cold soul, things that tempered him. Courage, honor, compassion, humor, desire. If Jim was flawed, he was no more so than she, who did nothing without first counting the cost, assessing the risks, weighing her desire against her security.

And if Jim didn't have the magical talent or the magical power that would fight off Lukas, he did, she now knew, have the single book she lacked and needed, and perhaps he had both the courage and the altruism to fight beside her to send Lukas back to the prison in which he'd been chained for over two hundred years—or to destroy him outright, if such a thing were possible. She hoped she was right about Jim.

Maybe there was still time to enlist his help. Maybe, in spite of her treatment of him, in spite of her rejection of his kiss, of his offered love, he would still listen to her.

She would call him when he got home from work, she decided. Talk to him, ask him to come over so she could explain things. He wouldn't believe her at first—how could he?—but she could show him things that might help him believe. Perhaps she wouldn't have to die after all.

Chapter Twenty-nine

Jim sweated and strained, staring at the candle, but nothing happened . . . again. He glared at the Ithnari, as though they were responsible for his failure. That's the second time, he thought. This is impossible.

"You're trying too hard," Gali said. "The first thing you have to do is relax. Breathe deeply, in through your nose, imagining warm water flowing up from your feet, over your legs, stomach, chest, and head—then out through your mouth, and feel it flowing down your back, towards the floor. Try to relax each muscle as you imagine the water flowing over you."

Jim sat there, breathing, feeling like an idiot. But slowly, gradually, it began to seem as though he were drifting in time to the cadence of Gali's voice.

"Good," she said. "Now, close your eyes, and imagine the candle wick getting hotter. Think of the hottest day you can remember, and send that heat and more into the candle. See the first faint spark, as the wick begins to light. Stay relaxed, or you'll lose it. . . . Now! Light the candle."

Jim *saw* the flame, springing forth purplish-blue at the base near the wick, and creamy yellow above. He smelled the first sharp, acrid smoke as the wick ignited, and then the smoother scent of wax warming and starting to melt. Then he opened his eyes, and—once again, nothing had happened.

"That was much better," Gali said. "Let's try it again."

It didn't look any better to Jim. He didn't *want* to try it again. He was tired, he was frustrated, he'd had a lousy day at work, and this wasn't working.

He *also* hadn't gotten to sleep until after two o'clock in the morning—the damned ghell kept charging him, and coming up through the mattress right beside him just as he was dozing off. The "through you" trick worked, but the monster was getting fast at dodging, and the last couple of times it had only stayed gone for a few seconds.

Finally, Jim had had enough. He took the book and tossed it in the trunk of his car, and drove to the abandoned Kmart three blocks from his apartment. He parked the car there, and walked back home. The ghell charged him a couple of times, and followed along. trying to scare him, but near the end of the second block, it stopped following.

When Jim realized the monster was no longer beside him, he turned, and saw the creature straining against an invisible barrier, trying to get at him.

Two blocks, Jim thought. He has to stay within two blocks of the book. Then he grinned, as an evil thought crossed his mind. He'd once seen his mother's cat walk to the outer reach of the chain that bound their neighbor's Rottweiler to a tree, and stand there, just out of reach, taunting the dog. At the time, Jim had thought Sheba was just being cruel—but he was beginning to see her point.

He studied the ghell for a second, and noted the exact boundary of the spot where the creature was struggling to move forward. Then Jim went right up to the edge of the barrier that held it back, and stood there, smirking.

The creature's face grew livid with rage, and it hurled itself at the barrier again and again. Jim watched and waited until the monster leaped, then stepped purposefully into the spot where it was going to land, and smiled. The ghell's expression went from rage straight to abject terror, as its body passed through Jim's. It immediately turned to flee, but Jim quickly reached out and waved his hand in and out through the center of the retreating monster's head. He laughed as the creature ran away. That ought to make him think twice before he messes with me again, Jim thought.

The memory of giving the ghell his comeuppance lifted some of the frustration from Jim's shoulders. That had been one of the very few good things to happen that day. He breathed a heavy sigh, and said, "Okay. *Once* more. But if it doesn't work this time, we give up, at least for today."

Gali talked Jim through the whole relaxation bit again. She assured him that once he had practiced a while, he would be able to enter the appropriate state of mind with a single breath in and a single slow exhalation. Considering that it had so far taken him no less than ten minutes each time, Jim was a bit skeptical.

Once he was relaxed, he began imagining the heat building up around the wick. She kept telling him to hold it back a bit longer. Jim was visualizing a day last summer, when it had been a hundred and five degrees, with ninety-eight percent humidity. He could still clearly remember the awful heat of that day, could feel the sun beating down, the back of his neck burning; he thought the memory into the candle. Sweat beaded his own brow, and trickled down the back of his shirt. He kept visualizing the heat increasing, as the sun rose higher in the sky.

Then he went through the whole stupid business of visualizing the flame catching on the wick, the smell of wax melting, smelling the smoke . . . he could *really* smell the smoke this time. He opened his eyes again. The candle wasn't burning—but he could *still* smell the smoke. In fact, he could *see* the smoke—coming out of the kitchen. Oh, no—

He jumped to his feet, and ran for the stove. He'd been baking a pound cake to take into work, but he'd forgotten it when the Ithnari started the magic lesson. He opened the oven door, then slammed it shut again quickly.

That's the first time I *ever* burned one bad enough that it actually caught fire, he thought, as he filled a pitcher with water. He threw open the oven and tossed the water on the pound cake. Steam and smoke poured out, making Jim cough and sputter.

The fire was out, but then the smoke alarm started blaring. Jim ran into the living room to turn it off, and was halfway there when the phone rang. He turned around and rushed back the way he'd come, then his right foot slipped in the water on the kitchen floor, and his feet came out from under him. He landed on the seat of his pants, right in the puddle of water.

He sprang to his feet, cursing, and ran to pick up the phone.

"Acme Detonators, R&D division, what can I do for you?" he shouted over the buzz of the smoke alarm.

"Jim? Is that you?" a female voice inquired.

Shit, it's Sharra, Jim thought. Why is it that the people you really want to talk to *always* call in the middle of disasters?

"Hang on just a second, Sharra. Let me kill the smoke alarm."

He laid the phone on the kitchen counter, and balanced on one foot while he took his tennis shoe off of the other. He ran into the living room and smashed the cover off the smoke alarm, then knocked the battery loose with his second blow. The raucous blaring ceased, and its dying note echoed in the sudden silence. Jim hurried back to the kitchen, and picked up the phone.

"Sharra?" he said. "I'm back." But she didn't answer. What is this, he wondered, some kind of a joke? He was about to hang up the phone when he heard a piercing scream in the distance on the other end of the line. "Sharra?" he yelled. "Sharra!"

Jim hung up the receiver in a panic. Something terrible was happening. He had to get over there. But he might need some help. He picked up the phone again, and dialed Willy's number. When he put the receiver to his ear, he heard only dead air.

Damn, he thought. I can't call out—Sharra's phone is still off the hook, so my line is tied up.

He let the phone drop to the floor, rummaging for his keys. He skinned out of the wet jeans he was wearing, and rooted around on the floor for the pair that he'd left his keys in last night. He finally found them and pulled them on, then ran out of the bedroom with one shoe in his hand, looking for the other one that he'd used to turn off the smoke alarm. He flopped on the couch and forced his shoes on without untying them.

"What's going on?" Mrestal asked.

Jim said, "Something's happened to Sharra—I've got to get over her house."

"Where's your backpack?" Gali asked.

"In the bedroom," Jim said. "Why?"

"Because we don't want anyone to see us, but we're going with you," she answered. Gali smiled, baring her tiny, pointed teeth. "They may be small," she said. "but you never know when an extra set of fangs might come in handy."

His car . . .

. . . was three blocks away in the bombed-out Kmart parking lot.

Bad timing, Jim, he thought. Good idea . . . but *bad* timing.

Chapter Thirty

Jim gunned the engine, and the Nova's tires barked as they left the rough asphalt for the smoother concrete of Sharra's driveway. He pulled around back, to the covered carport. Sharra's black Prelude was still there. Jim grabbed his backpack, and looked inside to make sure the Ithnari were all right. Then he sprinted for the back door, hoping fervently that Sharra's car being here meant that nothing was the matter, after all.

But the back door was standing wide open, and the clay geranium pots on the corner of the patio had been toppled and broken. The deck chairs were scattered and overturned, and the table and umbrella had been knocked over. It was clear that a struggle had recently taken place.

Jim crept nervously into the living room. There was a fireplace, and he took the poker from its rack on the hearth. The house was too quiet. He was fairly sure that whatever had happened, Sharra was gone. But he had to be sure, so he stepped cautiously into the hall.

He turned right first. Kitchen. Nothing in here, he thought. Dining room, also empty. He didn't see any sign of a recent struggle, either, so those two rooms were a dead end. He turned back the way he had come, started down the hall, and glanced into the first room on his left.

Jim looked about him in amazement. Somehow, he thought this might be what he was looking for. Dark walnut bookshelves were built into the walls, and the smell of old leather and old paper filled the room. But as beautiful as the library was, it wasn't what caught Jim's attention.

On a leather-covered table in the center of the room, there were two enormous pedestal candles, a clear crystal chalice, the sheath from a dagger, and a stack of leather-bound journals. All of this sat atop a black silk cloth, with symbols Jim recognized from the grimoire stitched into it in silver.

Two of the journals had fallen to the floor in the struggle, but Jim glanced at the one that was open on the table. The pages were worn and yellowed, and the ink had run in several places, where the book had apparently been water-damaged. And as Jim had half expected, the script was Lukas Smalling's now-familiar spidery scrawl.

The date at the top of the journal page was July 17, 1773. Jim studied the difficult handwriting, and wonder and fear warred within him, as he read:

Today, I know that I have failed. With the blood of my virgin bride, I summoned a ghell to the half-way point, and bound it as the spell required. The creature is truly hideous. It stares at me out of blind eyes and laughs at me.

The spell did not work properly. I now know that Sharra has been granted the immortality that I had intended for myself. For the first time, I begin to feel that my plans may be in jeopardy. I must find another way to draw back the veil of time. I will be there when the time comes. I must. The moment of conjunction has passed, but it will come again. When the two prime worlds again reach their nearest point, I will open the gate between them. With the power of both worlds at my command, nothing will stop me from ruling them both.

Below this line, there was a series of symbols, which had absolutely no meaning to Jim, but reminded him ominously of several equations he'd seen in the Advanced Math course he had flunked his senior year in high school. These were followed by a new date: July 20, 1773, and another entry:

Several of the primary sources indicate that Sharra's immortality can be transferred to me simply by sacrificing her to the ghell. *I will do it tomorrow.*

This was the last entry on the page. Jim flipped through the rest of the book. There were several blank pages, and then the text started up again, this time in a new hand. Jim had seen samples of this handwriting before—on her paperwork at the bookstore. The date was July 23, 1773—but the writing was unmistakably Sharra's.

Chapter Thirty-one

Considering what had been going on for the last week, Jim had been prepared for something weird. But he hadn't been prepared to discover that the girl of his dreams was slightly more than two hundred years old.

He began reading Sharra's journal entries.

July 23, 1773. Lukas came for me, as I feared that he would. I know not how I knew he intended to kill me, but somehow I did. He had kept me locked up in my room without feeding me for several days, so I pretended to be faint, so that he would have to carry me down the stairs to his work room. He has ever been of frail health, and I would need every advantage I could claim, if I were to survive that encounter.

The hideous creature which he had summoned with my blood sulked angrily in the corner of the room. It threw itself repeatedly against the invisible wall by which Lukas's spell held it prisoner. Lukas dropped me on the floor, and stood there, panting. I knew that if I were to kill him before he could kill me, I would have to act quickly.

While I pretended to be unconscious, he crossed the room and took a live rat out of a cage. He tossed it to the monster, and for the first time I realized that the walls of its prison were no barrier, save only to the creature itself. Before I could lose my nerve, I sprang up, and shoved Lukas across the lines that marked the boundaries of his protections. The beast leapt at him, but Lukas did something, and the beast skulked back, afraid. Still, Lukas could not escape, and he began to fade before my eyes.

Then he cursed me, and revealed the curse he had already laid upon me. He told me that I would never grow old, though all those that I knew would wither and die. Further, he also revealed that as it was my virgin blood that gave the spell its potency, I must remain ever chaste, or I will crumble to dust at the instant of consummation.

He said that he would return from the grave, and that I would pay for what I had done, and all the world would pay with me. He then spoke several words in a language I have never heard before, and disappeared in a blinding flash of light. I do not know if he lives or is dead, but he no longer torments me. Still, I wonder if he spoke the truth.

Jim flipped through dozens of entries relating to magical research, some spaced twenty, thirty, even fifty years apart. Then he reached a new entry.

I have feared for some time now that Jim Franklin is really Lukas. He looks almost exactly the same as Lukas did at the time when I married him. He is taller, of course, and sturdy and muscular where Lukas was always frail and sickly, but otherwise the resemblance is uncanny. He has asked me out, and I find him attractive, but I can't allow myself to feel for him.

And a later entry read:

I feel the taint of Lukas's magic around him. I no longer believe that Jim and Lukas are one and the same, but I can no longer doubt that Lukas is trying to return. Today I saw the ghell in the store. The time is nearing. If Lukas can be stopped, it will have to be soon.

Jim put down the book, and stepped away from the

table. He went down the hall, and hung up the telephone, trying to figure out what to do. Obviously, he couldn't call the police—they'd just get him a nice padded room. It might be exactly what he needed, but it seemed a few days too late for that now.

He decided to call Willy. The phone rang three times, and Karen's voice came on—he'd gotten the answering machine, and Willy hadn't changed the message yet.

Jim hung up. He always hated talking to those things—they made him feel like a moron, and generally drove him crazy. Which seemed a much shorter trip, lately.

Now what? he wondered.

He remembered the Ithnari. He'd left them in his backpack on the seat of the car. He ran outside and got them.

Gali looked angrily at him, and said, "It's about time. We can't be much help if you forget we're with you, you know."

Jim said, "I'm sorry. I was just a little tense, and I forgot . . . er . . . I was afraid you guys might get hurt."

Mrestal laughed. "*We* might get hurt," he said sarcastically. "Mister 'can't even light a candle' over here is afraid that *we'll* get hurt. So what did you find out, anyway?" he asked.

"Sharra is either the wife of the guy that wrote the grimoire, or else she and someone else have gone to a hell of a lot of trouble to convince me she is," Jim said. "I don't think she's trying to deceive me—it just doesn't fit. Which means she's got to be at least two hundred years old."

"Where is the book?" Gali asked.

Jim picked them up and carried them into the library. He put them both down on the table.

"Right here," he said, pointing to the journal.

Gali came over, and ran her hands along the edge

of the page. Her eyes closed in concentration. After a moment, she opened them, and said, "The journals are real. The tree this paper was made from died over two hundred years ago, and the ink is equally old." To Mrestal, she added, "They're probably valuable, too. Do you want to steal them?"

Mrestal said, "Now isn't the time."

Jim ignored the two of them. He looked around the room thoughtfully. "I kind of figured that, anyway. I couldn't think of any reason why someone would go to this much trouble to try and convince me, or anyone else, that Sharra was ancient and tied up with bad magic. It would be pointless if it weren't true." He thought for a moment. "I don't suppose you can do anything with your magic to figure out where Sharra is, can you?"

Gali shrugged. "It's really not the kind of magic we do well," she said. "Ithnari location spells are very slow—they can sometimes take several days to work."

"That's no good," Jim said. "Maybe there's something in the book—"

The telephone rang, and Jim ran to get it.

"Hello," he said. "Sharra Mills residence, can I help you?"

"Jim!" said the voice on the other end. "It's Willy."

Willy's voice was still screwed up—whatever the spell had done, it hadn't been kind to his vocal cords.

"Willy! I've been trying to get you on the phone! Something's happened to Sharra. Her place is all trashed, and someone may have kidnapped her."

"Not someone," Willy said, "some*thing*. I was driving past the entrance to Aaron Lakes, and I saw your monster carrying her off into the woods. When did the ghell become solid?"

Oh, shit. Jim suddenly realized that he *hadn't* seen the ghell all day. And if the creature had Sharra . . .

"I didn't know that he had," Jim said. "We've got

to find them, before he does something terrible to her."

"I already know where they are," Willy said. "I followed the monster. I'll meet you at your apartment; it's closer. We can take my car, and go rescue Sharra. Be sure to bring your book—we're going to need it."

Jim said, "I'll be there in a few minutes. And thanks." Then he slammed down the phone, and grabbed his backpack.

Jim turned to the elves. "Sharra's in trouble, and Willy knows where she is. I've got to help her. If you're coming, then let's go!"

Chapter Thirty-two

Jim opened the car door, and Gali and Mrestal bounded onto the seat. They watched him curiously as he started the car and backed out of his parking space.

"Where are we going?" Mrestal asked.

"Back to the apartment," Jim said. "Willy's going to meet us there. He knows where we can find Sharra."

Jim turned into the apartment complex. He saw Willy's car parked in front of his building, but no one was in it. That's weird, he thought. I wonder where they could be? He was pulling into a parking space when the Ithnari went crazy.

"We've got to get out of here," Gali said. There's *something* in the apartment."

"What do you mean, something?"

"Big magic," the elf answered, "and more evil than even your ghell could create."

Jim took a deep breath. He could get to Aaron Lakes on his own. Willy would have to take care of himself. . . .

And then he thought—Hell of a friend I am.

Jim sat there, torn between running into the apartment to see if Willy was all right, and racing off to save Sharra.

Then he saw Willy come out of his apartment, dragging Sharra in front of him. She shouted something

Jim didn't hear—then Willy slapped her hard across the face, and Sharra spun into the wall. Jim turned off the car but left the keys in the ignition. "He's gone nuts. I'm going to beat the shit out of him for hitting Sharra."

"The man is not what you think—and the girl is his prisoner," Gali said. "The man is the source of the evil I sensed—he's a wizard."

"No," Jim said, "he's an old high-school friend of mine that's about to get his ass whipped."

Jim opened his door—and a low, grating voice rumbled from the back seat, "Now you give book to Lukas-master," and an arm gestured straight at Willy. The ghell was back, and its voice was stronger. Jim found this a bad sign.

The creature grinned evilly. "That one mine," he said, pointing at Sharra.

Jim leaned over the back seat and reached through the monster and through the rotted rear window ledge and got the grimoire out of the trunk. "Through you," he snarled. "And she's *not* yours. She's mine."

The monster melted through the floorboard. Jim fumbled around beneath the passenger seat, and came up with a tire iron.

He climbed back into his seat and handed the book to Mrestal. "Watch this until I get back. Guard it with your life."

Mrestal said, "Wait just one instant. I can give you a moment of stealth, so that, if you are quiet, you can move as quickly as you like and your enemy will not see you." The Ithnari wove a net of green light from his fingertips, and tossed it over Jim. "Hurry. On one your size, it will not last long."

Jim jumped out of the car, locked the door, and shut it softly behind him. He had no way of knowing if the elf magic worked, but it didn't matter. He was going after Willy anyway—for hitting Sharra . . . and for whatever else he'd done to her.

"I know you're out there, Jim," Willy yelled. His voice sounded oilier and more repulsive than it had over the phone. Jim ran across the grass through the darkness, trying to figure his approach. If he went up his own steps, he would know which ones to step on to maintain his silence—but if the magic wasn't working, he gave up any hope of surprising Willy.

If it was working, he didn't want to waste it.

He decided to go up his own stairs.

He had an idea of what had happened to Willy. The elves, when they looked over the magic book, had said the third spell had been designed to summon the wizard Lukas. Maybe it didn't summon all of him—just his spirit. Willy was the one who'd used the book the third time. If he'd accidentally done the spell to summon Lukas—or, a suspicious part of his mind offered, if the book had tricked Willy into doing the spell it wanted—then Willy might truly be the wizard Lukas Smalling, and not his old friend. It would explain a lot.

Jim went up the stairs as Willy shouted again, "Come on out, Jim! I'll start hurting her if you don't bring me the book." Then he looked over Jim's head and off into the distance and said, "Oh, there you are. Where have you been hiding?"

Jim thought, You don't fool me. You don't know I'm here at all.

Fire flew from Willy's fingertips, though not at Jim—he made it up the last of the steps. Sharra didn't see him, Willy didn't see him . . . it was just like shooting fish in a barrel. He thumped Willy on the head with the tire iron, hoping he hadn't hit him too hard—he just wanted to knock some sense back into his old friend and find a way to get Lukas Smalling's spirit out of his body.

He grabbed Sharra before she fell.

"Follow me!" he whispered, and she looked straight

at him, seeing him for the first time. They turned to go down the stairs . . . and ran straight into the ghell. Sharra gasped, and Jim bounced back against the railing. Jim suffered a brief moment of shock as he realized the monster was suddenly corporeal. Then Jim gripped the tire iron like a baseball bat and swung with everything he had. The metal tool connected with a thud and a sickening crack that Jim hoped was the sound of ribs cracking. The beast howled and backed up a step, and Jim and Sharra bolted down the stairs.

Chapter Thirty-three

Willy rose to his feet just as they started down the stairs. He came over to the railing, and looked over the edge; raised his hands, and said something that Jim couldn't hear. Suddenly, the next three steps disappeared. Jim never thought he would find himself thankful for the pitiful condition of the apartment's wooden staircase. But if he wasn't *always* expecting the rotting steps to come out from under him, he would have fallen when they did. Instead, he had most of his weight on the slightly sturdier handrails, and he swung down to the next step, then turned around to help Sharra past the missing steps. Together, they started down again.

Lightning struck the rail next to Jim, and he fell down the last four stairs to the landing. Twenty-six steps, he thought. These are going to be the longest twenty-six steps of my entire life. Sharra ran past him and reached the ground safely. Slowly, Jim raised himself to his knees. He got to his feet, picked up the tire iron, and was about to start down after Sharra when he had a bad feeling—and looked up. He saw the ghell jump over the railing on the landing above, and he realized that the creature was coming straight towards him.

Jim froze for an instant in blank terror. Instinctively, he bolted back up the stairs, then realized he should have run the other way. He turned to do that, but he was too late.

Jim paled as the ghell dropped into sight before him—and kept on dropping. There was a loud crash as the rotting wood of the landing collapsed beneath the monster's crushing weight. Splintered, broken lumber toppled to the ground in its wake.

The staircase lurched and shuddered, and Jim braced himself, afraid that the entire stairway would collapse. But after a moment, the structure stopped swaying. All that remained of the landing was the square of doubled two-by-tens that anchored the two staircases, held aloft by a four-by-four post at each corner.

He held on to the railing as long as he could, and walked across the beam to the stairway that led up to the back apartment. He glanced nervously down the hole where the landing had been, hoping that the ghell was dead, or at least unconscious, but the creature was already climbing out from beneath the debris.

Jim hurried down the steps, hoping the staircase would hold together long enough for him to reach the ground by the steps instead of by gravity. He had no desire to tangle with the ghell at all, but the idea of confronting the beast again in the narrow confines of the ramshackle, nearly collapsed stairway scared him even worse.

Jim expected the ghell to come around the corner and start up the steps after him at any minute. Instead, Willy stepped out of a circle of light that burst into existence at the bottom of the steps. Jim began to suspect some deep karmic significance to the fact that the apartment stairs were built in two flights of thirteen stairs each.

"Do not look so surprised," Willy said. "You are not the only one who can be clever. However, your cleverness and your meddling are over."

Willy held his hands about a foot apart. As Jim

watched, trapped, the air between Willy's hands began to glow, red and violent. An instant later, the crimson light transformed into a burning sphere of flame that grew larger by the second, and Jim swallowed hard.

He looked out over the edge, and decided that he was better off making the jump. Besides, it seemed likely that he would have a better chance surviving the fall than living through what Willy had in mind. He tossed the tire iron over the side and placed both hands on the railing. He waited until Willy threw the spell, then jumped over the edge of the stairway.

The ground was only about six feet below him, and Jim landed well, bending his knees slightly to absorb the impact. His left ankle hurt a little, but it was just a twinge from the sprain he'd gotten sliding into third in the state 4-A semifinal against Broughton High. It hadn't healed properly, and always bothered him when he overtaxed it, but at least he could still walk on it.

His shoulder, though, was another matter. He had put too much weight on it and twisted it when he vaulted over the railing, and now he was paying the price. White-hot pain burned through his arm. It took everything he had to keep from screaming.

But then he saw the ghell—it was standing with its back to Jim, slowly lifting Sharra off the ground, its massive hands closed vise-like around her throat.

Jim picked up the tire iron, and ran towards the monster, thinking furiously. He would only get one chance, so he had to make it good. Despite its size, the creature seemed to be put together pretty much the same way people were. So Jim should be able to take it apart the same way. And there was only one trick he knew that was virtually foolproof.

He clutched the tire iron in his left hand, got a running start, and struck the beast across the backs of both knees as hard as he could. The ghell dropped

Sharra in shock and fell to the ground like a marionette with its strings cut. It howled in pain and rage, and thrashed about with its arms, trying to hurt Jim as he had hurt it.

But Jim had darted out of range. "Sharra! Come on! We have to get out of here!"

Sharra ran to him cautiously along the apartment wall, being careful not to get too near the ghell. She gave him a quick, hard hug that left him stunned with surprise. "God, I'm glad to see you." Then she pulled away and turned towards the parking lot. Jim followed, right behind her.

"Ah, there you are," Willy said, stepping out of the shadows beneath the stairs. He stared hard at Jim's face. "You know, the resemblance really *is* remarkable. Now then," he said, his voice suddenly hard and cold, "where *is* the book?"

Chapter Thirty-four

"I don't want to leave him, either," Gali said, "but the wizard has them both. If we wait here, he'll get the book, too."

Mrestal shook his head, and his brow furrowed. "Even if you're right, which I suppose you are, how are we going to control this machine?"

Gali frowned, shaking her head. "You're losing your touch."

"What do you mean by that?" Mrestal asked angrily.

"While some people were enjoying the ride," she began, "*I* was watching Jim operate this car. Purely as an intellectual exercise, of course—even I wouldn't try to *steal* a piece of trash like this. Except as transportation."

"Fine, O master who knows so much—tell me what we must do." Mrestal gave her a hard look, and Gali thought perhaps she'd been too arrogant about her knowledge.

"First, we have to turn this key."

She jumped onto the steering wheel and tried to turn it. It resisted her best effort, and she turned and glared at Mrestal. "*Help* me!"

He jumped onto the steering wheel beside her, and the two of them got the key to turn. The car rumbled to life.

Mrestal nodded. "You were right. What next?"

"This lever—we have to move it down. They tried sitting on the column that held the steering wheel and pushing, but that didn't work. Mrestal climbed out on the lever, and his weight shoved it down. It slipped into the second slot, and the car began to roll slowly forward.

"Oh, no!" Gali yelled. "We need to be going back!"

Mrestal slipped from the end of the lever but caught himself with his fingertips as he fell. The lever jerked and moved another two notches downward, and the car moved forward slightly faster.

They were rolling onto the grass, toward the back yard they'd burned the night before.

"The other way!" Gali yelled.

She crouched on the shelf beneath the front window and grabbed the steering wheel. Looking over her shoulder, she turned the wheel until the car began to creep in the direction she wanted. They rolled through the grass, toward Lukas and Jim and Sharra—and Gali spun the wheel harder. The car responded, but now all the mehns were looking in her direction. "We need to go faster! Push down the pedal on the floor!"

"Which one?"

"I don't know," Gali shouted. "Try them both!" The ghell was running toward them—it was going to get them, Gali just knew it. "Hurry!" she screamed.

Mrestal jumped on one of the pedals with all his strength. The car slammed to a stop and threw Gali into the giant glass window in front of her.

"The other one!" she screamed. "Fast."

The ghell was at the car, trying to tear the door off—and Gali knew it was going to succeed. Then the vehicle shot forward with incredible speed, and Gali realized they were aiming straight for a tree. She grabbed the wheel again, and pulled hard—too hard.

They swerved violently, aimed now at the other car. She shoved the wheel in the other direction, and they scraped along the back of the wizard's car as they drove past.

The wreck had the salutary effect of forcing the ghell to let go of the door. Gali was pleased by that.

"How are you doing up there?" Mrestal called. He sounded worried.

"All right, I guess," Gali said. "We got rid of the ghell. But I can't really see where I'm going. I have to keep looking over my shoulder." She shifted her position to a sideways crouch, with one leg braced on the steering wheel column, turned the vehicle a little too far, then overcorrected. The car swerved viciously, and she heard a thud as Mrestal lost his balance, fell, and rolled hard into the driver's side door as the car veered sharply to the right. "Sorry! I hope that didn't hurt."

The grumpy voice below said, "Oh, no. It felt good. Why don't you come down and push the pedal, and I'll turn the wheel?"

The car was slowing down. Gali used the opportunity to look behind her, then she shouted, "Mrestal, the ghell is about to catch us. Push the pedal hard!"

This time the car went much, much faster. Gali held her breath and tried to keep from hitting things, though she got too close to another car and bounced against it on her way past. The awful crunching noise the two cars made when they hit frightened her.

The ghell was still gaining on them.

"Can you push harder?" Gali yelled.

"Maybe if I stand on the pedal and push on the ceiling down here. It's low. . . ." Gali heard Mrestal shift positions, and suddenly the car accelerated to a terrifying new speed. The world rushed past in a blur, and Gali discovered she didn't have to turn the wheel very far to get the car to do big things.

"Is that faster?" Mrestal asked.

Gali swerved just enough to avoid hitting a car that was coming right at her. The other car roared at her, and she screamed, and they shot by, missing by no more than the breadth of a hair. "Oh, yes," Gali said weakly. "This is much faster."

She heard a thump, and the crunching of metal, and the back of the car rocked. She glanced back only long enough to see that the ghell had somehow caught them anyway, and was climbing onto the roof.

The car she'd just passed had lights in the front that had blazed into her eyes—she wished she hadn't looked at them. She was nearly blind for an instant after it passed, until her night vision came back. She saw the red back lights of a car in front of her, swerved around it, and winced as that car, too, roared at her.

She didn't think she wanted to steal any more cars, and she prayed to the all the gods she knew, asking them to get her and Mrestal out of this alive.

Chapter Thirty-five

Damn. I'm too far away to hit him with the tire iron, Jim thought, but if I try to close the distance between us, he'll have time to stop me with one of his spells. And if I wait too much longer, he'll have enough time to use a spell anyway.

Just as Willy was starting to raise his hands, Jim threw the metal tool, and ran straight at the other man. Willy dealt with the tire iron first, turning it into a snake. But he had no time to deal with Jim, who rammed his left shoulder into Willy's chest, knocking the wind out of the other man and slamming his head up against one of the staircase's support posts.

"Run!" he yelled to Sharra. "The book's in my car." Willy sagged to the ground, and Jim was about to hit him one last time, to make sure he was unconscious, when the snake Willy had made from the tire iron dropped from the post it had caught on and landed across Jim's shoulders. He screamed, stood up, and tossed the snake against the side of the apartment building. That's when he noticed that the ghell was missing. Jim glanced toward the parking lot, and spotted the beast running alongside his Nova, trying to pull open the front door—*his* car, Jim realized, which was rolling through the grass toward the whole lot of them at that very moment.

How the hell did the creature get to the car? he

wondered. It was running with a limp—but it shouldn't have been able to walk at all.

Sharra chased after the car, too, but from the other side. The doors were locked! She couldn't get into the car, because he'd made sure the doors were locked.

So he knew who was driving.

The Ithnari! he thought. Those larcenous bastards are stealing my car. And the book, too, for that matter. He quickly glanced down at Willy, who still appeared to be unconscious, then dashed for the parking lot.

Naturally, he got there too late. Sharra had finally given up, and was standing there, sweating and out of breath.

Together, they watched the rear end of the Nova pass slowly out of sight, swerving all over the road.

"What do we do now?" Sharra asked.

Jim thought furiously for a second, then said, "We'll take Willy's car. He's out cold, he won't mind."

Sharra said, "Do you mind if I stay here, while you get the keys? I'd really rather not be around him any more than I have to, even when he's unconscious."

Jim said, "Sure, no problem. I'll be right—"

He was interrupted by the sound of a well-tuned engine turning over. When he turned to look, he saw Willy backing his BMW uncertainly out of its parking space. He grinned at Jim from behind the wheel.

Sharra frowned at Jim. "He doesn't *look* unconscious," she said.

Jim had expected Willy to tear out of the parking lot. He stood in front of the car, hoping that it might slow the other man long enough for one of them to jump on the trunk and steal a ride. Willy revved the engine, then, unexpectedly, let out on the clutch too suddenly, causing the car to bark its tires and stall out. Jim shouted, "Jump!" and Sharra, seeing what he had in mind, leaped up beside him, onto the trunk of the BMW.

Willy barely seemed to notice them, as he struggled with the car. After several false starts, he finally managed to get it going, and *then* he started trying to shake them off in earnest. Jim and Sharra wedged their feet beneath the rear spoiler and hung on to each other—and to the tacky boomerang-shaped antenna on top of the car. They probably would have fallen off quickly at high speeds, but Willy was keeping it ten miles per hour under the speed limit, and seemed terrified of driving even that fast. They were actually in greater danger of falling off when he tried to shift gears than when he was trying to throw them from the car.

"What's the matter with him?" Jim wondered aloud. "He's driving like he's never *seen* a stick shift before. But his old Galaxy 500 convertible was a manual, too. In fact, I don't think Willy's ever owned an automatic."

Sharra shook her head. "That's not Willy," she said. "That is Lukas. When he brought us over here, he made me drive."

"Weird," Jim said. "That may be Lukas, but it's also Willy, and Willy knows how to drive a stick."

Sharra flinched as the car jerked from one side of the road to the other, then snapped back. "I don't know if any part of your friend is still in there," she told him. "And even if some part of Willy remains, he isn't in control."

"No," Jim admitted, "he doesn't act like Willy at all anymore."

Sharra said, "That is not Willy. It may someday be your friend again, but for now, Lukas controls his body as surely as he controls this car. Or rather, more surely," she finished, as the BMW veered off the edge of the pavement and onto the shoulder, bumping and fishtailing in the loose gravel in its pursuit of the Ithnari and Jim's car. Both the elves and Willy were driving without lights on—which added another layer of thrill to the chase that Jim would have willingly done without.

The pain in his shoulder began to subside. I just twisted it, he thought. I didn't actually injure it again.

Willy accelerated, and they came up on the passenger side of Jim's Nova. Jim could see the outline of the ghell sprawled along the top of the car, hanging on to both sides. So they weren't rid of the monster yet.

Willy veered to the left, slamming into the Nova.

Jim and Sharra held tighter to the antenna—both of them nearly lost their holds at the moment of impact. Jim couldn't help but wonder how the elves were driving his car—he wished he could see them. The only glimpses he ever got were when they were charging down the throat of an oncoming car—and then he could only see one little shape silhouetted on the dashboard.

Then Willy jammed on the brakes, and swerved across two lanes of traffic, to come up on the driver's side of the Nova. He pulled ahead of the other car, then spun the wheel hard to the right, cutting across Gali's path. She veered even more sharply to avoid a collision. The Nova jumped a shallow ditch, and drove merrily through a carefully landscaped perennial bed, crushing the flowers beneath its wheels.

At the same time, the BMW careened into the ditch, and Jim finally lost his grip on the antenna. As the car came out the other side of the ditch, he went sailing through the air. The last thing he saw before he landed in the bushes was his Nova, out of control, driving through the front wall of a house, with the ghell now perched on the hood.

Chapter Thirty-six

Jim crawled out of the bushes with a groan and a grimace of pain. Those damned little pointy-leafed hollies ought to be outlawed, he thought. As he started towards the house, he pulled more of the sharp leaves out of his T-shirt, where they had stuck completely through and were lodged in his chest, arms, and back.

His battered old Nova had come to rest inside someone's living room. He could see no sign of the owners—they'd left the television on as they fled the room. Vanna White was gracing the studio audience with one of her patented saccharine smiles. Then the ghell lurched into Jim's line of sight, inside the house. He ran over and picked up the television, and smashed it into a million pieces against a wall—Jim, unnerved by the monster's insane violence, still had to credit it with a level of taste he wouldn't have otherwise suspected.

Jim didn't see Sharra, or Willy, or the elves. He looked around the yard, then turned back to the house as he heard a roar.

A middle-aged man burst through the living room door, pointed a double-barreled shotgun at the beast, and fired. Jim guessed that the man didn't practice with the gun very often; the recoil knocked him off his feet. He dropped the shotgun as he fell, and several extra shells rolled across the floor, out of his reach.

"Yes!" Jim yelled.

A spray of blood arced across the room, as the ghell flew backward and fell on its back. At that range, the shot wouldn't scatter much, so even a twenty-gauge should have done massive damage. The shotgun blast would have installed a skylight and a new ventilation system in a human. The ghell was clearly made of sterner stuff than humans. The monster, though clearly hurt, wasn't even unconscious. In fact, Jim saw with amazement, it was getting back up.

"No . . ." he muttered.

The man's eyes went wide, and he groped desperately for the shotgun. He grabbed it by the barrel, turned it around, and leveled it at the ghell. He didn't remember that the gun was empty until the trigger fell with a feeble click. He reached in his shirt pocket for ammunition, but his hand came back empty. Then he scrambled across the floor on all fours, trying to reach the shotgun shells before the monster reached him.

Jim saw that the man wouldn't make it, and tried to quickly think of something he could do to distract the ghell. He was awfully far away from the beast, and he doubted he could cross the distance between them in time, but he couldn't just stand by and watch the ghell kill the man. He ran to try to stop the monster, crossed a cobblestone walkway in the dark, tripped on a loose rock, and fell on his face.

He looked up at the tiny house.

Stupid walkway must have cost as much as the whole damn house, he thought. You can't find a rock to kill a snake with in this part of the state.

Except, he thought with a smile, right here. He hefted the rock he had tripped over, and was thankful his shoulder had only been sore before.

The rock was almost round, and only slightly smaller than a baseball. The doctors who'd put his shoulder back together had told him never to throw anything again with that arm—had pounded it into his skull that the joint was ruined and the muscles were held to the bones with scotch tape and baling twine, and that if he ever pitched another baseball, they weren't going to be able to put him back together at all. But the rock would slow the ghell down—or at least get its attention—and Jim pitched it. He wound up, he aimed, and he released. It was a beautiful pitch. To even get the ghell's attention, he needed power. So he'd thrown his fast ball. He'd given it everything he had, and now it flew straight and true, like every winning strike he'd ever thrown— even though he was three years out of practice, and his shoulder hurt *before* he threw the rock. But with the release came another snap—this one inside. The blinding white heat of pain that followed the pitch nearly made him throw up.

He saw the stone hit the ghell's head with a deep, resonant thunk, and the creature turned and roared in rage. Jim staggered for the side of the house, hoping to hide in the trees there before the monster could see him. But the beast was fast, the pain was impossible—and Jim dropped to his knees as the agony swallowed him; he doubled up on the ground, vomiting. Spots of light swam in front of his eyes, and when he tried to stand, the sky whirled and spun, and dizziness pulled the world out from under him. He broke out in a cold sweat, and shivered and spasmed.

The vomiting passed, though the pain didn't. He looked up helplessly as the ghell slowly advanced toward him. Behind the beast, the man he had saved had finally managed to get the shotgun loaded again, and was creeping up to shoot the monster from point-blank range. The shotgun hadn't slowed the monster down greatly the first time, so Jim wasn't expecting much, but he was grateful for any help he could get.

But just as the man was raising the shotgun, Willy stepped out from beside the car, and raised his hands.

For a moment, time stood still. The ghell stopped where it stood, waiting. A sickly, greenish-blue light sprang up between Willy's hands, and the man with the shotgun froze. His eyes glazed over, and the shotgun drooped. Willy strolled over to the man, gently lifted the gun out of the man's unresisting fingers, and flung it away from him, up against the house on the other side of the car. He spoke softly in the man's ear, and after a moment, the man turned away and walked slowly back into the house.

"Now where were we?" Lukas asked. "Oh, yes. Getting rid of a thorn in my side." He glanced at the ghell, and said, "By all means, continue."

The creature sauntered towards Jim, grinning. "Kill you," it said.

Jim did the only thing he could think of—he rolled to his left, and kept on rolling—right under his car. Rolling on his injured shoulder made it hurt even worse—and Jim thought he heard crunching in the joint each time his weight rocked onto the injured shoulder. He had intended to hide beneath the Nova, but he smelled gasoline, and crawled out the other side—pulling himself with his left arm, pushing with his legs. Then his shirt snagged on the straight-wire repair job he'd done on the Nova's starter switch and pulled loose the electrical tape. Just as Jim was scrambling out the other side, the bare wires fell, and a stray spark ignited the puddle of gasoline Jim had just crawled through.

A blast furnace of heat and flame followed Jim out from under the Nova, and the gas on his shirt caught fire. Jim kept rolling until he'd managed to put out the fire on his back, smashing into the hurt shoulder again and again and again. The pain was incredible; he felt the world crash down around him, the agony of his burned skin and battered shoulder a solid, heavy block that pressed him into the ground. He fought against it, and raised himself to his knees, then vomited again until he felt like his head was going to explode from the pressure. He flopped facedown in the grass, and wished it would.

He lay in the cool damp grass, waiting for the ghell to finish him off. When the death stroke didn't come, he stood on wobbly knees and looked back toward the burning car. The monster and Willy were gone. The elves pressed themselves against the window nearest him, and pounded, and screamed.

Chapter Thirty-seven

Sharra lost her grip on the back of the car and slammed face-down into the ground—and the ground sucked up around her, and tried to swallow her.

Mud!

She pulled her head free, caught her breath and sat up, then scrambled out of the ditch. The fall had ripped holes in the knees of her jeans, and one tennis shoe was gone—lost in the mud or somewhere else.

Her knees and the palms of her hands were skinned and she felt a nasty bruise already beginning to form on her right thigh; she'd hit something harder than mud in her fall. For an instant she imagined herself a little girl again, with her mother stepping out of the darkness from behind a tree to scold her for ruining her clothes and trying to outdo the boys.

Then the feeling passed, and tears filled her eyes. She hadn't though of her mother in a long time. Bitterness and cynicism and years of watching friends and acquaintances grow old and die without her had scabbed over some wounds, dulling the pain of individual losses. She had forgotten how hollow the space in her heart that her mother once filled still was—after two hundred years, she had forgotten how very much she missed her mother.

Not much longer now until I join you, mama, she

thought. Lukas is back. It's almost over. Even if he wins, for me it's almost over.

She crouched low to avoid being silhouetted against the streetlights behind her, and moved towards the flower bed where Jim had fallen. She'd heard gunshots earlier, and until she knew who had the gun, she'd rather assume that Lukas was armed more than just magically. She didn't see Jim, so she started toward the house, along the stepping-stone path through the flowers.

There was a sudden flash of light to her left, and Sharra turned to look. Flames blossomed beneath Jim's car. The ghell backed away from the car, then turned and fled, obviously afraid of the fire. Lukas called out to the beast, but its primal fear of the fire had overcome whatever control he had over it. *Something* came rolling out from beneath the car, sheathed in flames. As it rolled, the flames died down, and Sharra realized it was a person. Since she'd just seen Lukas and the ghell, it almost had to be Jim. She abandoned stealth, and sprinted towards the place where Jim had fallen.

Running towards the blaze, Sharra saw Lukas weave a spell, then open the door of Jim's car. He reached in and took the book, slammed the door closed, then went chasing after his monster.

The cool night breeze brought a sudden reek of carrion to her nose. She heard a low growl, and came to a halt. She saw nothing at first, but she had drawn the golene through the gate to herself, and she knew its nature. She unfocused her eyes, looking for a shadow or a moving spot where her vision blurred— and she found it. Once she had a location, she concentrated until she could see the golene completely.

It stalked slowly toward her, its fur gleaming warm gold beneath the streetlights. But she saw dark spots where the blood of its recent kills caked and matted in its fur. It lifted its lip and growled again—its bared teeth terrible to see.

Sharra fled, trying to put some distance between herself and the creature while she thought of some way to stop it. Her most effective spells, like the one that had summoned the golene in the first place, required a great deal of time and preparation. She couldn't throw fire, she couldn't bring something else through the gate, she couldn't create a shield sturdy enough to hold it back. She could create illusions; she would have to hope they slowed the golene.

While she ran, she concentrated on the illusion of self—if she could cast it into the golene's mind, it would trick the golene into seeing a mirrored image of itself. The self-spell would move when the golene moved, fight when the golene fought . . . for as long as the creature believed it to be a real opponent, it would fight like one. Her pace slowed and became automatic as she concentrated her will, crafting the illusion. When the illusion was perfect, she forced the image into the golene's mind.

Her pursuer stopped suddenly, baring its teeth and growling at its invisible attacker. Sharra let out a sigh of relief, and put on a burst of speed, while the golene waited, challenging it opposite. When her illusion failed to attack, the golene launched itself at the shadow creature's throat. Sharra could imagine the shadow-golene lunging at the same instant.

The golene backed and screamed. She heard the one-sided battle behind her, the golene growling and snapping and snarling. To her own ears, it was answered with silence. It, however, heard its own voice bounced back at it, amplified—and it reacted with frenzied rage. It would catch on eventually, she knew. She planned her next illusion while she ran.

She was desperate enough that she decided to try an illusion so seemingly powerful that she hoped it would cause the golene to turn tail and run. She knew just the image she wanted. Jim had been trying to get her to read fantasy novels again, and had tried to convince her by playing on her love for Arthurian legend. The book he chose had a striking cover, with a twisting black dragon that snaked along the ground, climbing over a gnarled tree to threaten a knight that protected a golden-haired maiden.

She heard the golene coming up behind her, and cast her illusion. Her dragon was perfect, from its baleful green eyes to the tip of its obsidian tongue. But she was too tired to sustain the illusion for long, and the golene quickly discovered the dragon's nature and left it behind to chase its flesh-and-blood foe.

Sharra heard sirens approaching in the distance. One of the neighbors must have called the police when he heard the gunshots. A bitter smile crossed her face. The police weren't going to get to her in time. She was too far off the road and too far from the streetlights for them to see her before it was too late.

Sharra knew she had no chance. The golene was stronger than she was, and faster, and much better armed. It was probably just, on some sort of cosmic level, that she was about to be devoured by the very killing machine she had created to be her protector—but Sharra wasn't feeling philosophical. She'd finally found something worth living for, and now her only chance for happiness was being taken away. But she wasn't giving up yet.

She ran with everything in her, ran as though there were nothing in the world but her legs, the ground, and the golene behind her. Her left side ached, and every labored breath burned her throat and her lungs; her legs were solid lines of pain that weighed a thousand pounds apiece, moving in slow motion. She gave everything she had, and when that wasn't enough, she reached deep inside herself and gave a little more.

Then she smelled the stench of the golene, getting closer, and knew that more than she had wasn't going to be enough.

She glanced over her shoulder just in time to see the golene slam to a halt, eyes wide—to see it whimper and back away from her. She stopped, gasping for air, and stared at it, bewildered . . . and then she looked back in the direction she'd been running.

The shadows resolved into twelve feet of angry, hideous monster, and Sharra sobbed with exhaustion and fear as it reached out and grabbed her. It slung her over its shoulder, took two enormous running steps, and kicked the golene twenty feet across the yard.

In a thunderous rumble, the monster growled, *"Mine."* And while she kicked at it and pummeled the side of its head with her elbow, the ghell carried Sharra into the night.

Chapter Thirty-eight

"Get us out! Hurry!"

The Nova's interior was filling with smoke. Jim dashed over to the driver's side of the car. He tried the door, but it was still locked.

"Lift the latch!" he yelled. "Lift it!"

The two elves struggled to pull it up—but the old Nova had stiff, heavy locks, and the doors had been wrecked—Jim remembered Willy ramming the car. The elves couldn't get the locks to budge.

He backed away. He needed something to smash open the window—a baseball bat, a tire iron . . .

"Kick it," he muttered "I can kick it in." Jim motioned for them to back away. He took a run at the window, and suddenly, a part of him was in another time, another place. He was back in that dark alley, reliving the night that he'd lost his dream, lost his pitching arm, lost his career in baseball—all for the sake of trying to do the right thing.

He was running toward trouble again—toward someone else's trouble. And this time the trouble was probably going to get him killed for his effort.

That, said the little voice in his head, is the ultimate reward of do-gooders. Back off. Stay out of it. Survive! You never asked to get involved in all this.

Neither did the elves, Jim thought. They're here because of me, and they need me.

He kicked and the window cracked—kicked again, and it burst inward with a crash. The elves bounded out of the car and away from the flames . . . and Jim realized something it had taken him three years to figure out.

He was right to save the elves—but he'd *also* been right to help that man in the alley. Those guys who were beating him up had taken the law into their own hands—and they had been no better than the guy they'd attacked.

If it hadn't been for me, they would have killed him, Jim thought. Maybe that wouldn't have been a great loss to humanity, but it still would have been wrong.

Jim picked glass out of his leg with his good arm. He ought to go to the hospital—his burns were bad and his shoulder was a constant, grinding agony. All he needed to do was find Sharra . . . but he hadn't seen her since the two of them fell off the back of Willy's car, and he didn't see the monster or Willy anymore, either. No sooner had he realized that than he heard the sirens.

My car is parked in that guy's living room, Jim thought. Once they run the plates, they'll want to hold me for questioning—if I'm anywhere near here when the police arrive, there's no way I'll be able to help Sharra stop Lukas.

Fear gave him strength, and he managed to increase his pace. He jogged painfully towards the sparse cover of the row of cedar trees alongside the house. He was nearly there when he tripped and just barely caught himself. He felt around on the ground to see what had tripped him, and his hand fell on the stock of the shotgun.

He tucked it under his left arm. With the elves following behind him, he sprinted around the corner of the house, just as the first of the police cars pulled into the drive. From the deck lights and yard lights scattered through the neighborhood, he could make out a narrow strip of woods that ran for at least two or three blocks. He saw the lights of other houses through the sparser trees, and realized that they separated the neighborhood he was in from the next one over. Jim figured the police would eventually search it, but it was big enough to offer him a safe place to hide and rest for a few minutes.

He found a stand of pines growing close enough together to provide good cover, and sagged to the ground.

Jim laid the shotgun across his lap, then picked it up and examined it closer, amazed. No wonder that guy was knocked on his ass! The gun was a Davidson 10-gauge. His dad had shot one like it on a hunting trip the year before, and had been lusting after one ever since. He broke it open one-handed, and pulled out one of the shells. Three and a half inch magnum buckshot—couldn't have had more than a six-inch spread at that short a range, he thought. There should have been two huge holes in the ghell, and two matching holes in the wall behind him.

I don't even want to think of what that thing's made of, Jim thought. And I sure don't want to tangle with anything that took that and then got back up. How the hell did I get involved in this mess?

Jim had been afraid before, but as long as he'd been running, he hadn't had a chance to think about the danger. Now fear coiled around his stomach, an icy snake eating its own tail. He was tired, he was badly hurt, and he was alone—well, except for the elves, and he didn't think they were going to be much help. His breathing was harsh and ragged from the exertion and heat. His arms were blistered and the skin on his chest and back was raw and red. New blisters were forming on his stomach, and he would bet that his back was just as bad.

He couldn't lie down—the pain was too bad. Sitting hurt, moving hurt worse—fighting was going to hurt the worst of all. But if he wanted to save Sharra, he was going to have to fight.

He readjusted his glasses, grateful to still have them, and tried to figure out how to find Sharra.

He was probably going to lose, but at least, after years of regrets and doubts, his doubts and second thoughts were gone. He'd been right before. He was right again.

Chapter Thirty-nine

Sharra winced and the breath whooshed out of her as the sharp bone of the ghell's shoulder jabbed her in the stomach—again. The monster carried her through the trees. Branches slapped the backs of her legs and scraped her arms and back, snapped back from the creature's body and hit her face. She had a good grip on one of the huge spines that grew out of the monster's back, and she used that grip for leverage, to try to get away. The ghell had a solid grip on her, too, however, and her struggle was in vain.

This is it, she thought. I've tried to kill myself, but it has never worked. I will finally learn whether the immortality curse still works when someone else attempts the killing.

She fought to get free, but she didn't know if she really needed to. Jim hadn't been moving when she looked—the odds were high that he was dead. He was the first person who had ever given her hope, the first who had made her want to live. If he was dead, she wasn't sure she wanted to go on. Until she knew for sure, though, she intended to keep trying.

She heard a second set of sirens and saw red lights pass between two of the houses. Someone called the fire department because of Jim's car, Sharra thought.

There must have been at least ten or fifteen people at the accident scene by then, gaping at the fire. Why couldn't just one of them come into the woods? It would only take one to find her and get her away from the ghell. She prayed that one of them would see her, that someone, anyone, would save her from the ghell, that someone would intervene.

Her prayers were answered instantly.

"Looking for someone?" asked a cold voice.

It was definitely time to give up religion.

Lukas stepped behind the monster onto the path it had been following, and drew a sigil in the air—before it even had a chance to turn at the sound of its master's voice, the ghell froze in place. Sharra was still draped over the ghell's shoulder; she twisted around so that she could see Lukas—and froze. In his left hand, he held the grimoire.

"Hello, Sharra," he said. She couldn't make out the details of his face in the darkness, but she could hear the smile in his voice. "My lovely wife, the prime worlds approach their nearest point and, as I had planned, all of us are once again united. I think it is time we finished this game."

Lukas said something to the ghell, words Sharra didn't know, and the monster turned and followed him docilely, still carrying her on its shoulders.

He led them to a clearing, and told the ghell to put Sharra down. The ghell swung her down from its shoulder and pushed her to her knees in the dirt, and Lukas reached behind his back, and pulled a knife out of his belt. It was the art dagger Sharra had made to order by Salamander Armory for her own use as a ceremonial knife. Evidently Lukas had stolen it when he kidnapped her from her house.

"Very pretty," he said, looking at the blade. He bent and inscribed a large circle around her in the dirt, and another one around the ghell. "Sadly, it, like you, will not survive this night. Still, you both will be destroyed in a good cause. For the minor expense of an excellent blade and a beautiful woman, I will gain the primacy of two worlds and a legion of servants with so much power that nothing will be beyond my reach."

"Sounds like you're getting quite a bargain," Sharra said, sneering. She didn't try to move—the ghell would catch her, Lukas would hurt her, and as long as she appeared to cooperate, she might have a chance to escape later.

"I've always thought so." He smiled at her, and even on the stranger's face, the smile was the same one she'd known and fallen in love with. Now that she saw it again, she compared it to Jim's smile, and she couldn't understand why she had ever thought Lukas was wonderful.

Lukas moved his fingers in a complex dance and whispered a spell, and an eerie green fire sprang up along the line he'd drawn around Sharra. "So good of you to wait faithfully for me," he added. "I confess, my greatest fear was that you would unmask my two little lies—for at the moment you did, my dear, I was undone.

A chill ran down Sharra's spine. "Lies?"

He nodded, and his eyes glinted in the green light—his face, in that light, lit from beneath, was the face of a devil unchained. "Lies. Just two little ones, and I thought them terribly transparent. They were the weakest part of my plan—though when things fell apart and you won the immortality I was to have, I thought it fitting you should get no happiness from it."

"What lies?"

"My darling immortal, can you not guess? After so long? First, the lie of your trapping me in the gate. I planned it so that you would push me through, because I could not do it myself once my bid for immortality failed. Only between the gates of the worlds could I hope to survive until the next time the worlds aligned correctly. And the second lie—that of your death at the hands of a lover." He laughed at the expression on her face and shook his head. "I can see you never guessed, but how not? Stupid child, you are an immortal. You could have fornicated with the legions of Rome and you would have lived . . . and if you had, you would have been free from me, for only a virgin will suit my needs."

He smiled at her, and shoved his hands into his pockets.

Sharra lunged at him in a blind rage—and slammed into the barrier he'd built around her.

He shook his head and sighed. "You never learn. The time to run was before I bound you to this circle. Now you are mine." He cast a tiny light that hung in front of him in the air, twinkling like a star.

Then he opened the book.

Chapter Forty

The fire truck pulled away, and behind it, two tow trucks followed, yellow lights flashing. One dragged the burned husk of Jim's Nova, while the other pulled the dented, muddy wreck of Willy's BMW off into the night.

They're going, then, Jim thought.

But not all of them. He heard voices coming nearer, and flashlights began to play along the ground in the direction of the woods. Jim struggled to his feet. The police had evidently decided they needed to look for the disappearing drivers of the two wrecked cars.

Jim slipped behind a tree, and the elves bounded up into its branches.

One of the cops stopped along the back fence of one of the yards next to the house the elves had crashed Jim's car into. "Shit," he said.

The other one ran over to join him, and for a moment the two of them stood playing their flashlights over the ground.

Jim thought, Uh-oh. They've found something. He hoped it wasn't something that would lead them to him.

"You know what that looks like?" the first one said.

"No." There was a pause. "And I don't want to know."

"Looks a lot like the photos and plaster castings I've seen of footprints' of those Bigfoot monsters out in Washington . . . Oregon . . . out that way."

"I told you I didn't want to know."

Another pause, and the first cop said, "I reckon not, though."

"You reckon not, what?"

"Thought you didn't want to know." Silence. Then, "You see where the toes dig in . . . right along there?" Jim could see one uniformed officer kneel and run his finger along the ground.

"Yeah."

"Seven toes . . . and claws dug into the dirt. Prints I saw of the Bigfoot monsters—ain't any claws on them, and they had the same number of toes as you and me."

Jim heard one of the two men sigh deeply. "Watched that crap on television, didn't you? You watch more of them damned television specials than anyone I ever did know."

"And I have a theory because of it. So what do you think this is?"

"Some damn kid playing around."

A snort from the first cop. "Which just goes to show you ought to spend more time learning things. Some damn kid couldn't get enough weight on him to make an impression that deep. That's how they knew the Bigfoot monster was genuine—the footprints was dug in too deep to be made by a prankster."

"Jesus. You'd believe anything."

Both cops stood and began following their flashlight beams across the yard. "All I know is, when the shit comes down, I'll be ready, and *you'll* be standin' there with your mouth hanging open, wishing you knew what to do."

"And what would you do, if some Bigfoot monster come out of the woods and tried to eat you?"

"I'd shoot 'im in the eye, Larry. That's what I'd do. I'd shoot 'im in the eye."

They were following tracks along the ground, and

Jim knew what those tracks belonged to. And he thought, I hate to say it, guys, but I saw that sucker take two belly shots from a ten-gauge and keep right on coming. You shoot him, all he's gonna do is get pissed and eat you.

The cops were following the tracks, moving away from Jim, still arguing—rather loudly, as men do when they are scared but don't want to admit it—and Jim was ready to start looking for Sharra, when both cops stopped.

"Now that was weird. I woulda' sworn I saw another track heading that way." He pointed in the direction the two men had been walking.

"Yeah," the other cop agreed in a thoughtful voice. "But look—it doubles back right there, and heads back almost exactly the way we came."

"You think there's two sets of tracks?"

"No."

The thoughtful pause again. "Nope. Me either. I reckon it turned around and went the other way." Both officers turned around and began moving back at a slight angle from the way they'd come. They were moving, in fact, right toward Jim. His heart began to pound, and he slipped deeper into the woods. He moved quietly through the underbrush, being careful not to hit the shotgun against anything. He couldn't go fast, but he didn't think he was going to get caught, either.

Then he found a path—nice smooth ground under his sneakers, no debris to crunch—no dry twigs to snap under his feet and give him away. He wouldn't get caught the way Natty Bumpo and the "redskins" in *The Deerslayer* and *Last of the Mohicans* were always getting caught.

Gali bounded past him. "This way," she said, and vanished down the path ahead of him. Mrestal passed him, too.

On the path he made a little better time. He was moving into the woods at an angle, heading in about the same direction as the first set of the ghell's tracks had run. He stopped long enough to listen for the cops; he didn't like what he heard. They were closer than they'd been.

He wished he could see the path more clearly. It was so damned dark in the woods. He started to run, and the movement bounced his shoulder—he'd tucked his thumb into the belt loop of his jeans to keep from jarring the shoulder too much, but at a run, his stop-gap excuse for a sling was about worthless.

"Hey!" one of the cops yelled. "I see something!"

The elves raced past him in the other direction, heading back toward the cops. "Run, idiot," Mrestal told him on the way past.

Jim knew the cops saw him—and he couldn't help but think of the first cop's solution to monsters. "I'd shoot 'im in the eye." He figured two cops who'd been tracking something that was in no way human were going to shoot first and question the corpse—if they were calmer than that, he apologized mentally for misjudging them. But he couldn't take chances. He charged off the path into the woods and ran faster.

Behind him, something growled, and he heard the *bang* of a large-caliber pistol. Oh, God, he thought— what if they shot the elves? He turned to look, lost his footing, and fell to the ground.

"Did you get it?"

"No!" the other cop yelled. "There it goes!"

Jim recognized elvish laughter—the two officers went haring off after it.

He lay in the leaf debris while little twigs and clumps of humus and leaves poked holes in his blisters and rubbed filth into his wounds and the butt of the shot-gun pressed against his ribs so hard Jim was afraid they'd snap. As much as he hurt at that moment, though, he knew the pain would just get worse when he moved. It would be very easy not to get up.

He lifted his head, though—he wasn't going to let Willy and the ghell have Sharra without a fight.

Lying on his belly in the dirt, he saw something he hadn't been able to see at all while he was standing. Eerie green light played along the ground—three thin lines of it that shimmered and danced and glowed like cold fire. He sat up higher, but when he did, the light disappeared. He lowered his head again, and could see it, but only from that one angle.

He marked the direction, stood, and walked toward it as fast as he dared.

He heard the police still running in the opposite direction, and whoops and laughter, and he grinned. At last he'd found something the elves were good for.

And then he found himself approaching a clearing. Sharra knelt inside a circle of the cold green fire he'd seen earlier. The ghell was inside another. Willy stood outside the circles and grinned, and opened a book. *The* book.

He remembered what the elves had said about the book.

The third spell is supposed to bring Lukas himself. The fourth . . . the fourth will bring the demons of a hundred planes to do Lukas's bidding.

The ghell, according to the elves, was a minor demon. Just one minor demon, from one plane. A spell that brought the demons of a hundred planes, the worst nightmares of creation or evolution from a hundred interlocking universes—that spell had to be stopped.

Jim moved through the woods just beyond the clearing until he was right behind Willy. The sky had grown as green as the flames around Sharra and the ghell, and lightning stabbed in long, jagged arcs across the sky. It was, Jim noted, still a cloudless night.

He flipped the safety off and brought the shotgun

up left-handed, and stepped forward into the clearing. He jammed the gun against the back of Willy's head, and said, "Drop the knife, and let Sharra out of the circle, or I'm going to blow your head off."

Willy's shoulders stiffened, and he turned his head slightly. Jim could see the beads of sweat on his forehead and the look of fear in his eye. Willy looked back at the book and kept reading.

"Now!" Jim yelled, and shoved the barrels into the back of his head, hard.

Willy swallowed hard, and faltered in the passage he was going through. He dropped the knife, and with a wave of his hand banished the green-glowing circles . . . but he picked up where he had left off in the text.

"Stop that!" Jim bellowed, and flicked the safety back on, and smacked Willy on the top of the head as hard as he could left-handed.

The book dropped from Willy's fingers and landed at his feet. He turned and stared at Jim, and in a gravel-throated voice, a voice devoured by fear, he said, "Bad idea, Jim." Then his knees gave beneath him, and he toppled to the ground and lay still.

Then Jim felt it—the screaming horror that had enveloped him when the spells *he'd* done were left uncompleted. It was the unmistakable feeling of impending doom. The demons were on their way— Jim felt their approach in his gut and in his blood and in his bones. He hadn't stopped the magic fast enough to stop them. Streaks of green lightning ripped through the sky—hundreds, even thousands of them, and the ground beneath his feet shook as if in the throes of an earthquake from the roaring, battering shock-waves of the resulting thunder.

Sharra was shouting something at him, but he couldn't hear her over the noise. He stood there, frozen, terror-stricken, waiting for hell to devour him.

Then both police officers burst into the clearing— the ghell and Sharra and Jim, who was still holding the shotgun, turned to face them. One of the officers saw the gun and drew his own. Jim couldn't hear what he said either, but he had a pretty good idea he knew what it was. He dropped the gun and put up his good hand.

The officer's shoe burst into flames and he shouted and started kicking the ground trying to put out the fire or get the shoe off; almost immediately after the fire started, Mrestal ran out of the woods and grabbed the leg of Jim's blue jeans. He pointed toward the woods and pantomimed haste.

The other officer was staring at the ghell with an expression of awe on his face. It was only a few feet from him, and evidently he hadn't realized what it was when he came charging out of the woods. As he came closer, Jim realized that it was Frank Ray. Slowly, without taking his eyes off of it, he began pulling his service revolver from its holster.

"Frank?" Jim called the deputy, but he didn't respond. His eyes were round, the pupils dilated, and they were locked on the ghell with an almost religious fervor.

The lightning stopped, and for an instant Jim's ears rang in the silence. Then, with a slow, hideous, ripping sound, the sky began to tear; a vein of insane, colorless power grew in the rent between the two halves of normal space and time. The people in the clearing froze, staring. The ghell, however, set to screaming—a high, womanish scream loud enough to compete with the ripping noise.

"The book, Jim!" Sharra bellowed. "Throw me the book."

Jim stepped over Willy, picked it up, and threw it with his left hand. Sharra lunged for it—his throw had been lousy—and caught it.

The ghell suddenly turned and fled into the woods, still screaming. The second officer had buried his shoe in the sand, putting out the fire; both policemen were staring gape-mouthed after the retreating monster. Jim yelled, "Sharra, something awful is going to happen! We have to get out of here!"

Sharra's fingers glowed as she spun a web of light in front of herself; then she thumbed through the pages, glancing over them by fingerlight. "I can't leave, Jim," she yelled back. "Somebody has got to stop this spell—or there won't be enough world left for us to find a place to run to."

Gali jumped onto his left shoulder and shouted in his ear, "You *can* leave, Jim! You *should* leave! You don't want to see what's coming. Come on, come on, come *on* . . . let's *go!*"

Jim ignored the Ithnari. "I thought you didn't know how to do the magic!"

"I know better than anyone else! If I don't try, who will?"

Mrestal bounced up level with Jim's face. "Let's go!" he yelled.

"I'm not leaving Sharra," Jim snapped.

Frank and the other deputy were looking from Jim to Sharra to the two elves, the expressions on their faces indicating they were considering retreating after the ghell, when a golden retriever came cringing out of the woods towards Sharra, crawling on its belly with its tail tucked between its legs and its head low.

Mrestal saw it and yelled. He threw a bolt of fire that caught the dog on the rump.

"Don't hurt the dog," Jim yelled. "He's scared!"

"He killed that mehn in the bookstore!" Gali yelled.

Jim looked at the dog, and then at the elves. He didn't understand—too many things were happening at once, and he just didn't know how to handle it.

The ripping noise grew louder, and both cops looked

up. Jim saw their expressions change from bewildered disbelief to horror, and he looked up, too.

Gali had been right. He didn't want to see what was coming. It was too late now, though.

An arm reached through the rent in the sky, a leprous, fish-belly white arm banded at wrist and biceps with chains—and from the chains hung the remains of things Jim didn't want to identify. The hand at the end of the arm was rotting, the skin fallen away in places to reveal bone and tendon and graying, oozing flesh. The fingers were tipped with long, yellowed, horn-like fingernails filed into needle-tipped claws.

It was impossible to estimate the size of the arm—other than that it was huge. It reached down, and down, and down, and Jim realized it was coming straight for them. He started backing up; then Sharra glanced at the sky and he saw her jaw tighten. She didn't move. The policeman with the burned shoe sagged against the nearest tree, his face glowing gray and slick with sweat in the faint light cast by Sharra's spellweaving and the glowing hand from hell.

The hand touched the ground in the clearing, and Jim could estimate the thing's size—his immediate response was "too big." The hand was as tall as one of the Budweiser Clydesdales he'd seen on a visit to Busch Gardens when he was just a kid. Those moments of his life flashed in front of his eyes and vanished, taking all their warmth and happiness with them, and he realized these terrible events could easily be the last memories he was going to get. He found the gun at his left shoulder and tears running down his cheeks. His hand was on the trigger. He was pulling and pulling, and nothing was happening; the deputy with the burned shoe turned and ran screaming; an eye peered through the rent in reality and the hand flashed over to the officer who fled the clearing. The deadthing demon's fingers wrapped around the running man and tightened—Jim heard crunching—and the deputy made a bloodcurdling, gurgling scream in the back of his throat.

The safety, Jim thought. Flip the goddamned safety.

His thumb fumbled—one-handed, and off-handed at that, with a ten-gauge shotgun that had its safety on the right, he was damned near helpless. He lowered the barrels to the dirt, shoved the gun butt against his hip, crouched to move the safety, brought the gun back up—too late. Too late to do anything. The hand with the fallen deputy in it whipped up into the clouds again before he could shoot—and Jim looked down to see Willy back on his feet, stalking Sharra with a knife.

She was standing there reading, holding the book high in front of her with her face lifted to the sky. The dog was curled at her feet, cringing and shivering. The air around the two of them glowed faintly. The ripping sound had stopped, but the tear in the fabric of reality stayed open, and the arm was descending again.

The eye peeked out of the hole in the sky—a hellish red demon eye, lashless and unblinking—and Franklin Ray raised his service revolver, aimed, and emptied the weapon into the demon's eye. Six shots in quick succession—and at least one of them hit. Jesus, he's shooting at something real, Jim thought, and that fact surprised him; he'd expected the shots to be futile, but the shriek that erupted from the heavens blew down trees. The hand was still coming—but now it fumbled blindly.

Frank had reloaded, and was covering the demon's arm—shooting it if it came near anyone. Jim turned away to help Sharra. The dog at her feet was watching Willy, and its hackles rose. Willy stepped closer, and it came up to its feet slowly with its head lowered and its ears flat to its skull, and it snarled—Jim realized he'd never seen a golden retriever that big, or with teeth that large. Willy stopped, and pointed the knife at the dog, and said, "Attack her."

The dog shivered—Jim could actually feel the force behind the spell Willy used on the animal, but it never took its eyes off him, and it never backed down. Slowly it began stalking forward, growling low in its throat.

Willy backed up a step. The giant, stinking hand fumbled past him—he sidestepped it. It fingerwalked, spiderwise, past the deputy, who was reloading his revolver again with shaking hands. Frank moved out of the way, and the hand missed him, too.

Sharra never took her eyes off the book. She kept reading, kept her attention focused on the spell that would shut the gate to a hundred alien hells. The fumbling, seeking hand touched the faint glow in the air that surrounded her, and electricity crackled against it. Its flesh scorched—smoke roiled from the places where it had touched the lightfield and a worse stink than before washed through the clearing.

Willy muttered something and fire splashed out of the point of his knife, and surrounded the dog—but it didn't touch him. The wall of light that surrounded Sharra protected the dog, too. Willy cursed, then raised his arms above his head and wrapped himself in a wall of the green coldfire he'd called up before and shouted, in a voice that rang with power no human lungs would ever have, "GHELL! Bondslave! By your blood and bones, I command you *come here, now!*" He added words of magic, low and sibilant, and when he finished, the wall of fire shimmered around him and fell away into glowing scales that tumbled glittering to the ground. In the woods, Jim heard the crashing of heavy footsteps; heard the voice of the ghell, screaming in terror, drawn back to the clearing, to the end of the world, against its will.

The monster burst out of the woods, and the dog

saw it coming and charged out of the protective
cocoon that surrounded Sharra, straight for the ghell's
throat. Then Jim saw that whatever it was, it was no
dog. It vanished in mid-leap, and when it reappeared,
the beast was behind the ghell, clinging to its back
with taloned hands that had been hidden beneath its
fur, and biting and slashing through the leathery skin
for an artery. The ghell reached behind its head and
wrapped its fingers around the dog's throat. They
fought—and while they fought, Willy was free to go
after Sharra again.

Jim raised the gun and put Willy's head in his
sights—and then he lowered the gun. He couldn't shoot
Willy—not while there was a chance he was still in
there somewhere underneath the wizard Lukas. Not
while there was a chance he could still be saved. Not
while there was any other alternative. Jim clenched
the gun in his hand and charged; he slammed into
Willy with his left shoulder and sent him sprawling
onto the dirt. He pushed the gun away from himself
and dropped, on his knees, onto Willy's back. He heard
the air whoosh out of Willy's lungs.

"Leave her alone!" he shouted. "Dammit, whoever
you are, leave her alone!"

Willy writhed beneath Jim's weight, twisted, and
somehow rolled himself face up while holding the knife
underhanded. He slashed—but Jim was an athlete, with
fast reflexes and strength even in his left arm. He
caught Willy's wrist, and twisted; Willy paled and the
knife dropped to the ground—and Willy's knee came
up and slammed Jim in the back. Burned, blistered
skin took fresh abuse, and Jim cried out.

"She's going to be sacrificed, and I'm going to be
a god—and then you're going to die slower than anyone
has ever died before," Willy snarled in the stranger's
voice.

He started muttering a spell. Jim punched him in

the mouth, and his knuckles came away cut and bloodied, and Willy spat blood. He didn't try the spell again.
He did smile, though, and slammed a fist into Jim's
right shoulder.

Jim screamed.

Willy swung again, and Jim fended off the blow with
his left arm, but Willy came across Jim's chest with a
hard right, and slammed the shoulder again. Jim collapsed backward as the pain burned straight into his
brain. Willy levered himself up, grabbed his knife again,
and kicked a knee into Jim's gut.

"You should have shot me when you had the chance,"
he said. "I'm not going to kill you—yet—but I swear
I'll make you wish you were dead." He smiled through
bloodied, swollen lips and punched Jim in the face,
smashing his glasses into the bridge of his nose. Then
he jammed the knife into Jim's shoulder.

One of the Ithnari jumped onto Willy's back and
bit him on the ear. Willy, swearing, backhanded the
elf across the clearing—

Jim blacked out for an instant—long enough for Willy
to be on his feet, knife in hand, charging Sharra when
he came back around.

The gun was on the ground next to Jim. He reached
for it, dragged it close, pulled the butt into his arm-
pit and rocked it back and forth in the dirt, digging
it in so that when he fired it, it didn't shatter his shoulder. He slid his left knee under the barrels to act as
a rest. He got Willy into his sights . . . but Sharra
was there too.

The walking demon hand fumbled in front of him—
the ghell and the dog scrambled out of its way, and
the ghell leapt over Jim with the dog at his throat,
then staggered backwards. The fighting monsters
toppled into Willy; Willy jumped to one side; he was
no longer in line with Sharra.

Jim, with tears in his eyes, pulled both triggers.

Willy went down—Jim didn't have time to see where he'd shot him, though, because he'd also hit the ghell in the back—and the monster turned and got a grip on the dog, and ripped its head off. Ignoring the twitching body that still clung to its back, the ghell came after Jim.

The shotgun was empty—Jim couldn't move. This was it.

Then Frank was there, standing right over Jim's head, with his revolver gripped in both hands.

He pulled the trigger once—

"I'd . . ."

—and again—

". . . shoot . . ."

—and again—

". . . 'im right . . ."

—and again, and again—

". . . in the eye. . . ."

—and again, and again.

The ghell stepped forward.

No, it wasn't a step. The monster, its face blown off, was falling—slow as a giant tree—and Frank grabbed Jim by the good arm, and dragged him across the ground out of the way, and the monster crashed, dying, to the ground, and cried out. And twitched. At last, it was still. And the hand fumbled past, felt the monster lying there, and wrapped rotted fingers around its body.

A sucking sound filled the air. Jim, on his back, looked up and saw the rent in the sky beginning to draw closed. It puckered and shrank . . .

. . . and wrapped around the arm . . .

. . . and the arm thrashed.

"Can you stand up?" Frank asked Jim.

"I can try," Jim told him.

The deputy gave him his hand, and pulled Jim to his feet. "Now come on." He pulled Jim toward the trees.

"Sharra—" Jim protested.

"She's as safe as she's going to get—not that we could help her anyway—but something big is about to happen, and you and me don't have any magic wrapped around us." He let Jim lean on him, and pulled him to relative safety out of the clearing.

The sucking sound continued, and the screaming started again, as bad as when Frank had shot the skydemon in the eye. The arm began to thrash back and forth, taking trees with it, and the screaming got louder.

"She's trapped it," Frank said, and pointed at the sky.

Jim looked up, and saw the web of reality tightening around the single writhing arm. A sudden loud pop replaced the sucking sound, and the scream cut off as if it had never been. The arm toppled to the ground, and the rent in the sky was gone.

Sharra shuddered. The light around her died, and Jim staggered toward her. The Ithnari were ahead of him.

The giant hand dragged the arm around the clearing, still grappling for anyone it might reach.

Sharra shouted to Jim, "I need a match! Hurry! I have to burn this book!"

"Don't burn the book," Willy yelled—and his voice was still the stranger's.

Jim felt his heart sink—Willy's body lived, but the magic was over, and Willy was still gone. He dug through the pockets he could reach with his left hand—but he didn't have any matches and he knew it.

Frank was fumbling through his pockets. "I have a cigarette lighter in here somewhere," he muttered.

"Hurry!" Sharra yelled again.

Mrestal bounded back to her side, shooting over the grasping, stinking undead arm. "Drop it," he yelled.

Sharra stared at him for an instant—and Jim realized he could actually see the expression on her face.

"Morning," the deputy whispered, almost reverently. "We lived to see another one."

Sharra dropped the book, and Mrestal pointed at it, and closed his eyes, and flames danced out of his fingertips. The book caught fire—and Willy began to scream—the scream of the damned, hollow, hopeless, and fading, as if the wizard inside of Willy were falling down a tunnel.

Finally, the scream died.

And then Willy groaned. He put his hands over the gunshot wound in his stomach, and he winced, and said, "What the hell happened? How did I get here?"

And this time, he spoke in Willy's voice.

Chapter Forty-one

WEDNESDAY

Frank drove Jim, Willy, Sharra and the elves to the ER, and called in a few favors while he was doing it. He had a doctor who was a friend of his waiting when they pulled into the hospital. He covered their stories—including the one about Jim's car being stolen, and the one about Willy helping fight off the things in the woods, though one story was only sort of true, and the other wasn't true at all.

But Franklin Ray now knew the things he'd always suspected were true. He'd fought hell and won—and the proof that he'd won lay rotting in a clearing in an unnamed patch of woods with police photographers and county sheriff's gathered around it. He'd earned the right to be magnanimous—and he used it.

The doctor wanted to know what had happened—but the cop told him not to ask questions. Obviously eaten alive with curiosity, the doc and the ER nurses catalogued the injuries and cleaned and patched—and never asked. The cop was a pro. So were they.

The elves kept out of sight until Jim came back from surgery. He lay in his room, swathed in bandages, with most of the pain dulled by medication. Gali bounded onto his bed and grinned at him. "We were good, weren't we?" she asked. "We saved the book, and helped you, and fought off the ghell and the wizard, and even burned the book when it was all over."

"You were good," Jim agreed.

Mrestal jumped up onto the bed beside Gali. He clutched a shield in one hand—it was only when Jim had studied it for an instant that he realized it was Frank's badge.

"Where did you get that?" he asked.

Mrestal grinned. "The policeman was wearing it . . . but he didn't need it."

"You stole his badge while he was *wearing* it?"

"Pretty good, huh?" Gali said.

Jim closed his eyes and groaned. "That's not good. That's awful."

"It was hard," Mrestal said. "But fun. You should try it some time."

The door opened, and both elves shot off the bed into their hiding places. Jim had no idea where it was that they went.

Sharra walked in. She smiled at him, but it was a tired smile. She kissed him lightly and said, "I talked to the doctor and he said you're doing better than he could have expected."

Jim sighed. "That means my right arm isn't going to fall off. They say I may not be able to do much of anything with it, though."

"I know." Her eyes were dark with worry.

"It's okay," he told her. "I've got my future planned. When I get out of here, I'm going to go to college and get a degree in business, and then I'm going to open my own bookstore. I'm going to make a life for myself, Sharra . . . a life for *us*, if you'll have me." He gave her a confident smile. "It's all taken care of."

"Jim . . ."

Something in her voice stopped him.

"I went by your place like you asked. It isn't there."

"The beer can isn't there?"

"There was a can full of warm, moldy beer right where you said the gold can would be. So I went ahead and looked through the rest of the apartment—it's not there."

"Someone must have broken in and stolen it."

"Well, it seems like the sort of thing that would be pretty hard to pawn. When did you get it?"

"I made it . . . the night I did the spell that brought the ghell through the gate."

"You . . . made it?"

"Yeah. The magic spell I did was for turning things into gold—why are you shaking your head like that?"

"I told you once before, you can't use magic to make someone love you, or to create or transmute matter. Those were the things the alchemists tried the hardest, but they're the things that simply can't be done."

"But the can was sitting on my bedside table. It was solid gold—"

"The spell was an illusion—set up to make you think you had succeeded, so that you would do more spells in the book. Lukas planned ahead in that regard, very carefully." She frowned. "He planned a lot of things very carefully."

Jim sagged back in the bed. "That was my chance," he said. "That gold would have paid off my hospital bills, and I'll bet there would have been enough to pay for two years at business school, too." He felt like crying. Without business school, he was going to be stuck in the bookstore again—and he would never be free of the medical bills. He couldn't ask Sharra to marry him if it meant taking on that kind of burden.

But Sharra was smiling, and she didn't look worried. "Two hundred years of prudent investments add up to a pretty nice pile of money," she said. "It's scattered all over the world, in different accounts and under different names—but I can get my hands on as much of it as I need whenever I need it."

"You don't owe me anything, Sharra."

"I wasn't offering because I owed you. I was offering because I wanted to."

Jim patted the edge of the bed, and Sharra came over and sat down beside him. He reached out with his good hand, pushed aside an errant strand of Sharra's raven-dark hair, and traced the soft, smooth line of her upper lip with one finger. She opened her mouth and closed her teeth lightly around his finger, mock-threatening.

She kissed the finger lightly, then bit at it again, and Jim withdrew his hand, and ran his fingers through her hair. He stared into her eyes, then pulled her to him, bent his head to the side and kissed her gently. His injuries made the position awkward, but neither of them noticed. Gradually, the kiss became more serious, and Sharra pulled away from him.

"What is it?" he asked, worried.

"For so long, I watched others grow old and die, while I never aged. I had no reason to live, and I envied them death's warm embrace—I longed for that release from my pain."

"Don't," Jim said. "All that is past you now."

"Yes," Sharra said. "I've found something worth living for, something worth clinging to—you. But I spent so much time hiding from life. I'm not sure I know *how* to live."

Jim cupped her face in his hand, and wiped a tear from her eye with his thumb. He bent forward and kissed her on the forehead, then pulled away.

"You've been hiding from life, and I've been living in the past," Jim said. "We both have to learn how to live—we might as well teach each other."

He paused, torn between the desire to take her in his arms and the need to have a commitment from her, without any pressure from him.

"What we do—how far we take this—is your

decision. I will be yours for as long as you will have me, no matter what you decide. If you told me to leave, and never come back, in time I would probably eventually see another woman—but I could never love another woman. There is no other you out there. And you are all that I want, for the rest of my life. I would be greatly honored if you would be my wife."

"Jim, I . . ." Sharra's voice broke. She leaned into him, and hugged him tightly. Then she leaned back, and looked into his eyes. "Yes."

They were married a week later. It was a double wedding. Both brides were beautiful; both grooms were nervous. Willy's tuxedo looked like he'd been born in it. Jim's just looked like he'd slept in it.

The elves stole the rice.